Beautiful Lies

Kiffany Dugger

Beautiful Lies

Cover Design: Okomota – The Design Lab: Book Star
Editor: Nikkea Smithers

Printed in the United States of America

I dedicate this book to the loving memory of my heartbeat, my rock, my grandmother - Ada Dugger.

To Brandon Aaron and Derrick Clayton.

Love Always!

Acknowledgements

When this book was conceived in my mind, I had no idea what lay ahead. This has been the most challenging season in my life, but I thank God for his strength, faithfulness, and favor. My heart breaks for those grieving the loss of loved ones amid the COVID-19 pandemic. I am grateful to have loved and been loved by those I continue to mourn. Through it, all my hope is built on nothing less than Jesus' love and righteousness.

Rest Safe in His Arms:

Ada Ethel Dugger

Chandra James

Christopher Townsend, Sr.

Dale Nash

Walter Nash

Rose Perkins

Introduction

Dragging her bare feet across the yard making indentations in the freshly fallen snow, Tyger's toes grew numb. Struggling to reach the servant's entrance in the back of the house, the frigid winter breeze briskly swept across the lake stealing her breath. The weight of her unborn child pressed against her pelvis weighing her down, Tyger's breathing became labored. No longer able to feel the baby moving inside her, her heart raced with regret. Stopping to catch her breath, Tyger squatted with her rear end raised and knees bent. With her face almost touching the ground, she leaned down and saw fresh traces of scarlet making spatter patterns in the snow. Tyger reached between her legs and felt the warm blood dripping from her body. Almost blinding her, fresh snow continued to fall clinging to her eyelids forming tiny ice sickles. Treading through the snow squeezing her eyes tight and gritting her teeth, Tyger prayed that she could make it back to the house without passing out in a bed of snow.

Finally, approaching the entrance to the house, Tyger stopped on the steps, looked over her shoulder and scanned the back yard. In an instant everything was covered in a fresh blanket of snow. There were no traces that she'd ever been to the lake dragging her husband Spencer's dead body behind her.

Entering the house, Tyger stood in the laundry room and stripped down to nothing. She found a washcloth in the hamper and held it between her legs to absorb the flow. She reached in the dryer and grabbed a clean pair of underwear and the gown that she'd washed earlier. The pain was so intense that she could not lift her arms or legs to change into dry clothes. Tyger desperately wanted to scream, but she didn't want to wake her daughter Nina. She grabbed another washcloth, balled it up and placed it in her mouth. Biting down on the cloth, she tightened her eyes and screamed.

After dressing herself Tyger slowly made her way into the kitchen. Creeping through the house trying not to stumble, sweat poured from her face and flashes of fire rolled through her body. Holding on to the walls unable to stand, her legs grew heavy and her knees buckled sending her tumbling to the floor. Hitting the floor like a ton of bricks, a sharp piercing pain cut through her spine like a piece of jagged glass. The impact was so intense that she bit through her bottom lip. Lying on her back blood began to pour from the corners of her mouth. Trying not to drown in her own blood, Tyger coughed vigorously. With every cough, her belly burned like fire. She could still feel her flesh stinging from the hard kick that Spencer had landed on her backside earlier in the evening.

At last count Tyger's contractions were coming every seven minutes. She clinched her teeth and tried not to scream again. All she could do was lie on the floor staring at the ceiling praying that somehow she would make her way to the phone to call the paramedics.

Finally, Tyger raised one leg and pushed herself backward on the heels of her feet over to the telephone. Tyger reached her hand up and yanked the phone from the table. Landing on her chest, Tyger gripped the receiver tightly in her hand and dialed 911. A calm voice answered, "911 what's the nature of your call?"

"Please help me, I'm pregnant, I slipped and fell. I'm in labor… My contractions are now five minutes apart… I'm bleeding and I can't move!"

"Ok ma'am, calm down can you tell me your name?"

"My name is Tyger Benedict... My address is 5629 Lakewood Hills Drive... I live in Lakewood Hills Estates... Please... I think I'm losing my baby... Please help me!"

"Ok ma'am we're dispatching someone there right away... Mrs. Benedict are you alone? Is there anyone there with you?"

"Yes, I have a **ten-year-old** daughter Nina, she's asleep ... Just please send someone now!"

Tyger continued to lie there and listen while the lady on the other end asked her one meaningless question after the next. Tyger knew she was trying to keep her on the phone but listening to the woman's voice was making the pain more unbearable.

Tyger started to feel cold; there was a chill in her bones. Struggling to breathe, she looked at the ceiling urgently batting her burning eyes trying to stay focused and awake. Suddenly, the 911 operator's voice grew distant. Tyger could hear the sound of her own eyelids fluttering deep inside her ear canal. Trying to hold on, Tyger could feel herself fading. Tyger closed her eyes tight and begged God to spare her baby's life. This child, this life growing inside Tyger and her daughter Nina were the only good things that had come from her marriage to Spencer Benedict.

The room started to spin and everything around her was dark. The entire room was shrinking and soon all Tyger could see was a small round space with a tiny beacon of light surrounded by nothing but darkness. Tyger could hear the woman's voice on the other end of the phone moving further and further away. Suddenly there was nothing, no sound, no darkness... Nothing.

Chapter One

O n the morning of Friday, April 4th it was like Christmas at the Beaubien Station. The body of Spencer Benedict II surfaced after a warm front swept across Silver Creek Lake in lavish Lakewood Hills Estates. Spencer had been missing since late November of the previous year. He'd gone missing on one of the coldest days of the year and there had been no traces of him. It was as if he vanished into thin air.

It was officially Spring, but Michigan weather is unpredictable, it was still freezing. When the police fished Spencer out of the lake, his body was frozen solid. Spencer was butt naked with his hands tied behind his back and rope tied around his feet. He looked like a fat hog ready for slaughter.

No one had anxiously anticipated this day more than Detective Aiden Arias. This was the detective's lucky day. With the help of a willing benefactor, Detective Arias arrived in Detroit from New York nine months prior. The Detective waited patiently for a chance to get up close and personal with one of Michigan's most influential families. It seems that Detective Arias had become obsessed with Spencer's wife, Tyger. Tyger would not only be his ticket into the world of the

Benedicts, but he also knew she would lead him straight to Ace Del Toro. Along with several other miscreants in the city, Detective Arias wanted Ace dead. Ace was the real reason that he moved to Detroit. Detective Arias would do anything in his power to destroy Ace, meeting Tyger Benedict was just the icing on the cake.

Almost giving himself away, Detective Arias eagerly jumped at the chance to handle this case. The Detective had become quite taken with Tyger during Ace Del Toro's murder trial held in September of the previous year. Tyger showed up on the last day of the Del Toro trial and nearly took the detectives breath away. Since that day, the detective had been trying to find a way to inadvertently put he and Tyger within eyesight of each other. Now that Spencer's body had surfaced, Detective Arias would be the one to go and inform the grieving widow of her husband's demise.

Aiden knew he had to be careful. He knew that despite Tyger's marriage to the late Spencer Benedict, she had been having a ten-year affair with Ace. The detective was all too familiar with the rambunctious and sinister nature of Mr. Del Toro. It was also no secret that Tyger and former attorney turned corporate thug, Picasso Kennard, were best friends. Aiden knew neither of these men would let him within three feet of Tyger. Aiden would have to use his time wisely, walk hard and carry a huge firearm to get out of this alive.

After leaving the crime scene, Detective Arias gathered Gavan Cavanaugh, a young officer eager to make a name for himself and headed out to talk to Mrs. Benedict.

Approaching the gate leading into the Benedict Compound they paused briefly at the gate to announce their arrival. Officer Cavanaugh pushed the intercom button and informed the voice on the other end of the speaker of his request to enter the premises. After a few seconds passed the gate opened.

Cavanaugh drove up the cobblestone driveway lined with trees that seemed to reach the heavens. As the shade from the trees covered the driveway, small rays of sunlight danced through the thick branches and shined through the car window. Approaching the end of the driveway, a magnificent mansion with marble pillars and a massive fountain sitting in the center of the circular drive greeted the two men. The house was magnificent and even in 30-degree weather, the landscape was gorgeous.

Tyger knew exactly who the men were and what they wanted. From the upstairs window, she watched the two men exit their vehicle. Her contact at the police station had already informed her that Spencer's body had been recovered at the other end of the lake three miles from her home. Tyger put on her game face and prepared her statement in her head. She refused to play the role of the grieving widow. Everyone knew their marriage was a sham, so there was no use pretending.

Approaching the front door Detective Arias rang the doorbell. A few moments passed and they were left standing on the doorstep with no host in sight. Extending his index finger to ring the doorbell again, Detective Arias heard the lock click. The door sprung open, Detective Arias stood there trying to catch his breath and remember the reason for being on this beautiful creature's doorstep. Within two seconds, he had already compromised the case by mentally lusting after the dead man's wife.

Tyger Benedict was statuesque with curves in all the right places. She had a small waist, a round plump rear end and hourglass thighs. Walking like a prize Philly with her head held high, Tyger's legs were a mile long. Dressed in a silk Kaftan that hung off her left shoulder, the flesh-tone fabric clung to her plump breast. Her smooth chestnut skin made her deep blue eyes sparkle like brand new silver dollars. Her long lashes and thick eyebrows made her eyes command attention.

Standing in the doorway allowing the breeze to take control, the wind swept through the house blowing her cold black hair across her face. Carefully moving the small strand of hair that had fallen over her eye, Tyger had rendered the man standing in front of her speechless. In an instant, it had totally slipped the detective's mind that he was there to tell this woman that her husband had washed up in the lake a couple of hours prior to that moment.

Detective Arias cleared his throat and gathered his thoughts. He quickly reminded himself of who he was and why he was there. In a strong tone he asked, "Mrs. Benedict?"

"Yes, I am Mrs. Benedict."

Tyger wore a stern unyielding look that masked her admiration for Detective Arias' smooth olive colored skin and his cold wavy black hair. He was strikingly handsome and possessed an exotic mystique. Staring into his almond shaped amber colored eyes, he seemed familiar to her.

In a matter of five seconds, she'd carefully scanned Detective Arias' entire body. He was impeccably dressed in a black suit and a black button-down dress shirt with a herringbone cashmere topcoat that hugged his body perfectly. Tyger was a sucker for a fine well-dressed man and the detective was definitely fine as cat hair. His strong broad shoulders and powerful arms screamed *take me now*. His pearly whites were perfectly straight, and his plump almost flesh toned lips were like an invitation to openly admire all he had to offer. Detective Arias was smooth and confident. His thick New York accent and deep voice made her awkwardly curious.

The detective reminded her of Ace. Staring Detective Arias in his big brown eyes, Tyger silently reminded herself that any other man other than Ace Del Toro was off limits to her. Besides, there was something strange about the detective that stood before her. He was no ordinary Detroit cop. His eighteen-hundred-dollar cashmere coat had given him away. The man that stood before her had a story to tell and she had a sneaky suspicion that she was about to become the next chapter in this story.

Trying not to appear to be fazed by the detective, Tyger stood in the doorway with her arms folded, her neck stretched, and head erect. She was almost intimidating. Like a schoolboy, Detective Arias' belly fluttered as he stood on Tyger's doorstep.

Breaking up what appeared to be an awkward moment; Detective Arias flashed his badge,

"Mrs. Benedict, I'm Detective Aiden Arias and this is Officer Cavanaugh. I need to speak with you regarding your husband Spencer Benedict II. I think it would be best if we could step inside for a moment."

Tyger stood aside and extended her arm for the men to enter her home. Officer Cavanaugh declined the offer. He stood outside on the porch as if he were guarding the house. Once they were inside Tyger closed the door and turned to Detective Arias,

"May I offer you a cup of coffee or tea?"

"No thank you."

After standing in the midst of an awkward silence, Tyger broke the ice, "How may I help you detective?"

In a compassionate tone Detective Arias delivered the news. "Mrs. Benedict, I'm sorry to inform you that your husband's body was found this morning in Silver Creek Lake."

Detective Arias waited for her to shed a tear or show some type of emotion; instead, she just stood with her arms folded. The detective waited for a delayed reaction. Finally, he broke his silence. "Mrs. Benedict is there anything I can do for you?"

With her arms still folded, "Come on Detective, did you really expect an overloaded display of emotion from me? My husband was Spencer Benedict III the most hated man in Michigan. He's been missing since November. Neither you nor I expected him to be found alive."

Stunned by her candor, Detective Arias responded, "Well, Mrs. Benedict we always hope that we find those that have gone missing alive."

"So detective, would you like me to come down and identify the body?"

"Yes. We also have a few questions that we would like to ask you. We can wait while you get dressed."

Tyger unfolded her arms, "If you don't mind, I would prefer to drive myself, I have an appointment this afternoon."

"That will be fine, Mrs. Benedict. You can follow us, that way we will avoid delays."

Tyger displayed a coy smile, "Thank you, please call me Tyger."

As the words escaped her lips, Detective Arias imagined that Tyger was flirting with him. Walking toward the sitting room adjacent to the foyer, she offered the detective a seat, "You are welcome to sit in here while I get dressed."

Detective Arias took a seat on the stool in front of the baby grand piano. He tried to gather himself and erase the image of Tyger from his mind. Watching her hips sway with a rhythmic motion as she exited the room, the detective lowered his head and placed his palms on his face; he was thrown off balance and reduced to the immaturity of a teenager. He was almost hypnotized by her.

When the detective raised his head, his jaw dropped at the sight of Tyger standing before him. A vision of perfection dressed in black lace lingerie, she stood like a magnificent statue. As Tyger stood in front of him with her five-inch stilettos, Detective Arias rose to his feet with a lump in his throat and that was dry as a bone. Watching Tyger walk toward him, the detective felt his pulse quicken and his knees grow weak. Finally, they stood before each other breathing the same air. Locked in an unyielding embrace, Tyger could feel his hard and inviting manhood pressing against her leg. Feeling her warm bare skin, Detective Arias continued to hold Tyger close to him breathing in her intoxicating fragrance. Releasing a low and sensuous moan that traveled through Detective Arias' body like an orgasmic earthquake, Tyger ran her fingers through the detective's soft black hair. Detective Arias leaned in and passionately parted Tyger's lips with his tongue.

Engaging in a wet sensuous tug of war, Detective Arias slowly kissed Tyger. The scent of her perfume danced on his nose sending him into another world as their tongues continued to explore each other. Detective Arias ran his hands up her thighs and caressed her round firm cheeks. Palming her bottom like a perfect fitting glove he caressed her neck with the tip of his tongue. His fingers softly danced up Tyger's thighs sending a shiver up her spine. As the sound of unadulterated lust filled the air, Detective Arias' fingers caressed her flesh, Tyger felt her body quiver. Her body throbbed as he gently parted her with his fingers and messaged her flesh; she could feel her heart beating between her legs.

Feeling Tyger's body surrender, Detective Arias whispered, "That's it, just let go." Falling against the wall, Detective Arias lifted Tyger into thin air making her feel light as a feather. Spreading Tyger's legs apart entering her, he became weak as her warm nectar flowed all over him. Wrapping her legs around his body the detective moved deeper and deeper inside of her exploring every single inch. As he explored her warm flesh that gripped him like spine tingling suctions he was mesmerized by the passionate look in her eyes. Tyger's lips griped him tightly almost making it impossible for him to hold on.

Running her fingers through his silky cold black hair, Tyger whispered, "Go deeper." As the words escaped Tyger's lips and made him drunk with excitement, Detective Arias felt the tips of his toes tingle and a shiver traveled up his strong backside. With her nipples like provocative chocolate kisses, Detective Arias marveled at her perfect round breast and profound nipples. Tyger watched his veins pulsating between her legs and moving slowly inside her making her weak with passion and wild with desire. Detective Arias' knees grew weak as a warm wave ran through his body. He grabbed Tyger and held her close to him. He placed his massive hands on her back and delivered hard commanding thrust as her lips quivered and rained excitement that gushed all over him.

As he felt her wet juices flowing, he yelled, "Damn... Damn... Damn" and finally, "Got Damn, Tyger." Releasing an earth-shaking orgasmic climax, he began panting and trying to catch his breath.

Hearing her call his name, his heart raced. "Detective... Detective... Are you ok?" Just as he felt a warm release touch his hot flesh, he opened his eyes and found Tyger Benedict standing in front of him fully dressed and commanding his attention.

Standing in front of Tyger with his heart beating like a drum, Detective Arias realized he'd just let his imagination take him to a place that he wished reality would soon follow. Embarrassed, he quickly pulled his coat closed and turned toward the window. Realizing his embarrassment, Tyger calmly tried to avoid any further awkward moments, "I'm going to grab my coat and I'll be ready to leave in just a few minutes."

Walking away, Tyger peeked over her shoulder, "If you need to use the restroom before we leave it's down the hall to your left."

Tyger walked upstairs leaving Detective Arias to gather himself. After he was certain that Tyger was upstairs, Detective Arias ran to the restroom. After freshening up, he stood in front of the mirror trying to make sure there were no obvious signs of the imaginary tryst. It was all a vision of grandeur; there were no obvious signs. After checking and double-checking, he exited the bathroom and made his way outside. Detective Cavanaugh was still standing in front of the house as if he were guarding Buckingham Palace. Looking over at Detective Arias, he asked, "Man are you ok? You're beet red,"

"Yeah, I'm good. This cold air has me feeling a little flushed."

Cavanaugh reached in his pocket and retrieved a stick of gum from its pack and offered Detective Arias a piece, "So, how was it?"

Detective Arias nervously answered Cavanaugh, "How was what?"

"Talking to Tyger Benedict. She's gorgeous..."

Accepting the stick of gum, Detective Arias placed the gum in his mouth and looked over at Officer Cavanaugh and laughed, "She's just a woman. It's my job not to notice her."

"She might be just a woman to you, but she is major. She used to be the Assistant District Attorney."

"I didn't know, I must have missed that little piece of info."

Officer Cavanaugh made it his mission to school Detective Arias on Tyger Benedict 101.

"Tyger Benedict was a better lawyer than her husband Spencer, she never lost a case. After her daughter was born, she stopped practicing law and devoted herself to being a full-time mother."

Officer Cavanaugh paused for a moment, "You know this isn't going to be an easy case to solve. Spencer wasn't exactly the guy next door. He had enemies everywhere. Not to mention right before he went missing, he'd just finished the Ace Del Toro case. He tried to send Ace away for life. Even though Ace is the perfect suspect, I don't think Ace is the killer."

Slowly turning toward the window putting his sunglasses on, Detective Arias peered out into the yard,

"What makes you so sure Ace didn't kill Spencer Benedict?"

"I just don't think Ace is dumb enough to kill Spencer right after his own murder trial."

Savoring the flavor of the gum, Detective Arias turned toward Officer Cavanaugh, "Cavanaugh, you're young, you have a lot to learn. I've been doing this a lot longer than you. I know guys like Ace all too well. I'm one hundred percent sure that he's our man."

Officer Cavanaugh laughed, "You might be right, that woman in there is reason enough. I'd kill for a piece of that."

Detective Arias looked over at Officer Cavanaugh, raising his left brow he stated, "Maybe you can help me understand why a man like Spencer would allow his wife to carry on with Ace Del Toro…?" Officer Cavanaugh gave Detective Arias a matter-of-fact stare.

"You have to pick the battles you know you can win. Let me give you a brief lesson in Benedict/Del Toro 101. First of all, Ace Del Toro is not the one to mess with. He has killed men with his bare hands. Everything caught up with Del Toro last year when he killed two men and a so-called witness came forward to testify. It looked like Ace was going away for life and out of nowhere on the last day of the trial, a mistrial was declared due to evidence tampering. Word on the street is that Spencer tampered with the evidence in order to get a conviction. That was his way of finally getting rid of Del Toro. Rumor has it, after some strong convincing with a loaded gun, Spencer's law partner Kyle Cane told Ace that Spencer set him up to get car jacked the night the murders were committed. Ace was supposed to be killed; instead, he killed the guys that tried to jack him. Cane also snitched just to make sure Ace would be convicted, Spencer paid a witness to testify they saw Ace pull the trigger and it wasn't self-defense. When the trial was over and Ace walked, Spencer got scared after Cane's body parts started showing up; he thought he was next. Ace had a $100,000 price on Spencer's head; he wanted Spencer delivered directly to him so he could watch him die."

Detective Arias' mouth flew wide-open, "…A hundred grand?"

Cavanaugh tapped Arias' on his arm, "Man think about it, Spencer married the woman Del Toro has been in love with since they were in high school and then he tried to take away Ace's freedom. Both men wanted the other gone by any means necessary."

Listening like an inquisitive child, there was a question that was burning in Detective Arias' mind, "If Ace is involved in all this illegal activity and Spencer was the District Attorney and Spencer's father is a judge then why can't Ace be stopped?"

Cavanaugh laughed, "This is deeper than street money, this is about gentrification. Ace funneled his money into real estate, restaurants, and a few other business ventures. Even though he still had his hands in the streets, that shit can't touch him now, that's the last thing that will take him down. Ace or Picasso Kennard will never get their hands dirty. The real deal is a land development project that Spencer and Ace were bumping heads on. A company was trying to buy property in Ace's old neighborhood to build condominiums. Most of the buildings were rental properties, which would force tenants out into the streets with no place to go. For people that owned their homes outright, they weren't being offered enough money to relocate. Ace was against the land development and of course, Spencer was for anything that would make him money. Ace stood in the way of Spencer making millions."

Like a sponge, Detective Arias soaked up everything he heard. He had learned a wealth of information in just five minutes. He was the new kid in town and no one, not even the person that brought him there trusted him enough to tell him the real dirt on what was going down. Officer Cavanaugh had just turned into the Detectives personal 411 operator. The Ace Del Toro that he once knew had evolved into a beast and he knew that it was kill or be killed.

It took Tyger thirty minutes to get ready. Just as Detective Arias was getting ready to go see what was taking her so long, Tyger sauntered out of the front door. Cavanaugh's mouth flew open, "Damn!" She wore fitted leather pants, a black cashmere cowl neck sweater with a leather overcoat. Like a graceful gazelle, she stepped out on to the driveway in her black calfskin booties with the iconic red bottom soles.

Walking toward the detectives' car with her hair cascading in the wind, her dark oversized sunglasses enhanced her glamorous charm.

Stopping to address the detectives, Tyger asked, "Are we ready?" Nodding their heads "yes", both men were at a loss for words. Satisfied with the answer that she needed, Tyger walked to her black sports car parked in front of one of the garage stalls, settled in and waited for the men to take the lead. Watching her through the passenger side mirror watch him, Detective Arias couldn't shake the fact that the thought of her made him literally lose control. The fantasy of being with Tyger seemed so real that he knew the reality of being with her would blow his mind.

Chapter Two

Driving through the Motor City on her way downtown, Tyger reminisced about her days in *The Hole*. Tyger Blackwell-Benedict was born with a smooth cocoa hue, soft curly hair, and big, beautiful doe eyes. Tyger and her brother John Paul were the only two of the four children born to Napoleon and Delilah Blackwell that had their father's rich sun kissed skin, Napoleon Blackwell is a tall, strapping, coffee colored Geechee from the Georgia-Carolina border whom everyone called Whiskey. Delilah's family is from the Solomon Islands; many would say this is what caused her exotic beauty to be intoxicating. Delilah's smooth caramel skin, deep blue eyes, and beautiful natural blonde hair that grew from her roots made her seem enchanted. Since she was a teenager Tyger worked hard to maintain a darker hair color.

Tyger's parents got caught up in the seventies and somewhere between Roots and smoking too much marijuana they named her sisters Piper and Bella. Tyger's brother John Paul never abbreviated his name or answered to a nickname. He was called by his entire name, John Paul, every day of his life.

Tyger and her family moved to Detroit from South Carolina when she was in the fourth grade. The big city was different from what Tyger and her siblings were used to. Detroit was cold not only in temperature, but with relationships as well. The people were rigid and uninviting. Between the oil refinery and the other factories surrounding the area, the smell of rotten eggs lingered, the air was funky and unclean.

The Blackwell children were like palm trees in Alaska, odd and out of place. When Tyger started school, dark skin wasn't exactly in. She got caught up in the old slave politics of lighter skin being better. The kids at school totally mutilated her name calling her Black Tyger for most of elementary school. Tyger was tall for a nine-year-old. She was long and lanky. She wore glasses and her oddly colored curly hair made up eighty percent of her body weight.

In order to survive their first year in the city, Tyger and her siblings stuck together like glue. Tyger grew up on the Southwest side of Detroit off Liddesdale and Fort Street just a few blocks from the oil refinery. Every day of her life until she was seventeen, she inhaled the putrid air that smelled exactly like burned rubber and rotten eggs. Tyger lived in a neighborhood known as *The Hole*. Her street was a dead end where people dumped everything from furniture to dead bodies.

Once upon a time, the neighborhood was decent with hard working people and families that actually knew each other. In the eighties, the crack epidemic invaded the city and everything went downhill from then on. Like most neighborhoods, Tyger watched as her section of the world became infested with base-heads and small-time dope dealers standing on the corner selling poison rocks.

When Tyger and her family first moved to Detroit, they lived in a six-unit apartment building. The building was old and dirty. The halls were filled with the strong smell of piss and rats scurried from corner to corner anytime a beacon of light shown through. A few months later, Tyger and her family moved to a three-family flat that was owned by an old woman from their church. After the woman died, her parents inherited the building. Tyger's best friend Picasso Kennard lived in the basement of the Blackwell home with his brother Shakespeare and their mother Beverly. Picasso and Tyger were the same age and Shakespeare was six years older than the two of them.

The second semester of her fourth-grade year, Tyger and Picasso officially met on the playground and became fast friends. As a joke, Tyger was being pulled through the iron gate on the playground by two boys who wanted to see if she was skinny enough to fit through the bars. Picasso heard her screaming and saw a crowd gathering around her. Since John Paul wasn't around to defend his sister, Picasso felt it was his duty to come to his neighbor's rescue. That day marked the beginning of a lifelong friendship between the Kennard's and the Blackwell's. Picasso taught Tyger and all of her siblings how to survive and adapt to their new environment.

Picasso's mother Beverly was a promising singer that moved to Detroit from Alabama to follow her dream of becoming a singer and dancer. She was only sixteen when she had Shakespeare and twenty-two when Picasso was born. Soon after she had Picasso, Beverly discovered heroine and that was the end of her dreams. After crack hit the scene, Beverly found a new drug that was even more lethal than her original drug of choice. Smoking crack had become Beverly's number one priority, nothing else mattered, not even her children. She turned the basement into a brothel and drug den. Picasso spent most of his time with Tyger's family. Shakespeare followed in the footsteps of the rest of the boys in the neighborhood whom he idolized that drove big body Benzos, with the gold dookey rope chains draped around their necks, tracksuits, pagers, and fresh white sneakers. On any given day he could be found hanging out on the corner or a nearby stoop with the other dope boys.

When Tyger and Picasso were thirteen crack cocaine changed their lives forever. On the hottest day of the summer, Tyger and the rest of the children returned home from the community pool to find the Wayne County Coroner wheeling a body out of the basement on a stretcher in a big black body bag. Shakespeare haphazardly made the statement that one of Beverly's boyfriends probably OD'd. As they approached the house, they saw Delilah walking up from the basement steps. The look in her eyes confirmed that the body in that black bag was Beverly's.

Before the body was hoisted into the coroner's van, Picasso ran to the gurney and ripped open the zipper on the bag. Beverly's arm fell out and hit Picasso in the center of his chest. It was as if it knocked the life from his body forever. Living down there at the end of the earth, they'd seen plenty of dead bodies, but Beverly was the first dead person they actually knew and loved.

Beverly's death changed everything and everyone in that house. Picasso and Shakespeare were forced to grow up whether they were ready or not. Since Beverly's family didn't want to take responsibility for Picasso and Shakespeare they stayed with the Blackwell's. Napoleon let them live in the basement and he watched out for the boys. Napoleon began working harder and pushing himself like a madman. Soon he opened his own bar across the railroad tracks closer to Jefferson and Shafer and called it Whiskey's. From then on Napoleon Blackwell disappeared and he became known as Whiskey, even to his children.

Whiskey was a musician by trade, but a hustler by nature. He was a friend to every drug dealer, hustler, thief, and cop in the city. Whiskey had the police in his back pocket. He never had to snitch on anyone to get what he needed. Whiskey taught his daughters to be independent and street smart. He taught his son how to gain respect and still instill fear. After he made a name for himself, no one dared to mess with Whiskey or his offspring.

For the next few months after Beverly's death Delilah was always on edge. For the first time her children noticed the sadness in Delilah's eyes. She became obsessed with looking at pictures of her days as a dancer. She would sit on the stoop or in the window and gaze into thin air. Whiskey and Delilah fought constantly about everything. Day by day Delilah blamed Whiskey and the kids for ruing her life. She constantly called him a no talent musician and a two-bit hustler.

The day Delilah left, the kids returned home from school to find Whiskey's saxophone and sheet music burning in a garbage barrel on the back porch. Delilah was gone and she didn't bother to say goodbye or leave a note. Delilah disappeared around the same time as her employer, District Attorney Kyle Grey.

As time passed, they forgot Delilah existed and never spoke of her until she showed up at Tyger's college graduation. Since the day she left, Delilah had been in Chicago with Kyle Gray enjoying the comforts of being a kept woman. When she returned, she was no longer Delilah, she was Dee Dee and he was now Judge Gray. The two had gone their separate ways but remained friends. It seems that the judge traded Dee Dee in for a younger whiter model.

After John Paul graduated from high school, he moved out of Whiskey's house and into the streets with Shakespeare. They both started pushing major weight and moved to a suburb one step up from the ghetto. After graduation, Piper moved in with Shakespeare. Shortly thereafter, Piper and Shakespeare were happily married until he was killed in the middle of the night inside the home they shared.

The morning after Shakespeare's funeral, Piper disappeared and hasn't been seen by her family since the day she left. Although Tyger and Piper have not seen each other in over fifteen years, they communicate through letters. Tyger has never visited Piper and she has no idea of her sister's physical address. Tyger sends letters to a different PO Box each year. Every so often Piper will call from a restricted number just to hear her sister's voice. Piper does not ask about Bella or her mother. Piper calls both Whiskey and John Paul once a month to check on them; she has severed all ties with Bella and Dee Dee. Piper has provided no explanation for her elusiveness or her estrangement to her sister Bella.

Tyger's sister Bella fell into a series of unfortunate events. She was found beaten and unconscious at Shakespeare and Piper's the night Shakespeare was killed. She witnessed the murder, but to this day she won't talk about it. Since that night Bella has been snortin, shootin and smokin anything she can get her hands on to numb the pain. The only difference between Bella and a textbook crackhead is she has Tyger and her money to take care of her. On the surface, Bella appears to be the beauty that she has always been.

After high school Picasso and Tyger went away to college and on to Law school. After passing the bar, Picasso spent a few years as a criminal defense attorney. Ironically, he retired from practicing law and followed in his brother Shakespeare's footsteps. Tyger asked Picasso why he wasted so much time in school if he was going to end up throwing it all away. Picasso told her the most successful criminals knew the law inside and out.

College is where Tyger met her husband, Spencer J. Benedict III. Spencer and Tyger were both Pre-Law and from Michigan so, they often traveled in the same circles. At first glance, there was nothing special about Spencer. Spencer was of average height and weight. His skin tone was a warm shade of chestnut. He was always neatly groomed and wore his hair close with a flawless line. Spencer wore his clothes well and gave the illusion of having a nice physique. Physically Spencer was not Tyger's type. She was never physically attracted to him until she heard him debate. There was something confident and powerful about him and Tyger wanted to know more.

Spencer was pretentious and arrogant. He was smart and determined to out-shine everyone in the class. He was so damn smart he was annoying. Spencer was destined to be a top-notch lawyer; it was in his blood. Spencer's father, Spencer J. Benedict II is perhaps the most crooked judge in the country. Affectionately known as S.B., Judge Benedict has made a fortune by getting the vilest human elements off scott-free, for a hefty price.

Spencer wore Tyger down until she agreed to go out with him. Spencer offered her security, which was more than her true love, Ace Del Toro could ever offer her. Tyger saw them as the power couple, taking over the world together.

Spencer and Tyger's union caused a rift in her relationship with Picasso. Spencer and Picasso loathed each other, but they tolerated each other because of Tyger. The instant Tyger and Spencer said, "I do" Spencer changed. Three weeks after they were married Tyger said something to Spencer he didn't like, he stopped speaking to her for weeks. Soon the periodic bouts of silence turned in to verbal abuse, shortly thereafter, Spencer hit Tyger across the face with an open hand during an argument.

When Spencer first hit Tyger, her natural reaction was to defend herself. Tyger picked up the closest thing she could get her hands on and hit him over the head. That night they beat the hell out of each other until no one was left standing. The next day Tyger filed for divorce. By the time Tyger returned home from seeing her attorney, Spencer and his parents were waiting for her. Spencer's father explained to Tyger that Benedicts did not divorce, it was unacceptable. Spencer's father told Tyger that the only way she would leave the marriage was in death. Judge Benedict expressed his regret over the possibility of Tyger meeting with an untimely accident.

The hair on the back of Tyger's neck stood up; she knew she would have to figure a way out of her marriage. For the first time, Tyger looked over at her mother-in-law Genoa Benedict, and saw the look of sheer terror in her eyes. Tyger knew then that she or Spencer would have to die in order to end their union from hell. As Tyger and Genoa grew closer, they realized they both possessed the same goal, to rid themselves of the Benedict men.

Tyger never told Picasso, John Paul or Ace about Spencer's physical abuse. Fighting with Spencer became a normal part of her marriage. Everything about their life was a farce; they were the Benedicts she had to keep up appearances. Although, her home life was a mess, she liked the prestige the Benedict name afforded her. Tyger promised herself that she would hang in a little while longer with Spencer and plan her departure just right. After finding out she was pregnant, Tyger knew that a child would guarantee that even after Spencer's death she would be taken care of for the rest of her life.

After Nina was born with Down's Syndrome, Tyger realized that she could not trust Spencer to honor his parental commitment. Spencer was hoping for a healthy son capable of following in his father and grandfather's footsteps. The state of Tyger's loveless marriage void of passion and excitement sent her back into the arms of her high school sweetheart Ace Del Toro.

Ace, Picasso, John Paul and even Spencer were all wrapped up in the streets in one way or another. After Spencer became the District Attorney, things took a weird turn. Spencer spent most of his career being paid to look the other way when it came to Picasso, John Paul and even Ace. As much as Spencer loathed the three of them, he was not foolish enough to turn away stacks of cash. It was a dysfunctional oxymoronic family made of order and chaos. Spencer of course was the outside stepchild who thought he held the key to their freedom. The sad thing is that Spencer knew at any moment they could say to hell with him and end his life. Spencer was a criminal, but he was not gutter and did not respect the rules of the street like Ace, Picasso, and John Paul.

It didn't matter that Ace, Picasso and John Paul had poured their filthy money into legitimate moneymaking opportunities; they still knew how to get down and dirty. Their hands would always be stained with blood and their hearts made of stone. When they were boys, they cooked rocks and wrapped robust herbs in crisp white paper that made one travel beyond this earth. They pimped pure white ladies that traveled through awaiting nostrils delivering intense pleasure. They made dirty boys travel through tight veins leaving sons, mothers, and daughters helpless. They bought fast cars, lavish homes and on the surface lived a life that dreams were made of. Tyger was no different from the men she loved, she reaped the benefits of their exploits and they would always protect her. Although she tried hard to deny who she really was at her core, given the opportunity she would do whatever she needed to protect those that she loved. In the beginning, they were all young flashy and fly. As time passed and everyone grew older, they became hardcore wealthy men and women that would never mentally escape *The Hole.*

Chapter Three

Before heading to the police station to answer questions about the last time she saw Spencer, Tyger and the detectives were rerouted to the coroner's office so she could officially identify the body. Although it seemed a rather morbid way to spend the afternoon, Tyger was anxious to identify Spencer's body. The events surrounding Spencer's death seemed surreal. At any moment, Tyger was expecting to wake up and realize the past six months had all been one big, twisted dream. Spencer's death was inevitable, no one really knew when or where it would happen, but he was on everyone's hit list. No one expected Spencer would die the way he did.

Tyger exited her car and walked toward Detective Arias and Officer Cavanaugh waiting to escort her to identify Spencer's body. Entering the building, she was greeted with sympathetic stares from her former colleagues. In the midst of handshakes, hugs and remorse-filled greetings, Tyger played the role of the grief-stricken widow as best she could.

Standing in the middle of a sea of familiar faces, Tyger acknowledged those that wished her well and those who wondered if she killed her husband or if she hired someone to do the dirty deed. Nevertheless, like the wife of a politician, she breezed through shaking each person's hand and addressing him or her by name. Tyger's days as the Assistant District Attorney trained her to never forget names or faces. Those names that she did not know, she quickly scanned their badges and addressed them personally. Whiskey taught his children to never meet a stranger and to make even the smallest person feel larger than life. People are more inclined to help you without question when you treat them well.

Growing tired of Tyger's fanfare, Detective Arias reminded her that the coroner was waiting. Turning quickly without making eye contact with the Detective, Tyger walked toward the double doors marked "Authorized Personnel Only." The detective pressed the red button on the wall and waited for the doors to open.

Almost immediately, a gust of wind blew Tyger's hair as the door's swung open. Hesitating for a few moments, Tyger placed one foot in front of the other crossing the threshold. Tyger stopped mid-stride and stared down the corridor void of any signs of human life. Suddenly, her legs grew weak and she was unable to move. She was experiencing an uneasy unexpected sentiment in the pit of her stomach. Was it the shock of seeing Spencer's lifeless body? Was it guilt for the role she played in his inhumane disposal? Was it the fact that this was just the beginning of what could be a long investigation or was it genuine remorse for the loss of Spencer's life? Whatever was going on inside her was real, but she could not tie her physical apprehension to a particular emotion.

Detective Arias reached out to Tyger, "Mrs. Benedict, are you ok? Do you need to sit down?" Tyger placed her hand on her chest and inhaled, taking two deep breaths.

"Thank you Detective, I'm fine. Just a little overwhelmed. I guess I'm not as prepared as I thought. I just need to catch my breath for a moment."

"Just take all the time you need…"

Tyger nodded her head, "I'm fine now, please let's just continue."

Tyger cleared her throat, took one deep breath and walked through the double doors and down the long hallway. The corridor was narrow with gurney's and other medical equipment lining both sides of the wall. Tyger was no stranger to the morgue; during her early years as a public defender, she made several trips to see the coroner. Walking down the distant hallway with the light bouncing off the tile floor listening to the sound of her heels echo in her eardrum, Tyger could not help but think of the aftermath that was sure to come.

Up until that moment, Tyger was sure that Spencer's murder was an open-and-shut case. There were no witnesses willing to come forward with the truth about what happened that night. Tyger was eight months pregnant the night Spencer went missing and could not conceivably kill a grown man and throw his body into the lake. Everything appeared to be circumstantial, but Tyger knew she had won cases with much less.

With her heart fluttering in her chest like a caged butterfly needing to escape, Tyger slowly continued down the corridor. The sound of her heels hitting the tile floor echoed in her ear almost piercing her eardrum. Looking down at the beige tile with specks of ghastly green and uneventful shades of yellow, Tyger could see the shadows of her two companions lurking behind her. Finally, reaching the door to where her husband's body was held, she stopped and waited for one of the men to open the door for her. She held her stomach in close and arrested her breath to prepare for what was to come. This was no ordinary identification process. Tyger was getting ready to see the raw and gritty image of what her husband looked like after being trapped at the bottom of the lake for six grueling winter months. She knew that this was an old tactic that had been used on suspects in the past. They wanted to see how she would react to seeing Spencer's body, but she was no stranger to seeing fresh bodies being pulled out of the most horrid conditions.

Anxious to enter the room, Officer Cavanaugh reached out and opened the door for Tyger. Tyger entered the room to find one of her old colleagues Dr. Milan standing across the room waiting to greet her. Dr. Eugene Milan and Tyger had been old friends. She had known Dr. Milan since she was in law school. Dr. Milan taught a Forensic Science class that, Tyger, Picasso and Spencer were all enrolled in. Tyger smiled at the sight of Dr. Milan. She felt more relaxed and confident that this would be a quick visit. Walking into the room, Tyger reached out to hug the doctor.

"Eugene, it's great to see a friendly face." Dr. Milan embraced Tyger.

"Tyger, I'm so sorry that we had to see each other under these circumstances."

"I know, this has been such a difficult time these past few months. It's hell not knowing where someone is, if they're alive or dead. Hoping they're ok and then this, but we can't say we didn't know it was a possibility..."

"You know I've known Spencer for a long time. Longer than you have as a matter of fact."

Not wanting to let the police know just how close Dr. Milan and the Benedict's were, Tyger quickly diverted attention back to the body lying a few feet away.

"I'm just glad that Spencer is in your hands. I know you'll do everything possible to get to the bottom of this, so we can let him rest in peace.

"Yes, well then I suppose it's time." Dr. Milan walked over to the metal table where Spencer's body lay with a sheet draped over him. Tyger followed behind him, without flinching she turned her attention toward the body under the sheet appearing not to notice the ropes she used to tie her husband's hands and feet lying on the table next to the body. To add a little improv to the moment, Tyger simply asked, "Ropes?" Dr. Milan nodded his head and pointed toward the table, "Spencer's hands and feet were tied together with those ropes."

Pretending to express her disappointment, Tyger took a deep breath and pursed her lips together. The detectives stood a few feet away from Tyger on the opposite side of her. Detective Arias kept his eyes glued on her waiting for her reaction. With his hand resting on the sheet, Dr. Milan looked over at Tyger. "Tyger, please understand when Spencer was found early this morning, his body was practically frozen. He's probably been in that lake all winter..."

Tyger, interrupted Dr. Milan, "Doc, I've prepared myself for what I'm about to see, let's just get this over with, please."

Dr. Milan slowly uncovered the body revealing the body of Spencer Benedict III. Spencer's body was surprisingly well preserved. The icy water had kept Spencer's body as if he'd been preserved in a museum. There he was, the man of the hour, naked as the day he was born. Tyger stood over her husband staring at him trying to conjure up a tear or two, but she had nothing to give. Deep down, all she really wanted was to confirm Spencer was dead. She wanted to make sure his murder wasn't all just one bad dream. With her hands tightly gripping her purse, they started to burn like they did the night she dragged his heavy dead body across the yard in a blizzard. Staring at him she thought of how volatile their marriage had been. She thought of what an asshole he'd been to everyone he knew, even his own mother. Realizing that her facial expressions could never hide her true feelings, Tyger figured she needed to shut down quick.

She looked up at Detective Arias, "This is my husband, this is Spencer Benedict III, he looks just like he did the last time that I saw him."

Detective Arias nodded his head, "Thank you Mrs. Benedict we can go now. I know you're anxious to put this day behind you."

Tyger nodded in agreement, "Yes detective, we still have to make a stop at the station so I can make my official statement.

"Actually, Mrs. Benedict that won't be necessary. I'm quite sure we'll be seeing you again soon. Please make yourself available…"

Tyger narrowed her eyes and looked straight at Detective Arias, "You know where you can find me and I'm quite familiar with how to get to the police station. You have my full cooperation."

Tyger did not wait for a response from Detective Arias, she turned toward Dr. Milan. "Eugene, how soon before you complete an autopsy?"

"Spencer is top priority. I should have something conclusive by tomorrow before five p.m. The toxicology reports will take longer, but we will know what we need to know by tomorrow. I've already done some preliminary examinations and I'm quite sure I will have a definitive answer fairly quickly."

Detective Arias quickly interjected, "Mrs. Benedict, this is still a murder investigation, Dr. Milan will let me know the exact cause of death and I will contact you."

Turning toward Detective Arias and locking eyes, Tyger changed her tone, "Detective Arias and Officer Cavanaugh, this is *my* husband lying on this table, unless I am a suspect, as his widow, I have the right to ask the medical examiner anything that I choose. If I am a suspect, as counsel representing myself at this moment, I have the right to know the victim's cause of death. Now, if I have graduated from person of interest to suspect, please do tell so that I may seek appropriate legal counsel."

Not giving either of the men a chance to respond, Tyger abruptly turned her back to the two men and focused her attention on Dr. Milan. "Eugene, I think this is just a bit much for me. I have developed a terrible headache. I will need to go and make funeral arrangements for my husband. Thank you so much for your help and please take care of Spencer. We will talk soon." Walking toward the door, Tyger turned toward both the men, "Gentleman, I'm sure I'll be seeing the two of you sooner than I'd like. Until then, take care."

Tyger tucked her clutch under her arm and walked toward the door with her heels hitting the tile floor like horseshoes hitting asphalt. The sound was more confident than before. Tyger had come to see what she needed to see, now she had to make sure she could handle whatever came next. She knew the coroner's report would say *blunt force trauma*. There were two things Tyger knew that the police did not; Dr. Milan was more than just an old professor and familiar colleague. He owed Tyger his life and he would do anything to protect her. Tyger also knew that after the cause of death was determined, the police would come to her home to determine if that's where Spencer was killed. The house had been treated like a crime scene cleanup; everything had been erased, burned, painted, and replaced. There was no indication that a crime had been committed. The object that had been used to render Spencer's fatal blow would never ever be found and everything seemed to be in order just in case the house would be searched. All of the physical evidence had been taken care of. All Tyger needed to do was sit back, watch and play the game.

Chapter Four

A fter leaving the coroner's office Tyger felt relieved; she would no longer have to watch and wait for Spencer's body to wash up in her back yard. Now more than ever she needed to figure out her next move. Tyger knew she would see more of Detective Arias than she wanted. The only thing keeping her above suspicion was the fact that she was eight months pregnant and in labor the night Spencer went missing. The city was experiencing a winter storm that night and there is no way that a woman who was eight months pregnant could throw a grown man in the lake. When she arrived at the hospital, she told them she had fallen down the stairs. Tyger rehearsed this defense over in her mind since that night. She had erased all evidence of the murder-taking place in the house, but that was not enough to keep the detective at bay.

Tyger's mind was racing with what "if's" and "should haves" she almost forgot she needed to get back home to Nina. Tyger reached out to call Genoa to inform her that she was on her way back home. Before the thought escaped her head, the screen in front of her lit up with "Ace" flashing. Tyger yelled, "answer" and waited anxiously to hear Ace's voice. Hearing Ace's voice on the other end made her melt.

"Hey there!"

Tyger could hear Ace smiling through the phone. Ace's voice was masculine and strong. Tyger's body quivered from the power in his tone. Ace was excited to speak with Tyger. Her soft and sensuous voice always made him feel warm and reassured. After realizing he was turning into a big wuss, Ace changed his tone,

"So, I hear you had a pretty interesting morning, everything ok?"

"Yeah, everything is ok for now…" Tyger paused, "I was escorted to the Coroner's office to identify Spencer's body."

Being careful not to discuss any details, Ace revealed a cynical laugh, "That doesn't surprise me. I think everything will be fine."

That was code for, *"we'll talk about it in person later."* Tyger and Ace continued to engage in ambiguous chatter. Finally, Ace asked, "So what time will I be expecting you tonight?"

Tyger hesitated to answer Ace. Although she could not honor his request to see her, she still reveled in the idea that he missed her. With reluctance and regret Tyger explained, "I'm sorry I can't make it tonight. I promised Nina we would spend the evening eating popcorn and watching movies. I couldn't dare disappoint her." Ace retracted his request; he would never put himself before Nina.

"Well of course my little princess is more important than my burning loins…" Ace laughed at his own humor as he continued, "Why don't I come by and join you ladies?"

Tyger immediately wanted to say yes, but she hesitated once again, "That does sound nice, but I will have to ask Nina if it's ok first."

"Well, I have nothing to worry about; my girl loves her uncle Ace. Just call me and let me know what time to be there."

Tyger knew Nina wouldn't mind Ace joining them for the evening. Nina loved Ace more than her own father. Nina and Ace had a special relationship. Even though her needs were special and sometimes challenging, in her mysterious way she understood to never mention Ace's name in front of Spencer. Tyger had taught Nina about secrets and how important it was to keep secrets. Ace was a treasured secret that Nina kept close to her heart.

Nina was born with Down's Syndrome. She was beautiful with brilliant brown eyes and long black braids. When she smiled, her eyes closed and became small creases beneath her brows. Her smile lit up the entire room. She was a ray of sunshine and a definite reassurance that Tyger's entire marriage to Spencer was not in vain. Ace doted on Nina; he wished he were Nina's father.

After engaging in fifteen minutes of flirtatious chatter, Tyger and Ace ended the call. Immediately, after hanging up, each of them reminisced about the first time they met.

Even at seventeen, Ace Del Toro was perhaps the most beautiful creature Tyger had ever laid her eyes on. At six-foot-four Ace stood perfectly erect with a broad chest. His cold black hair highlighted his olive-colored skin. His strong chiseled jaw line was a clear indication of his power and strength. Ace's only physical flaw was the four-inch crescent shaped scar on his right cheek that curved at the top of his lip. The scar made him even more desirable.

Ace was smooth and quiet with impeccable style. His clothes were finely tailored. He wore diamond cufflinks and handcrafted shoes imported from Italy. Ace had never been seen in a sweat suit or much leisurewear. At first glance in a finely tailored suit one can never tell that this perfectly fine specimen of manhood could rip your heart out of your chest with his bare hands.

Ironically, Ace was a God-fearing man and attended Mass and confession faithfully. He was never without his rosary beads. Ace said he knew who he was and what he has done; only God can judge him.

Ace was born to a Puerto Rican mother and a Cuban father. He had an older brother that he loathed. In all the years they've known each other Ace had only spoken of his family twice that Tyger could remember. All Tyger really knew of Ace's family dynamic was that his mother and brother were still alive living somewhere in New York.

The name on Ace's birth certificate was Asa Del Toro, when he arrived in Detroit, he had a strong New York accent so people started calling him Brooklyn Ace and it stuck with him.

Ace and Tyger met when she was fifteen and he was seventeen. They met at a neighborhood party that Tyger was forbidden to attend.

Ace was from an area of town that was off limits to Tyger and her siblings. Tyger and Ace were from the same, yet different worlds. They lived in separate communities within different cultures in Southwest Detroit. Ace grew up with his grandmother in a two family flat in Mexican Town near I-75 and Vernor. Tyger grew up with her family a few miles down the freeway, neither welcomed with open arms in the other's community. Ace was sent to live with his grandmother as a means of discipline when he was thirteen. Both Ace and Tyger were from and end of the earth that the world had forgotten about.

Against Whiskey's wishes, Tyger and Bella followed John Paul, Picasso and Shakespeare to a late-night party. Standing on the wall watching everyone in the basement grind and wind around the dance floor, Tyger felt an uninvited voyeuristic gaze. When she looked across the room, she found Ace staring at her. When their eyes met Ace slowly walked across the dimly lit basement with the glow of the red light following him. Once he approached Tyger he licked his full ripe lips and introduced himself, "My name is Asa, but my friends call me Ace."

Without displaying a smile, Tyger replied, "Well Asa, you can't call me at all." Tyger and Bella walked up the basement stairs and left Ace standing alone.

That Monday after the party Tyger walked out of her school to find Ace standing on the sidewalk waiting for her. From that moment, Ace and Tyger became a part of each other. Ace is like a bad habit that Tyger cannot and does not wish to break. Ace is as much a part of Tyger as the warm blood that flows through her veins.

In a perfect world Tyger would have married Ace Del Toro and had a house full of half -breed babies, but the streets is the one thing that Ace loved more than Tyger. Spencer was Tyger's chance to be the person that she always wanted to be, or so she thought.

Ace has never accepted the fact that Tyger chose to marry Spencer instead of him. For a long time Tyger tried to forget that Ace existed, but it was damn near impossible. Ace and Picasso had become business partners and there was no avoiding him. One day Tyger found out that Ace planned to marry a neighborhood girl named Maria Padilla in a private ceremony at St. Stephens off the Boulevard. Tyger dressed in the most tastefully revealing dress allowed in the House of God and strutted down to the church. Once she arrived Ace and Tyger disappeared into a private room for approximately three minutes. After Ace and Tyger exited that private room, poor Maria Padilla left the church with nothing. Ace and Tyger left the church with an understanding; she would leave Spencer and be with him when the time was right. Unfortunately, keeping that promise would take a bit longer than Tyger planned.

Ace was a different type of man than Spencer. Spencer played the role of a wanna be gangster, but Ace was the real deal. Ace was like a quiet storm, he didn't believe in arguing or repeating himself, but he believed in severely punishing those who crossed him. He didn't mind getting his hands dirty.

Spencer was totally white collar. He would never get his hands dirty. Spencer was greedy and careless. He was motivated solely by money. He talked a good game and sold a shit load of wolf tickets. Spencer bought his power, but Ace earned respect and commanded power. Spencer was loud and loved to be seen. He would argue his point until he was exhausted, or he thought you were defeated. Spencer was arrogant and flaunted his wealth. The truth was Tyger was never afraid of Spencer, the real demon in the family was Spencer's father S.B. Tyger never believed that Spencer would kill her, but she was certain that S. B. would.

Spencer was aware of his wife's lifelong love affair with Ace, but he never confronted Tyger or Ace. Tyger was his smart and beautiful trophy wife that he needed to help him earn his robe and gavel. With her brilliant mind and incredible street smarts, Tyger was his secret weapon. She was the one that helped him win his cases. Spencer and Tyger had a marriage of convenience and one had something that the other one wanted. Tyger and Ace remained discreet so no one could ever confirm their affair. They had become masters at their little love game, they found creative ways to spend time together.

Tyger has never told Ace that Spencer physically abused her. That was an embarrassing secret that she kept tucked away. To avoid the discovery of her bruises, she would schedule her visits with Ace in-be- tween the fights with Spencer. The fights between Spencer and Tyger were often intense; the way Tyger handled Spencer, you would think he was just as tired of getting beaten as she was. But nonetheless Spencer's alcohol fueled rages continued leaving Tyger no choice but to defend herself.

Spencer knew he could never beat Ace, Picasso or John Paul, so he tried to do the next best thing; take away their freedom. On a hot summer night in July, three men attempted to rob and carjack Ace. Ace shot two of the men and the third fled the scene. The third man testified that there was no robbery and Ace killed his friends in cold blood. A witness testified that Ace called the men to meet him and shot them over drug money. When the car the men were driving was searched drugs were found at the scene. Ace was being tried on two counts of first-degree murder. Spencer was hopeful Ace would finally go to jail; His legitimate real-estate ventures and role of a businessman could not protect him. Years of evading the law had finally caught up with Ace. The entire setup was sloppy and appeared to be orchestrated by an amateur, but most of the judicial community was happy to catch Ace anyway that they could.

While Ace was on trial two men rolled up on Picasso at his club and attempted to kill him. Picasso got away with a flesh wound, but the two men were found dead twenty-four hours later. One of the men was found lying on the hood of a car with his index finger covered in blood. Inscribed on the hood of the car in blood was Picasso's name misspelled staged to look like he was identifying his killer. There was no doubt Picasso planned to avenge his shooting, but someone had beaten him to it. Picasso was not the one who pulled the trigger, nor did he hire someone else to do it.

Ace and Picasso were on the chopping block being setup; the dynamic duo would soon be cellmates. There was only one more loose end to tie up. Everyone scattered about nervously trying to figure out John Paul's fate. But he was one step ahead of the game. John Paul laid low for a while, not making waves of any kind. Tyger and Whiskey decided to call in a few favors to get to the bottom of who was trying to destroy them.

They all knew low-level bottom feeding criminals couldn't keep their mouths shut for the right price. They knew a snitch would always sell out to the highest bidder. Everyone who wanted to be somebody was itching for a chance to get in Whiskey's good graces. Whiskey was well connected; he knew just about everyone that was anyone. People were more than happy to sing like beautiful blue birds. It didn't take long for Tyger to find out Spencer's law partner Kyle Cain helped Spencer arrange the unfortunate incidents that had befallen Ace and Picasso.

Typically, where you find a man in power that has no idea how to treat people, you will find an unhappy driver or personal assistant itching to spill the beans for a few bucks and a promise of a well-connected position. Thanks to Kyle Cain's driver/personal assistant, Tyger learned all she needed to know about Spencer's plan. Tyger, John Paul and Whiskey paid Kyle a visit one afternoon, the following day a nicely wrapped box in neat brown paper packaging showed up at the Benedict home addressed to Spencer. Inside the box was a recording of a conversation between Kyle Cain and Spencer accompanied by Kyle Cain's right ear.

Unfortunately, because of his partnership with Spencer and willingness to destroy Picasso and Ace, Kyle Cain had been thinly spread all over the state of Michigan. The assistant who graciously spilled the beans about Kyle and Spencer's plan met his demise as well; you can never trust a snitch no matter how resourceful they may be. Tyger's family had been saved, the charges were dropped against Ace and Picasso.

Fortunately, Tyger learned among the names on Spencer's list to be destroyed was hers. There was no indication how she would meet her gruesome fate, but there was something waiting for her. Spencer planned to eliminate anyone who stood between him and a multi-million-dollar land development deal.

Picasso, John Paul and Tyger had purchased most of the houses within 3 blocks of where they grew up. They were planning to build affordable housing, just as Ace had done in his old neighborhood. Spencer was set on developing those areas into something more lucrative for him. Spencer and Kyle Cain purchased other houses in the area under another company. Spencer had a two-million-dollar life insurance policy on Tyger. He knew upon her death she would leave all of her assets to their daughter Nina. Spencer assumed he would care for his daughter after her mother's death and have access to all that was left to her. Spencer thought there was no one else Tyger would entrust Nina to. Tyger's sister Bella was a dope addict. Her mother Dee Dee was an irresponsible whore. Her brother John Paul was out of the question. Her father Whiskey had the heart of hustler and couldn't devote his life to caring for a special needs child. Her best friend Picasso, well there was really no explanation needed.

These were all the reasons Spencer had conjured up in his mind why he would never question the validity of the will Tyger had shown him. For face value, Tyger and Spencer Benedict had locked their wills up in the safe deposit box for safekeeping. They both appeared to be open and honest about the contents in both documents. Fortunately, the will belonging to Tyger that was housed in that safe deposit box wasn't worth the paper it was printed on. Upon Tyger's death, everyone would be surprised to find out Tyger left everything she owned not to her child but to her sister Piper. Not even Piper had knowledge of this. Picasso Kennard was the Executor of Tyger's estate, he would ensure Tyger's wishes were carried out. Tyger understood Picasso could not physically care for her child, but she trusted he would do every-thing in is power to make sure Nina had everything she could ever need and want.

After tying up all the loose ends surrounding the Kyle Cain and Spencer debacle, John Paul decided he needed to disappear; he relocated without leaving a forwarding address. Unlike his sister Piper, John Paul never writes, but he calls from time to time from an "Unknown Number."

The next few weeks after Ace's trial was priceless; Spencer spent many nights pacing the floor wondering when, where and how Ace was going to seek revenge. Spencer had no idea it was his own wife that he should be afraid of. Spencer stopped sleeping and eating. He was so desperate he asked Tyger to intervene on his behalf. Shit had gotten real and the game that he attempted to play had played out. His nerves were so bad any little unexpected noise would send him into orbit. Night after night Tyger was amused by Spencer's nervous antics. Spencer hired a bodyguard and increased security around the house. Not even Spencer's father S.B. could save him from Ace Del Toro and Picasso Kennard.

After weeks of staying out of sight, Ace warned Tyger of Spencer's upcoming demise. Ace wanted to make sure she nor Nina were anywhere near Spencer when he was killed. Tyger reminded Ace why he wasn't sitting in a 6x6 prison cell calling his new woman Larry. He owed his freedom to Tyger; all she wanted in return was to be the one to take Spencer out. Ace was adamant about Tyger not getting her hands dirty. He didn't want her to get caught up in anything that would cost her freedom or her life. Tyger begged Ace to be patient and let her take care of Spencer. For the first time Tyger confessed to Ace what her life with Spencer had truly been. She told him about the emotional and physical abuse, she shared every detail hoping Ace would understand her overwhelming need to take Spencer's life. Tyger explained her one true pleasure in life was to watch as the life drained from Spencer's eyes as she took his life. Just when it seemed Ace was going to leave everything up to Tyger, she walked out of her restaurant one afternoon and found a note on the seat of her car that read, "No deal, one bullet for every time he put his hands on you." Every day Spencer left the house, Tyger waited to get the phone call that he'd been found dead. Instead, he walked his ass through the door every night alive. Tyger never imagined it would all come to an end on that cold and stormy winter night in November. Only three people were present the night Spencer was killed. The third person was Spencer, and dead men tell no tales.

Chapter Five

Arriving home carrying the burden of what was yet to come, Tyger remained focused on Nina and her safety. She wanted to be alone with her daughter and enjoy a quiet evening with just the two of them. Tyger gave Lillian, the housekeeper, the night off and sent Genoa and Dee Dee out on the town. Genoa and Dee Dee had become fast friends. Sadness and regret was a common bond that they both shared. Both women were immensely unhappy with the choices they'd made so, they chose to live vicariously through Tyger. Genoa and Dee Dee both secretly competed for Tyger's attention. Genoa cherished the time she and Tyger spent together. Her own son was a no-account demon seed that treated Genoa like trash. When Tyger came along, she'd finally had the child she longed for. Dee Dee spent most of her days wishing her own children loved her unconditionally without reservation, but her little vacation with Judge Grey and her self-centered attitude had proved her unfit and untrustworthy.

Genoa and Dee Dee left as Tyger and Nina retired to the theatre room to enjoy their girl's night. After settling in for a night of mommy and me time, the sound of the doorbell rang throughout the house. Tyger winced in disgust and tried to figure out who could be on the other side of the door. Spencer's death had become a welcome mat for house guests. Before John Paul left, he and Picasso were regular visitors at the Benedict home. Tyger made huge meals in the middle of the week and invited friends and family. With the exception of a dead husband floating in the lake behind the house, Tyger's life was normal for once. The only link in the chain left to be cut was her father-in-law, S.B.

S.B. and Spencer had a strange relationship that only the two of them understood. There was no real warmth or father-son love between the two. Genoa expressed on more than one occasion her deepest regret for giving birth to Spencer. Since Tyger entered her life, Genoa was able to have some sort of life outside of trying to maintain her sobriety and sanity. Spencer was morally deviant like his father. S.B. and Spencer were so much alike, one couldn't stand to look at the other. No matter how they loathed each other, when it came to chaos and destruction they still stuck together like glue. Tyger had escaped the stench of the hole by bearing the Benedict name, but her intellect and inbred street smarts kept her on top. Tyger knew at some point she would need Genoa in order to escape the clutches of the Benedict men. As powerless as Genoa believed she was, Tyger taught her to be resourceful and use her position in society to her advantage. Spencer and S.B. worked hard to preserve the family name. Spencer was heartbroken when Nina was born with special needs; he needed a son to carry on his name. Tyger's pregnancy was Spencer's second attempt at preserving his legacy.

Traveling to the door with Nina by her side, Tyger wondered who could be on the other side of the door. Approaching the door, she peered through the glass, but there was no one there. Opening the door and carefully sticking her head through the opening, there was still no one to be found. Startled by Nina's cry, "It's cold" Tyger gripped the handle to close the door. Just before the door closed, Tyger noticed Detective Arias' car parked across the courtyard. Almost camouflaged by the darkness of night, the detective's midnight black SUV was hiding in plain sight. Grabbing Nina's hand, Tyger stood in the foyer trying to figure out where this man could be.

Tyger led Nina through the house by her hand peeking through the windows searching for Detective Arias through the yard as she hurried through the house. She knew he was outside somewhere snooping around. Realizing Detective Arias was behind the house peering out at the lake, Tyger dashed to the back of the house with Nina in tow.

Standing in the kitchen hidden by the absence of light, Tyger stared out the French doors leading out back. Tyger watched as Detective Arias stood on the boat dock staring into the water. Anxiously needing to confront the detective Tyger leaned down and kissed Nina on the forehead. She instructed Nina to stay in the house and remain in the window where she could see her. Walking to the billiards room, Tyger grabbed one of the barstools, placed it in front of the window and ordered Nina not to move a muscle. Pulling her sweater tight across her body, covering her hands with her sleeves, Tyger opened the door and headed into the night.

Landing on the boat dock, the sound of Tyger's footsteps startled the detective. Turning abruptly toward Tyger, he offered a quick explanation, "Mrs. Benedict, I didn't think you were home so, I thought I'd come out here and see what I could find."

Appalled, her words spat ice cycles as cold as the frigid Michigan spring temperature, "I'm assuming since you're snooping around in my backyard you have a warrant? This is private property; you have five minutes to leave before I have you removed."

Oddly aroused by her boldness in giving him an unexpected tongue-lashing the detective tried to redeem himself from his dreadful slip of the tongue, "Please Mrs. Benedict, I didn't mean to intrude. I'm just doing my job."

Realizing she needed to calm down before she made herself appear guilty, Tyger offered an apology, "Look Detective, I apologize for my tone, but you do realize you can't just lurk around my home in the dead of night. My husband was found dead this morning and we have no idea who did it. You're a live target out here alone in the dark. We really don't need any more dead bodies around here."

As the moonlight cast a shadow on Tyger's face, Detective Arias became lost in her eyes. Feeling uncomfortable from his pining gaze, Tyger inconspicuously danced to Detective Arias left and began to face her house. Now shining on Detective Arias, the moonlight revealed that familiar look in his eye Tyger noticed earlier in the day.

Moving a stray strand of hair behind her ear, Tyger lowered her head and looked back in the detective's direction,

"Listen detective it's freezing out here and I have to get back to my daughter, exactly why are you here?"

"Please, call me Aiden."

"Alright Aiden, what do you want?"

Paralyzed by Tyger's beauty, words escaped him. Placing his hands in his pockets and slightly tilting his head, he looked into Tyger's eyes and took a deep breath, "I know I'm out of line for saying this, but I can't understand why a woman as beautiful as you ended up with both Spencer Benedict and Ace Del Toro."

Boiling inside from his uninvited invasion of her privacy, Tyger carefully swallowed the venomous words that were forming in her throat. Trying to avoid saying something she'd regret, Tyger looked away for a few seconds. Looking toward the house, she saw Nina still waiting patiently in her chair; she took a deep breath and looked back at Aiden.

"Aiden, you seem to have no home training whatsoever. You come to my home at an ungodly hour and snoop around my property, then you stand out her in the freezing cold staring at me like I'm a gazelle and you're a hungry lion. To make matters worse you have the audacity to ask me why I married my dead husband that you fished out of the lake less than twenty-four hours ago? Detective Arias, excuse me, I mean Aiden, you seem to have some mighty big balls right now, but you need to watch your step, I would hate to have to deflate them. "

Tyger and Aiden stood there in yet another awkward silence. Feeling she needed to lay her cards on the table and leave no stone unturned, Tyger broke her silence, "My relationship with Ace Del Toro is no secret. So you won't be confused, let me run it down for you Detective. Ace and I have known one another since high school. I will make no apologies for our relationship. The fact is, this is grown folks business and what happens between a man and woman is between that man and that woman. Just so we're clear, unless I'm a suspect in my husband's murder my personal escapades are off limits."

Just as Aiden parted his lips to speak, Tyger interrupted, "Although my husband is dead, this is still his house and you will respect him in his absence. I can assure you I did not kill my husband and if you want to discuss that, then call me down to the station."

Not giving Aiden a change to respond, Tyger turned toward the house and walked back up the steps. Stopping in midstride, she turned and looked back at Aiden, "Detective Arias….Your crime scene is out there in the middle of the lake. I don't want to see you out here again without a warrant."

Watching Tyger walk back toward the house, Aiden yelled out, "I know you didn't kill your husband. But he didn't end up in the lake by himself and I just don't think a woman who was eight months pregnant put him there. You can tell Ace Del Toro and Picasso Kennard that I'll be calling on them soon."

Tyger turned back toward Aiden, stared him straight in the eye, "I'm certain they're already expecting you."

Chapter Six

With Nina no longer in her sight, Tyger trotted up the hill back to the house. Trembling and sweating, her heart almost escaped her chest. Walking into the house Tyger frantically yelled Nina's name. Just as Tyger swooned into full panic mode, a male voice bellowed through the house; it was Picasso. Trying to catch her breath, Tyger stood in the middle of the hallway staring at Picasso wearing a huge Dumbo grin.

"I heard we were having movie night."

Before Tyger could respond to Picasso, Ace emerged from the kitchen. Tyger couldn't believe how careless they were.

"Do you people realize I am in the middle of a murder investigation, where, by the way you two are also suspects? What the hell are you thinking? Didn't you see the big black SUV sitting in my driveway with a police light in the window?"

Ignoring her rant, Ace walked toward Tyger and kissed her on her forehead, "Yes, of course we saw it. We had just pulled in behind the trees and turned the lights off when he pulled up; he didn't see us. We sat in the car and watched him ring the doorbell and walk around to the house. We saw you open the door and look out. When we saw him walk around the house, we knew he was headed out back to the boat dock. We figured when you didn't see anyone at the door you would automatically check the back of the house. We've been here the whole time. Nina didn't move until she saw you coming back up the hill."

Like a light switch, Ace flipped from comfort to aggravation. Ace commanded, "First thing tomorrow morning you're getting a new gate. That piece of shit out there is no good. How did that detective just roll up in here anyway?"

"How the hell should I know? Maybe you left the gate open when you made your way through." Ace and Tyger began to argue; screaming, Nina put her hands over her ears. Picasso ran over to her and scooped her up in his arms. Nina wrapped her arms around his neck and laid her head on his shoulder. Picasso and Nina walked toward the theater room and left Tyger and Ace standing in the middle of the floor eyeballing each other.

Making sure Picasso and Nina were out of sight, Ace stepped toward Tyger, "Stay the hell away from that damn detective. I don't like the way he looks at you. Don't ever let him in this house unless he has a warrant. Tomorrow you get another gate and prepare to move out of this house. This house has too many bad memories for you and Nina."

There was something oddly different about Ace's angst toward Detective Arias. She could tell by the look in his eyes he was serious. Stunned, Tyger didn't know what to say, but she couldn't remain silent, "Ace!'

Ace narrowed his eyes and raised his brow, "Tyger this is not up for discussion. I don't want you near that man. Spencer is dead and you have no reason to live in this house. You can't use Nina as an excuse to stay away from me anymore. It's been ten years and I'm tired of waiting on you to make a decision about us. After this investigation is over and all this bullshit is said and done there will be major changes."

Confident that he'd just laid down the law, Ace turned and followed Picasso and Nina. Tyger called out to him, "Ace Del Toro!"

He looked back at her and spoke in a low commanding tone, "The discussion is over for the night, now come on let's go enjoy the movie…"

Remembering the way Spencer used to talk to her she folded her arms and flashed a disappointed yet devious look at Ace. Immediately realizing his tone had been less than desirable, he didn't know what to say to her. Ace worked hard not to treat Tyger like she was something he owned. Tyger was the one thing in his life he tried hard not to control. He afforded her more liberties than anyone else in his life. Begging her forgiveness with his eyes, he walked toward her and reached out to embrace her.

Throwing her hand in Ace's face, Tyger was furious, "Let's get one damn thing straight, I am not your property and you will not demand that I do anything. I love you Ace, but I cannot and will not allow another man to treat me like shit, not even you. Now, get the hell out'a my house, you and I have nothing left to discuss this evening."

Not waiting for Ace's response, she turned and walked toward the media room and never looked back. Burning a hole in Tyger's back with his eyes, Ace suddenly felt an unwelcome gaze fall upon him. With the hair on the back of his neck standing at attention, Ace glanced over at the window and noticed Aiden staring into the house. Aiden and Ace stood in the middle of a bizarre silent exchange; neither one of the men said a word. Just as quickly as he appeared, Aiden shot Ace a cynical wink and disappeared into the night.

The sight of Aiden sparked a fire inside of Ace that made his soul smolder with disgust. This was a feeling that had lived inside Ace for decades. There was something between this detective and this beast that could only be settled with bloodshed. Trying to control the animalistic rage that was roaring inside, Ace stood silently with his eyes closed breathing in the warm atmosphere of the house. Ace tried to think of Tyger and her beautiful cocoa skin. He thought of Nina and her sweet smile. He tried to think of anything good and decent that would stop him from devouring Aiden Arias. But there was no use, the damage had already been done, the image of Aiden standing a few feet away had already been etched on the lobes of Ace's brain.

Heading toward the door, Ace turned and opened the door almost ripping it from the frame and walked out into the dark Detroit night in search of redemption. Leaving Picasso behind, Ace sped down the driveway. As the gate opened, Ace's phone rang. Trying to keep his eyes in front of him and identify the caller, Ace looked at the screen to see who was calling. As the robotic announcement "Anonymous Caller" filled the air Ace grew frustrated. Failing to navigate the car and control his emotions, Ace almost crashed into the iron gate that was taking an eternity to open. Listening to the mind-numbing rings one after the other, Ace's blood started to boil. Aggressively yelling "answer", the phone would not recognize Ace's voice. He reached out and pressed *answer*. The voice on the other end answered, "I've been waiting for this day."

"I'm sure you have, meet me at Belle Isle in front of the old zoo in twenty minutes."

Ace hung up the phone without waiting for a response. Filled with adrenalin and riddled with the uncertainty of his meeting, Ace drove through the city at top speed. Holding on to the hope that he would spare Aiden's life he prayed aloud. Ace's prayer bellowed through the car, "Please Lord I don't want to kill him, please don't let me kill him… please don't let me kill him."

His lips vibrating from his fervent repetition, Ace quietly pulled into the space next to a black SUV with tinted windows absent of light. Exiting their vehicles, the two men met in the middle of the street landing within less than twelve inches of the other. Aiden extended his hand to Ace; Ace declined to shake Aiden's hand. Trying to figure out if he were real, Ace stared into Aiden's eyes. Breaking his silence, Aiden smiled, "It's been a long-time little brother."

"Not long enough."

"Is this how you greet your brother after all these years?"

"You stopped being my brother a long time ago."

Moving out of Ace's direct path, Aiden stepped back a few inches, sat on the hood of Ace's car, and placed his foot on the bumper, "I'm sure you don't mind if I have a seat, do you?" Without uttering a word, Ace calmly reached in his pocket and pulled out a pack of gum. Ace removed a stick from the wrapper, popped it in his mouth, and placed the pack back in his pocket. Slowly chewing the gum feeling the flavor on his tongue, Ace masked the bitter taste of Aiden's obvious gesture of disrespect. Making sure that they were alone, Ace surveyed his environment. Still wearing a sheepish grin Aiden mocked Ace, "Damn brother, are you paranoid? You scared to talk to me, you think I'm wearing a wire?"

Ace replied, "I know you're not wearing a wire, you're smarter than that. It looks like someone is going around dumping bodies in the lake, so I need to keep my eyes open at all times."

Aiden revealed a sarcastic laugh, "Come on Ace, you don't have to pretend with me, I'm not wearing a wire. I know you killed Spencer, but I just can't prove it right now."

"I'm not losing sleep over this Spencer Benedict bullshit. I don't give a damn what you believe, I called you here as my brother to give you a warning, you need to stay away from Tyger Benedict."

"Aww, isn't that sweet, my little brother wants to warn me to stay away from his girlfriend."

"There's nothing sweet about it. Don't get it twisted, I really don't give a damn about you, but I promised mama that I would respect our kinship and not rip your beating heart out of your chest."

"And how is mama, I haven't seen her since you sent her to some place where she won't even contact her own son. But I guess that's to be expected, you are her favorite."

"I don't control mama; she can contact whoever she wants. If she doesn't want to talk to her own son, that's something that you need to work out. Maybe you need to ask yourself what kind of son would stand around and watch while his father drug his mother around by her hair and beat her ass every day. You let Papi turn you into a monster that never respected mama.

Aiden let out a boisterous laugh "Monster, you call *me* a monster? Little brother, you forget that I know who you really are. I know where you come from and what you're made of. You're the one that was created by a monster. It was because of you that Papi treated mama the way he did."

Ace lashed out at Aiden, "That's a got damn lie, what happened to mama was Papi's fault. Papi was a weak, sick and twisted bastard that turned you into a weak little bitch like him."

Aiden jumped off the car and into Ace's face, "Is that why you killed Papi?"

"No, I killed Papi because I promised him that I would if he ever laid a hand on my mama again and I never break a promise, so back the fuck up out'a my face before I make good on this bullet that I owe you…"

"One way or another you're gonna pay for what you did to Papi."

"Papi got what he deserved, or did you forget that it was his debt that brought that man into the house to hurt mama. You seem to forget your father was a gambling drug addict that put his own family in danger. While you're calling me a monster, you forget that it was me who came back to New York to help you when there was a price on your head. It's because of me that you're not dead."

"So what you want me to thank you? Thank you for always making me look like a fool, like I can't take care of myself. Like my little brother has to always bail me out."

"If you want to be treated like man then act like one. You keep playing me for some cheap neophyte hustler. I been in this shit far too long not to be well connected. You can't hide your dirty little secrets behind that piece of shit badge, that don't mean shit to me. You think I don't know why you're here? You think I don't know that you're a fuckin snitch and that you had to leave New York? You think that I don't know that when you finally had the chance to put the bastard away that kidnapped and raped mama that you took money from him to keep him out of prison?"

Unable to speak, Aiden swallowed the lump in his throat. With a probing look, Ace starred into Aiden's eyes, "How could you let the man walk away that destroyed your mother's life? I gave him to you, I gave you the chance to be the hero, and you just screwed it up for money?"

Feeling his stomach churn in tiny knots, Aiden felt confused, "What do you mean you gave him to me?

"Before Papi died I made him tell me who attacked mama, I made him tell me who my biological seed was, and he told me, it was Jaivin Ortiz. I knew that Jaivin was in Miami and went to see him because I needed to see the monster that created me. I wanted to rip the breath from his body, but I left him for you to finish off. After everything you did to me, I knew that you needed a win. You were failing as a detective and everyone on the streets hated you. Mama saw you as the child that gave her so much grief and you needed to win. I'm the one that called you and tipped you off that Jaivin would be arriving in New York at the dock that night. I delivered him right to your doorstep and you let that man pay for your silence. You knew who he was because Papi said he told you who Jaivin was. He bragged that you were gonna put Jaivin away one day and I wanted that so badly for you. No matter how much I hated my own biological seed, I loved my big brother more. I wanted you to win, but you lost. I knew you didn't have the heart or the balls to kill Jaivin, but I at least thought you'd send him to prison. You busted him with enough powder to get the state of New York high, but you let him go for a few hits and a hand full of money, and he still put a price on your head. In the end I still ended up killing him for you and you stand in my face and look at me like you wanna choke the life out'a me."

Feeling full of the information his brother had just unloaded on him, Aiden clapped back at Ace, "So, I guess we're fucked up like both of our father's. I didn't need you to give me a win. I don't need you to save me from myself. Don't you get it? With every microfiber in my soul, I hate you! Ever since the day you were born you have been the center of mama's world. She doted on you and tried to hold you close to her, so the world wouldn't treat you like the bastard that you are. After you were born, Papi couldn't stand to look at you. For a long time, I couldn't figure out why he hated you so much, until he told me what happened to mommy. You were a constant reminder why Mama would never love me the way she loved you. Papi was so obsessed with making your life miserable he didn't give a damn about his flesh and blood. He paid no attention to me. The only time he spent with me was when we were both making you miserable."

Ace shook his head, "You're sick! I didn't ask for your crackhead daddy to put his family in danger and leave his wife vulnerable for an attack by the man that Papi owed money to. Did you know that Papi kept buying dope from Jaivin after he attacked mama? I guess it doesn't matter to you cause you're just like your father…weak and stupid!"

Aiden snapped back at Ace, "We'll see how weak and stupid I am when I send you to the chair for Spencer Benedict's murder. I really don't know if you killed Spencer Benedict and I don't give a damn. What I do know is you will go down for this murder and I will be left to console that fine piece of ass Tyger Benedict."

Ace reached over and grabbed Aiden by his throat lifting him off the ground with one hand. With his feet dangling in the wind, Aiden struggled to breathe. Ace tightened his grip on Aiden's neck and threw him on the hood of the car, "Stay away from Tyger or I will kill you with my bare hands. I tried to be nice and honor the fact that we are blood, but obviously that means nothing to you. Just as I saved your life, I can snatch it from you! You think you can break me by sending me to prison; hell prison ain't shit to me. A man like me knows prison is always a possibility. The only way you can break me is by killing me."

Dragging Aiden off the hood of the car like a rag doll, Ace stood him up on his feet and released his grip. Dazed and confused, Aiden wobbled trying to gain the strength in his legs. Fixing Aiden's clothes and slapping him back to consciousness, Ace stared into his eyes. Regaining his senses, Aiden grabbed his neck and tried to catch his breath. Breathing in massive gulps of air, Aiden was unable to speak. Ace grabbed him and delivered small thrust to Aiden's back demanding him to breath. Mocking Aiden, Ace reassured him that he would be fine, "You'll be ok in a few minutes, just breathe slow and try not to choke on your own spit."

Falling back on the hood of the car, Aiden was unable to gather himself. Ace reached out and grabbed him by his shirt and dragged Aiden over to his own vehicle. Opening the door and placing his brother in the driver's seat, Ace leaned into Aiden "Listen, it's obvious that either you don't believe that I'll kill you or you just don't care. Because you're still my brother and I promised our mother I wouldn't kill you, I'll make a deal with you. I won't come looking for you, but if you cross my path the wrong way and get between me and mine, I'll stop your breathing forever big brother. I need to know that you understand me, so nod twice for 'yes' so I'll know that you heard me."

Still holding his neck, Aiden nodded his head twice. Walking away leaving Aiden spindly legged and confused, Ace turned back toward Aiden and added fuel to the fire he'd created, "If I were you, I'd go to the hospital and get myself checked out. I think I felt something in your neck snap. I wouldn't want you to wake up dead in the morning."

Driving off leaving his brother struggling to breathe, Ace knew by the hand of the other one of them would soon die.

Chapter Seven

Tyger woke up at dusk to the elegant smell of a fresh Cuban cigar. The hint of dark chocolate, coffee bean and anise tickled her nose as the thought of Ace ran through her mind. Still pissed from their disagreement earlier that evening, Tyger pulled the covers closer to her body and tried to forget about Ace. Feeling the brisk Michigan spring breeze rip through her bed sheets, she struggled to understand why her room was so cold. Trying to find a comfortable spot in her lonely frigid bed, Tyger rolled over on her back and stared at the ceiling. Watching the shadows from the trees outside her window dance on the ceiling, she vigorously batted her eyes trying to convince herself to fall back asleep.

Realizing the cold wind ripping through her bedroom was coming from the open door leading to her bedroom terrace, Tyger was startled by the image of a man in the distance. With her heart racing, Tyger reached under the pillow next to her to grab her gun. The robust wind ruffled the sheer curtains leaving them flailing in the wind. With her finger securely gripping the trigger, Tyger slowly rose up focusing on the image of the stranger resting on her terrace. Crawling out of bed trying to calculate her next move, Tyger's heart sank to her feet as she identified the intruder. Ace was sitting outside on the balcony smoking a cigar and sipping on a glass of something strong.

Tyger could only conclude that there was single-malt scotch in his glass. Ace was not a drinker, but when he did indulge, his choice was always the same. Feeling relieved, she collapsed on her back and took a couple of deep breaths. Trying to gather her thoughts, she rose up once more and watched through a haze of smoke as Ace calmly took a drag of his cigar. Watching him roll the finely crafted Churchill through his fingers, Tyger was mesmerized. Tyger could not fathom why Ace was sitting on her terrace with the hawk blowing off the lake in the still of the night. If Ace was indulging in a drink and a cigar that meant he was trying to remain relaxed while mulling over a possible fatal matter. The fact that he was sitting outside her bedroom, led Tyger to believe that somehow she was directly involved in his obvious turmoil.

Struggling to make sense of the scene unfolding in front of her, Tyger was startled by Ace's voice, "I'm glad one of us could sleep peacefully."

Grabbing her robe form the edge of the bed, Tyger took advantage of her cue to engage Ace in conversation, "Would you please come inside and close my door?"

Ace extinguished his cigar and let the last drop of scotch glide down his throat. With much force he rose up from the chair and walked through the door. Walking into the bedroom caressing his Rosary beads, Ace's face was edged with tension. Nervously closing her robe, Tyger stood to her feet. As Ace vigorously caressed his Rosary beads, Tyger's stomach became twisted in knots. Tyger knew when Ace handled his beads, he'd just done something or was about to do something that he needed to repent.

Trying not to show her discomfort, Tyger took a deep breath and tried not to show discomfort, but it was impossible. Ace walked toward Tyger and she began to shiver. With a furrowed brow and an unyielding jaw Ace titled his head, "Tyger, what's wrong? Why are you acting like you're afraid of me?"

Tyger ran her fingers through her hair, "I don't know, could it be because you broke into my house in the middle of the night and sat outside on that cold ass balcony for God knows how long watching me sleep like a damn stalker? Now you're standing in front of me with a gun strapped to your side. You're gripping those beads so hard, you're about to rip them apart. Not to mention you're sitting out there drinking some shit that would put a hole in concrete. What the hell do you expect?"

Walking toward Tyger with his arms extended, Ace started to laugh, "Baby, I'm sorry. I guess you know me too well. I didn't mean to scare you and I didn't break in, Dee Dee let me in. I've been worried about us since you put me out earlier but most important, I don't like Detective Aiden Arias hanging around here. I don't trust him."

Tyger's heart dropped to her feet when Ace mentioned Aiden's name. "Yeah, Detective Arias just popped up last night lurking outside like a prowler."

Removing his jacket and placing it on the chair, Tyger almost became sidetracked by the sight of Ace's biceps bulging from his shirt. Feeling Tyger's eyes caressing his body, he walked over and placed his gun on the nightstand. With her eyes glued to Ace, Tyger's temperature continued to rise as he undressed. Tyger's addiction to Ace was so strong she needed some sort of patch, pill or shot to curb her dependence.

As if she didn't know, Tyger asked, "Ace, what are you doing?"

"I'm getting ready to take a shower so we can go to bed."

"You know you can't stay here."

Watching Ace drop his pants, a flash of heat shot through Tyger's body. Tyger stood there staring at his erection calling to her. Rendered speechless from the sight of his perfect form, Tyger tried to figure out why he couldn't stay. Her voice cracked as she tried to explain why Ace couldn't stay the night,

"Nina is in the next room and my nosey mother is somewhere in this house. It's just not a good time!"

Standing before her flawlessly naked, Ace aggressively responded to Tyger, "Let me tell you what's not a good idea, you ignoring my request." With his jaws tightly clinched, Ace looked into Tyger's eyes,

"I want you stay your ass away from Aiden Arias. Do you understand me!"

Ace had just become unhinged in a matter of seconds. His eyes danced with contempt as Aiden Arias' name escaped his lips. Ace was less than an inch away from Tyger with his nostrils flaring. There was a fire in his eyes that Tyger dreaded seeing. There was something different about Ace's body language, this wasn't business, it was personal. Tyger stepped away from Ace hoping he would gather himself soon, but he was still seething with anger.

With his left arm resting by his side, he raised his right hand and pointed his index finger at Tyger, "I saw the look in his eyes tonight; he wants to do more than solve Spencer's murder. I watched you when you were down at the boat dock. I saw the way that the two of you looked at each other and I don't like it at all. You need to remember that I am the only man in your life now. Of all people I'm not letting this muthafucka come in here and take something else away from me, do you understand?"

Feeing confused Tyger felt she was missing something. "Ace what's going on with you? What do you mean by taking something else away from you? You talk like you know Detective Arias. Tonight, he wouldn't shut up about you, what's going on, am I missing something?"

Walking into the bathroom Ace grabbed a towel from the cabinet and explained, "Tyger it's too complicated, I don't want to talk about it right now." Tyger immediately became angry.

"Hell, you are in my house and I demand an explanation now." Tyger snatched the towel from Ace's grip and stood in front of him.

"You come into my house and scare me half to death and then you dictate what we will and will not talk about. We've never had that type of relationship and we're not gonna start now. We've never kept things from each other no matter how bad or senseless. Now, tell me what's going on with you and Aiden."

Beating on the bathroom counter, Ace became enraged as his eyes grew wide like silver dollars. "Aiden? You and this muthafucka on a first name basis now?" Tyger threw up her hands and tried to walk away.

Ace grabbed Tyger's arms and pulled her back toward him, "Ai-den, is my brother!"

With her lip hanging down to the floor, Tyger was stunned, "What?"

"Yeah, that's right, my brother."

"Why didn't you tell me he's your brother?"

"I thought I wouldn't have to. I never planned for you to meet him. Last year after my grandmother's funeral he stayed around. I thought he would get tired of Detroit and move on, but he's still here waiting to catch me slipping. I think he stayed around thinking I was going to prison, but when I didn't, I guess the bastard tried another angle."

"Ace, I don't remember seeing him at your grandmother's funeral or your trial."

"He was there at the funeral, he was definitely at my trial, and I know he saw you at both because I saw him watching you."

"Well why didn't you just tell me who he was last night."

"I wasn't ready to talk about it. I hate that muthafucka!"

Tyger stood in front of the bathroom vanity staring into Ace's eyes watching hate fester in his pupils.

"Ace you don't mean that. He is your brother."

Ace snapped, "He *was* my brother!"

Walking toward the shower and turning on the water, he hesitated to enter the shower, Ace turned to Tyger. Feeling like he needed to give her some sort of explanation for his behavior, Ace revealed his family secrets.

"I came to live with my grandmother because my brother betrayed me."

Ace grabbed a towel from the rack and wrapped it around his body. He sat down on the stool next to the shower. Settling in the chair next to him, he grabbed her hand.

"I have always been the person you see in front of you. Even as a kid, I had an untamed spirit that I couldn't shake. Growing up I loved Aiden, he was my big brother, I idolized him. Between the two of us, I was bigger and stronger. I was quiet, but I wasn't a punk; I meant what I said and I said what I meant. Aiden was the weaker one, but he was always trying to prove to our father he was tough. He wanted to join a gang, but a part of the initiation included robbing and beating some random person. I was never interested in being in anyone's gang; I couldn't let some other dudes have control over me and tell me what to do. Aiden was always scared of his own shadow, so I told him I would stick up somebody and we would pretend like he did it. The agreement was no one would get hurt we were just gonna rob some store on the other side of town and take the owner's I.D. for proof. I told Aiden he had to go with me so he could say he was there and give details. Once we got in the store, I gave the gun to Aiden to hold while I took money from the register, some cigarettes, chips and other little bullshit. Aiden started dancing around waiving the gun in the air and Papin off at the mouth and threatening the man behind the counter; all of a sudden the gun went off. I almost pissed on myself, I was paralyzed at the sight of the store clerk's brains splattered everywhere. I looked over at Aiden and he couldn't move he looked like he was going to pass out. Still holding a fist full of cash and a pack of cigarettes, I grabbed the gun from Aiden and tried to calm him down. He just kept babbling about how it was an accident and we were going to jail. When I finally got him to calm down, we ran out the back and left the man lying on the floor in his own blood. We ran and didn't stop until we got home. Aiden ran straight to my father and sang like a bird, "*Papi, Papi Ace just killed a man, he tried to rob him.*"

I tried my best to explain to my father that I didn't pull the trigger. Of course, he didn't believe me. While Aiden watched he beat me until I couldn't stand up. Papi kept me locked in the basement for weeks until my cuts and bruises healed. After the visible bruises from my face and arms healed, he put me on a bus to Detroit with a broken arm."

Trying not to break, Ace took a moment and stared at the wall, "While I was packing my clothes Aiden told me I was used to getting in trouble so no one would believe he robbed the store. Aiden said he was glad I was being sent away because I was the reason why Papi always beat mama."

Tyger interrupted, "Why would Aiden say that?"

"Aiden and I have different fathers; my mother was raped by a man that came to the house looking for Papi because he owed him money for heroin. As a result of the rape, my mother got pregnant with me and she refused to have an abortion. Every time Papi looked at me, I reminded him of what happened to mama, so he beat both of us. Aiden got beat by Papi one time and he never wanted it to happen again, so he kissed Papi's ass every chance he got."

Tyger asked, "I never asked this before, but I guess this is a good time; when was the last time you spoke to your parents?"

"I go and see mama once a month. I moved her to Florida. That's where I go when I disappear sometimes."

"So, that's the other woman you disappear with every month."

"Yep..."

Bracing herself for the answer to her next question, Tyger took a deep breath. "What happened to your Papi?" Ace turned and looked at her

"Do you really have to ask?" Tyger, lowered her head and nodded 'no'.

Ace leaned in, lifted Tyger's chin and stared into her eyes, "I need you to stay away from Aiden. If he ever hurt you, I would kill him. Please don't put me in the position to break my mother's heart for killing my own brother."

Pleading with his eyes, Ace stood in front of Tyger. Seeing the passion in his eyes, she reached up and caressed Ace's cheek. She ran her fingers along his flesh tone scar and reassured Ace, "Baby, I could never risk losing you. You should know that I would risk my own life to keep you close to me."

Continuing to stroke his face, Ace grabbed Tyger's hand and kissed her palms. He leaned in close and softly kissed her lips, "I love you."

Engaging in a passionate kiss, Ace picked Tyger up and walked toward the shower. Entering the shower Tyger wrapped her arms around Ace's neck and held on for dear life. Standing under the waterfall the warm water trickled down their faces. Beads of water crowned their lips as Ace and Tyger's slippery tongues touched. Feeling Ace's massive hands slide over her body, Tyger moaned with orgasmic excitement. Tyger wrapped her legs around Ace's waist and held on as he gripped her thighs and lifted her from the floor. As Ace pinned her against the shower wall Tyger felt her back pressed against the hard wet marble. Thrusting himself inside her, Tyger's breath escaped for a moment as Ace kissed her neck. Tyger's body grew weak and her mind started to wander in no certain direction as she felt long gentle strokes in the depths of her soul. The water fell from Ace's chest and dripped between Tyger's thighs making it easier for Ace to extend his mind-blowing pleasure. Penetrating deeper and deeper Tyger could hardly catch her breath. As Ace stroked harder and harder Tyger glanced down and watched in amazement as she saw his long thick flawless caramel erection move in and slightly out of her inviting southern comfort. Ace gave Tyger every inch of him; with each stroke a feeling of excitement sent waves of pleasure up her spine. Tyger's body grew weak as she wrapped her legs around his waist and pulled him in deeper. As Ace shouted, "Damn, Tyger" she could feel him growing harder. Tyger felt him enter into what felt like the pit of her stomach. Tyger clinched her muscles tight and hugged him like a tight-fitting glove. As his gentle strokes turned into rapid precise thrust Tyger's walls began to quiver with the anticipation of an orgasmic eruption. Tyger grew dizzy as she pressed her fingernails into Ace's back and gently sunk her teeth into his shoulder. Tyger's legs continued to intensely quiver. Panting like animals, they both released a deafening wail as they exploded into an uninhibited full body orgasm. Still resting inside of Tyger, Ace parted her lips with his tongue and gently suckled her tongue allowing Tyger to release yet another eruption of sheer pleasure. Dazed and lifeless, Tyger relaxed her back on the wall of the shower and stared into Ace's eyes. For the first time in ten years neither Ace nor Tyger were worried about a thing; for a brief moment they were the only two people in existence.

Chapter Eight

The next morning Tyger woke up and rolled over landing on the spot where Ace slept. There was nothing there, but a cold empty space. His elusiveness made Tyger's head spin with contempt.

Running her fingers through her hair and lying her palm over the empty space on the other side of the bed, she glanced over at the clock; it was seven thirty a.m. Tyger needed to hustle so she could get Nina ready for school.

Disheveled, Tyger aimlessly walked into the bathroom and leaned over the sink splashing water on her face. Her hair looked like a lion's mane; she looked like she had been rolled hard and put up wet. Ace had left her feeling lethargic and unmotivated. Reaching for a towel to dry her face, she noticed a small box resting on the vanity. The box was made of blood red calfskin leather with her initials etched in gold on the top. It was a tiny little thing that was suitable for housing exquisite trinkets like diamond rings and earrings. With unruly excitement, Tyger threw the towel into the sink and grabbed the box. She carefully opened the box and marveled at what she'd uncovered. It was the ring that Ace had given Tyger the night he begged her not to marry Spencer.

Without hesitation, Tyger retrieved the ring from the box and placed it on the ring finger on her right hand. She stood in front of the mirror mesmerized by the flawless stone. She could not believe Ace had held on to the ring all those years. Remembering the reason she didn't marry Ace ten years ago, Tyger grabbed the ring violently twisting it off her finger. Holding the ring in her hand staring as if it were going to suddenly speak to her. Ace's late night family drama confirmed what Tyger had always known; Ace had demons that he would never conquer. Tyger loved Ace with all her heart, but was she ready to commit herself to yet another broken man?

Timidly placing the ring back in the box Tyger left it on the bathroom counter just as she'd found it. Stepping into the shower she washed away the memories of last night. Placing her hand on the wall, Tyger placed her head under the water and felt the water pierce her scalp and roll down her face. The hot water spraying from the wall behind her rolled down her back evoking images from the night she dragged Spencer's body across the yard. Images of his dead body lying on the metal table in the morgue danced in her head. Tyger wished she could wash away the last fifteen years of her life. She would go away to school and never return to the place she once called home again. Nina was the only good thing she could wrap her mind around. Drained by her never-ending thoughts of frustration, heartache and confusion, Tyger turned the shower off, toweled off and walked toward the vanity. Unable to take her eyes off the little box resting a few feet away from her, she couldn't stop thinking of Ace. Like a magnet she was drawn to the box. Like a woman possessed she couldn't help herself, she ran over opened the box. Prying the ring out of the box she slipped it onto her finger once more. If only for a moment, she would bask in the intoxicating fantasy of being Mrs. Asa Del Toro.

Preparing for the day, Tyger walked down the back stairs and into the laundry room to gather Nina's raincoat and goulashes. Gazing out the window, she paused for a moment wishing Spencer had stayed at the bottom of the lake. This was just another hellacious mess that had invaded her life. Tyger was not only in the middle of a murder investigation, but now she was caught up in a Cain and Abel battle with Ace and Aiden.

Now that Spencer's body had been found and the coroner was working overtime to determine the cause of death, Tyger had no time to waste. After dropping Nina at school, she traveled to Spencer's condo. It had been months since she stepped foot inside her late husband's home away from home. Spencer had a hideaway he thought was a secret. He kept everything in that den of sin that he didn't want people to find. Spencer had no idea Tyger knew about his condo. An accidental opportunity steered Tyger toward Spencer's hideaway. One morning Tyger misplaced the keys to her car, feeling unmotivated to search for keys to any of the other cars, she noticed Spencer's keys on the table. Chasing some out of the way boutique on the other side of town, Tyger became lost. Frustrated and needing to get home before Nina arrived from school, she programmed the GPS to take her back to her house. Unfortunately, Spencer's home wasn't programmed the same as Tyger's. The GPS drove her straight to Spencer's secret hiding place. Reveling in the fact that Spencer was traveling over a thousand miles away, Tyger tried her luck at the keys on his key ring

After her first visit, she made a copy of the key and waited for her next opportunity to use it. Unfortunately for him, Spencer died a few weeks later giving Tyger the opportunity to freely ramble through his house. Over the course of six months, Tyger had gone through the file cabinets and a few other hiding places around the house. She had uncovered stacks of cash, offshore bank accounts and deeds to property in other states. Over the course of their marriage Spencer had mastered the art of concealing vital information from Tyger, but one dumb ass mistake like putting the key to his secret spot on his key ring and programing the address in his GPS had proved to be quite lucrative for Tyger.

Over the past few months, Tyger had been careful not to spend too much time at the condo. She was sure Spencer's greedy airhead mistress Gigi Palmer had spent time at the condo when Spencer was alive. It was just a matter of time before Gigi came to pillage the condo for treasure. Each time she visited the condo she found more evidence of Spencer's greed. Tyger uncovered a two-million-dollar insurance policy on Nina. She found a hefty policy on herself, S.B. and Gigi. It was evident Spencer had big plans for the Benedict family. Each time

Tyger collected new documents she dropped them on Spencer's attorney Henderson Bishop's desk. Henderson was only loyal to the person holding the cash. Now that Spencer was gone and there was no need to honor his secrets, Henderson confirmed Spencer had a plan to get rid of Tyger, but he didn't know the details. Although Spencer's will revealed Tyger wound inherit everything, it was only for show. He was confident that Tyger would die before him and she would never get her hands on his money. Henderson spent many sleepless nights researching deeds and accounts to make sure Tyger could stake her claim. For those items she could not legally possess, she figured out a way to get her hands wrapped around them in spite of the legal red tape.

It had been approximately forty-eight hours since Spencer's body had been found. Tyger had turned that condo upside down and pulled every precious document she could find. She stopped by for one last walk through. There were two more areas that Tyger needed to tackle before her scavenger hunt ended. She parked down the street and entered the condo through the back door. Convinced she would find nothing new, she sat behind Spencer's desk to rest. Looking down under the desk she saw a piece of paper sticking out of a crack between the desk and the bottom drawer. She bent down and reached for the paper, but it was stuck. Falling on all fours she realized she would have to remove the drawer in order to retrieve the paper. She jiggled and wiggled and even tried to snatch the damn thing open, but there was something preventing the drawer from opening. Feeling defeated she rested on her heels and pondered the importance of recovering that piece of paper.

Determined to gain access to the drawer, she reached down and gave it one hard yank. Snatching the drawer out of the desk, it sailed out off track and landed on the floor. Tyger yelled out "cheap piece of shit." Turning the drawer over to see what was stuck to the bottom she found nothing. Pissed, Tyger stuck her head through the empty hole where the drawer was once housed. Peering through the hole she found a large manila envelope taped to the inside of the desk. Extending her arm, she reached in and peeled the envelope from the desk.

Throwing the envelope on top of the desk, she tussled her hair and tried to gather herself. Reaching toward the desk, she was startled by the sound of the door chime; someone was in the house. Stuffing the envelope inside her purse, she pulled her gun.

Trying not to make a sound Tyger slowly eased around the desk. Stepping into the hall she saw a woman with her back facing the opposite direction. Recognizing the woman, Tyger lifted her gun, "Is there something I can do for you?"

The woman threw her hands up and slowly turned toward Tyger, "Is that gun really necessary? I'm not armed."

Lowering her gun, Tyger stared at her husband's mistress Gigi Palmer with a puzzling look. GiGi had poor taste in everything; she was strictly low budget. She wore a distastefully tight suit that rode her thighs when she walked. Her jacket was so tight the stitching was unraveling. Her aging titties were bulging from her shirt begging to be covered. She wore a dime store weave with a fake part in the middle. She carried a faux crocodile clutch and plastic shoes masquerading as patent leather.

Tyger smiled, "I thought you were an intruder, I thought my life was in danger. Hell, it still might be."

"You don't have to worry about me; I'm just here to protect my own interest."

Tyger laughed, "Your interest! I should have known you knew about this place. I suppose you have a key?" Tyger was dumbfounded, she couldn't figure out how she and GiGi had not crossed paths at the condo over the past six months.

GiGi tucked her purse under her arm, "Are we going to stand here in the hallway and talk or are you going to invite me to sit down?"

Tyger extended her hand for Gigi to walk toward the office. She refused to turn her back on Gigi, she let her lead the way. Gigi walked into the office and placed her plastic clutch on the desk. Taking a nearby seat, she looked up at Tyger,

"You and I have some unfinished business to discuss. I have not received my payment for this month; I was supposed to receive it two days ago. I figured that since Spencer's body was found two days ago that you were just tied up, so I decided to pay you a visit, but when

I approached the house; I saw you leaving and I followed you. Yes, I knew about this place but, no I don't have a key, you left the door unlocked. Actually, I have never been inside this condo, I was never invited. I figured Spencer's real will must be hidden in here somewhere and I need for you to show me what's in it before you try and double cross me with some fake will you created."

With a calm tone Tyger remarked, "Gigi, you don't have to follow me around like a bloodhound. I will give you what we agreed on. And I have nothing to hide from you concerning Spencer's will. As a matter of fact, I had a copy notarized just for you."

Tyger took a seat behind the desk, "I have always been a fair, rational and realistic woman. You and Spencer spent a lot of time together and I am actually grateful to you for that. You kept Spencer away from home plenty of nights which left me available for other opportunities." Tyger reached over and grabbed her handbag. She reached in and pulled out an envelope that was stuffed inside her purse. She extended her hand and offered the envelope to GiGi, "You saved me a trip, you were my next stop."

GiGi reached over and grabbed the envelope from Tyger's hand. Counting the contents, she looked up at Tyger and smiled, "Thank you."

Without displaying any type of tangible emotion, Tyger reached inside her attaché case resting beside her foot. Thumbing through several envelopes, she finally located what she was searching for. She pulled out an envelope retrieving a document from inside; it was a copy of Spencer's will. Tyger leaned over and placed the will on the edge of the desk in front of Gigi.

Boiling over inside with devious excitement, Tyger parted her lips to break the news to Gigi, "I'll give you a moment to read through the will. But I can tell you that you're going to be grossly disappointed. Spencer didn't leave you anything. Your name isn't mentioned anywhere in the will, not even under miscellaneous property."

Tyger sat back in the chair with a snide grin waiting for GiGi to come unglued.

Gigi's grabbed the will from the desk and started reading through it like a speed-reader. Not finding her name buried in the midst of the legal jargon made Gigi furious. Feeling this was some kind of joke, Gigi wondered how Tyger cut her out of the will. She knew her beloved Spencer had left her at least the condo and the car that she was driving. Gigi snapped at Tyger,

"Tyger what bullshit are you trying to pull on me. I know Spencer left me the condo, he told me that he was leaving me the condo and money in his will."

Tyger laughed, "A man will tell you anything when you've got your legs wrapped around his neck."

Gigi looked like she was about to have fit. "Spencer didn'tleave the condo to you; I suggest you read it carefully to see who your new landlord is going to be. With wild eyes Gigi scanned the will, her eyes began to bulge and her breath became heavy. Spencer did not leave the condo to Tyger or Gigi, he left it to his cousin Vincent. Vincent had been Spencer's driver for over ten years. Vincent knew everything about Spencer. Ironically, Vincent did not care for Spencer and his insufferable arrogance.

Gigi was speechless; she didn't utter a word for three minutes. She continued to read over the will trying to make her name appear inside those pages. Tired of waiting on Gigi to realize she was shit out of luck, Tyger broke her silence, "My suggestion to you is that you work something out with Vincent to lease the condo to you or give you reasonable time to move out. The car that you're driving is in Spencer's name and is apart of Spencer's estate which of course goes to me and Nina."

In a sarcastically reassuring tone, Tyger leaned in toward her, "Gigi, I was just as shocked as you were. Honestly, I wasn't expecting Spencer to leave me anything, but the will is set in stone. He was a selfish son-of-a- bitch, but I guess you know that now. In light of our little secret, I will admit that I am in no position to bargain with you. In addition to the five-thousand dollars a month that I've been giving you since the night Spencer died, you can have all the furniture in the condo, the car that you drive and I'll buy you a house or condo of your choice."

Unable to contain herself, Gigi exploded, "You dirty bitch, I know you changed Spencer's will. I know Spencer left me the condo and a substantial amount of money."

Tyger calmly said, "Listen, Gigi the will has been the same for years. Considering that you were my husband's whore, I am trying to be more than diplomatic. Be smart Gigi, cut your losses. I don't have to offer you anything. Surely you cannot be stupid enough to think that a man like Spencer, hell or any other man would include you in an ironclad legal agreement to be read in front of his friends and family." Tyger took a deep laboring breath, "Look Gigi, the unfortunate thing is that I actually think more of you than Spencer did. Realistically, if you meant that much to him, he would have made arrangements for you to be taken care of, but it appears that he did not."

The two women sat across from each other with their eyes locked like lions ready to rip each other apart. There was one question that was on both of their minds. Even Tyger was curious to know why Spencer didn't make the effort to ensure Gigi was taken care of. He had enough money to set her up without a paper trail. There appeared to be nothing stashed away for her.

Feeling the conversation had gone farther than it should, Tyger stood up and walked around the desk, "Let me give a little advice for the next man. All gifts should be paid for in full and in your name. The condo you live in and the car you drive should be in your name. The extra money you get should be treated as income; you enjoy a little and save the rest or start a business. As a side piece, you have no security. Even in death, a man will never shame himself or his family no matter how bad things are at home. In the future keep your mouth closed, you talk too much; you spread you and Spencer's business all over town. You didn't respect him or yourself. Whatever was between the two of you was just that, between the two of you. You were too busy wanting to be seen, thinking you were making me look like the stupid wife. No one respects a whore. You weren't even an investment; you were just disposable income."

Tyger sat on the edge of the desk and looked down at Gigi. Gigi pointed her finger toward Tyger, "Do you think I spent all those years with that evil limp dick asshole to be left with absolutely nothing? You best believe somebody is gonna give me something. Spencer spent many nights talking to me about his client's business, I know all about Judge Benedict's dirty deeds, your precious Ace and that fine friend of yours Picasso Kennard..."

Gigi arose from her seat, "…but most important if you want to hold on to that little girl of yours and not go to jail then you better get me whatever I ask you for."

Fuming inside, Tyger swallowed the lump in her throat. Trying not to reveal the anxiety that just shot through her body she was two seconds away from spitting fire, but she maintained her composure. Gigi leaned in toward Tyger, "Never forget that I know what happened the night Spencer was killed, and I know exactly who the real killer is."

Without flinching, Tyger suggested, "So why don't you just go to the police."

"Please Tyger, this information is worth more to me than it is to the police. You see since Spencer's been gone, I've had to make a few adjustments to my lifestyle and I'm not too happy with it. The way Spencer died, I felt sorry for you. I was sure Spencer left me well taken care of, but that was my mistake. Since that evil bastard left me with nothing, I'll just have to get it from you. So, you see Mrs. Benedict side pieces have security when they watch their lover being rolled into the lake by his wife. You didn't even deserve to be called his wife; he spent more time with me than he did with you."

Tyger laughed, "And where did that get you? Even in death, Spencer screwed you with no intent to satisfy you."

Gigi took a deep breath, "You're right, it got me nothing, yet. I honestly thought that one day Spencer would leave you. The night he died, I just had to see what being Mrs. Benedict would be like. He was so drunk he asked me to take him home and drop him off at the gate. I was supposed to drive him home and let the cab that followed take me home, but he was so drunk I didn't think he'd make it up the hill, so I drove him through the gate and dropped him off at the door. After I made sure he was in I was more than curious to see how Queen Tyger was living. I went around the side and peeked through the window, that's when I saw you big and pregnant. Spencer never told me that you were expecting. I was standing in the window with my eyes glued to the glass watching you two argue like two strangers in the street and all of a sudden, I blinked and Spencer went down; that was it, just like that he was dead. After I saw what happened I stood there stunned. For a moment I felt this weird kind of peace and excitement came over me. I was tired of Spencer and just like that he was gone, I knew that if I waited and held on to what I knew, my ship would come in. You see Tyger, you're a mother. I do feel sorry for you, so I can't let you go to prison and leave poor Nina abandoned."

Tyger took in a few breaths of air, "If you did see what happened that night what makes you think that I will go to prison?"

Gigi let out a cynical laugh, "Don't be stupid Tyger there are several versions of the truth and I have a few scenarios in mind that I can repeat and I know you'd never sacrifice the person that really killed Spencer. That's why you are gonna deliver me one million dollars in cash by tomorrow at noon. If you don't, you will find yourself in a world of trouble."

Tyger sat in silence staring at Gigi without blinking. Gigi had no idea who she was really dealing with. She had no idea that Tyger could snap her neck with one twist of her wrist. The men in her life had taught Tyger things that the most experienced criminal didn't even know. Watching Tyger's eyes turn cold the hair on the back of Gigi's neck stood up. Her heart started beating faster and faster as her palms grew moist. Gigi began to regret the threats she made.

Closing her eyes, inhaling and exhaling, Tyger broke her silence, "I will not give you a million dollars. You will get what I think you deserve. After you leave this house there should never ever be a reason for you to contact me again. The only reason why I'm not gonna kill you where you stand is because I have no way at this point of properly disposing of your body. I am going to assume that you are so grief stricken that your senses have temporally abandoned you. So, I'm gonna let you slide on the threat. I need you to understand that I know more about you than you think, Gail Gardner from Cleveland, Ohio. I know your old poor gray-haired mama still lives in that three room project with the screen door half hanging on the hinges. I know it will be a cold day in hell before your daddy or baby brother get out of prison. So, Gigi if you wanna keep passing licks across the table like a little girl then keep it up but, remember my tags are a whole hell of lot harder. The difference between us is that I don't deal with the police. I believe in a different kind of justice. If you think I'm gonna let you fuck with my family then you're even more stupid than I thought you were. Now, please leave before I throw you out."

With sweat beads crowning Gigi's scalp she grabbed her purse and nervously stumbled toward the door. Tyger yelled out, "Gigi!" Gigi stopped and turned her head back toward Tyger, "You need to under- stand that even if you do tell the police, that won't keep me off your ass. Once you walk out that door you will never be safe again."

Gigi walked down the hall at top speed. She grabbed the door handle turned it and yanked the door open. Gigi put one foot in front of the other and tore out of the condo.

Standing in the window watching Gigi drive away, Tyger's chest heaved with anger. Feeling overwhelmed, she closed the curtain and walked back into the office. Realizing she never opened the envelope she found, she swiped it from the desk. Emptying the contents onto the desk, photographs fell out of the package. To her amazement and disgust she squinted her eyes as she gawked at photographs of S.B. having sex. Tyger picked up the photographs and saw the woman in two of the photos was Gigi. The mystery had been solved. Spencer left Gigi nothing because she had proved to be just that, worth nothing. On another photograph Tyger identified the woman with S.B. as Mayor Bilton's wife, Corrine. The final photo made Tyger's mouth drop and her stomach churn. She stood frozen as the sight of naked bodies of her father-in-law and her mother's lover Judge Kyle Grey made her ill.

Holding the photographs in her hand, she finally figured out how to get rid of S.B. and Gigi. Smiling to herself, Tyger placed the photo- graphs back in the envelope. Gathering her things and preparing to leave, she almost slid across the floor. She'd stepped on something slick. Looking on the floor, she saw another photograph lying face down near her foot. Bending over, she grabbed the photo from the floor and flipped it over. Breathing deeply with a furrowed brow, she stared at the picture in disgust. Holding a picture of S.B. and her mother in bed together made her want to throw up. Tyger could not take her eyes off what was in front of her. It was like a bad accident, too horrid to look at, but too fascinating to look away. How long had Dee Dee been sleeping with S.B. and who was taking all the pictures? The last thing she wanted to see was S.B.'s out-of-shape naked ass with her mother. The sight of all those old, wrinkled peckers made her head spin. Tyger thought, "Damn, these are some nasty folks." With her stomach churning with repulsion, she placed the picture in the envelope with the others. Her mind was racing with images that she wished she could burn. Now that her mother was caught up in the mess, Tyger knew she would possibly have to sacrifice her mother for her own benefit.

Chapter Nine

S till seething with anger from her encounter with Gigi and the blinding photos, Tyger locked the condo down and headed back to her car. Sitting in the driver's seat trying to catch her breath and gather her thoughts, she was startled by the sound of the phone ringing. She looked up and viewed the screen in front of her to see who was trying to reach her; Doc Milan flashed across the screen. Hoping that Dr. Milan was one-step closer to releasing Spencer's body, Tyger quickly answered the phone.

"Hey Doc."

"Hello Tyger, is this a good time to talk?"

"Yes, what's up?"

"I have the results of Spencer's autopsy and it's not quite what I expected."

Tyger's heart skipped a beat; She quickly played the night Spencer died over in her mind. What could she have missed? Taking a deep breath, Tyger questioned Dr. Milan,

"What's wrong? What did you find?"

"Well, the base of Spencer skull was crushed. There were still fragments of broken glass or crystal lodged in the back of his head."

Tyger waited with bated breath to hear more. So far, Dr. Milan's report was not a complete shock. She had previously shared in detail with Dr. Milan what happened the night Spencer died. Tyger interrupted Dr. Milan, "Is there more?"

"Yes, there is. Spencer's cause of death was not the injury to his skull. The autopsy showed there was water in his lungs; Spencer drowned. Spencer was still alive when he was thrown into the water."

Tyger closed her eyes and buried her chin in her chest. Spencer was alive when she threw him into the lake. She'd rehearsed her defense over the past six months just in case she was ever on trial for Spencer's murder. Her defense would now have to change; she'd thrown a living breathing body into the water. While her head was spinning with the reality that her husband was alive when she dragged him across the back yard, she could hear Dr. Milan's voice faintly calling her name. Realizing she'd mentally checked out, Tyger shook her head.

"I'm sorry Dr. Milan, I'm still here."

"I'm sorry, I know that's not what you expected to hear. I also found traces of cocaine. The drugs would explain why his behavior was as erratic as you described." Tyger was stunned.

"Cocaine? Spencer was many things, but he was not a drug addict. Are you sure?"

"I'm positive. Wherever he was before he came home that night, he had a good time. Judging by the stress on his organs and the lining of his nostrils, Spencer had been using for quite a while. The mixture of cocaine and liquor caused his heart rate to increase faster than normal, which caused him to have a heart attack before he ended up in the lake. The bottom line is Spencer's cause of death was drowning."

Still shocked, Tyger laughed aloud, "A heart attack, cocaine…this is insane. Have you shared any of this with Detective Arias?"

"No, I called you first. I'm sure a warrant will be issued to search the house to figure out where Spencer died."

"That's fine let them come."

Preparing to end the call, Tyger heard Dr. Milan calling her name before hanging up."

"Tyger!"

"Yes?"

"Now that the autopsy is complete, the body will be released soon. What are your plans for a funeral?"

Tyger took a deep breath, "There will be no funeral. Spencer will be cremated as soon as his body is released. A memorial will be held soon after."

"I will make sure there are no unexpected snags in releasing the body."

"Thank you Dr. Milan."

"Take care Tyger."

Dr. Milan and Tyger disconnected the call. Tyger could always count on Dr. Milan to come through for her. He and Whiskey were childhood friends in South Carolina. Dr. Milan had spent most of his life at the bottom of a bottle; he was drunk for breakfast lunch and dinner. During his stint as a surgeon in Los Angeles, he was able to mask his alcohol addiction. Unfortunately, during a surgical procedure, he cut a main artery and the patient died. Dr. Milan was fired, sued for malpractice and a criminal investigation followed. Tyger called in a few favors and got him an excellent defense attorney. When Dr. Milan moved to Detroit, Tyger helped him start a new life. Just like most of the men in her life, Dr. Milan would do anything for Tyger.

Pondering her next move, Tyger needed to visit with her father. Still feeling uneasy about her visit with GiGi and learning the results of Spencer's autopsy weighed heavy on her. Since Spencer's cause of death was no longer blunt force trauma, the real cause of death could no longer be seen as an accident if taken to trial. Tyger began to regret tying his hands and feet. Tyger knew in just a few hours or sooner, the police would descend on her house like a pack of vultures searching for fresh meat. The weapon used to crack Spencer's skull was long gone. The hit was clean and produced minimal blood, but Tyger made sure the so-called crime scene had been cleaned of any traces of ill intent ever taking place.

The last twenty-four hours had been like a destructive storm; everything was unraveling and getting swept away in a deceptive current. Like a retched disease suffocating the life from her she felt helpless. Releasing a boisterous scream that shook the car she laid her forehead on the steering wheel, she begged. "Lord, help me!"

Chapter Ten

After disconnecting from Dr. Milan, Tyger felt overwhelmed; she knew she needed to see Whiskey. She realized she messed up; she should have killed Gigi months ago. Driving to her father's lounge, the images of the last six months replayed in her head like a horrible movie. Spencer's murder, Gigi's blackmail, losing her son, Ace's trail; the horrid reality that her life was unraveling like frayed thread was too much. So much had happened, there were so many ragged ends that needed to be cut.

Tyger was dead set against involving Picasso or Ace in any of her plans. Now that Aiden had entered the picture, they were being watched like hawks, there was no room for error. Tyger knew she could no longer handle things on her own; she needed help to get out this mess.

Trying to locate Whiskey, Tyger fumbled through her contacts trying to dial him. They had not spoken in twenty-four hours and she needed to check in with him. She would need his help for the next phase of her plan. The loud ring of the phone bellowed throughout the car vibrating through Tyger's body. With the phone continuing to ring without an answer on the other end, she felt anxious. Suddenly, the sound of her father's voice as he answered made Tyger feel at ease.

"Hey Baby Girl."

"Hey Daddy." Hearing Tyger call him Daddy, Whiskey's tone changed to one of concern. His children never called him Daddy unless they were in trouble or hurt.

"What's wrong Baby Girl?"

"I need to see you now, where are you?"

"I'm at the spot downtown. I'll be waiting on you."

"Ok, I'll be there in twenty minutes."

Tyger disconnected from her father and made a u-turn in the middle of the street. Whiskey had an upscale supper club in downtown Detroit. Still off the beaten path, it was exclusive to members only. Each member needed a coded membership card to access the club. The card-carrying members ranged from the upper echelon of Michigan's elite high society to the gutter thug whose money granted entry. No matter who entered the doors, there were rules that must be obeyed, no one was above eviction.

Arriving at the club, Tyger reached in her wallet and grabbed her access card before exiting the car. With her card in hand, she quickly sprinted toward the door, swiped her card and entered her code. The club didn't open until seven o'clock, so she needed to enter her private code to enter the building. It was still early; the employees had not yet arrived. The room was cold and dimly lit. After making sure the door was secure, Tyger headed to the back toward Whiskey's office. The sound of her heels hitting the hardwood floor echoed through the empty club making it known that she had arrived.

Strutting through the building with a swift swagger, she finally reached her father's office. Opening the door to the office, Tyger smiled at the sight of Whiskey sitting behind the desk. Whiskey got up from his seat and walked around the desk to greet her. She ran into her father's open arms and buried her head into his chest. Gently caressing his daughter's hair, he asked, "Tyger, what's got you so shook?"

Pulling away from Whiskey, Tyger ran her fingers through her hair, "Dr. Milan called me with the autopsy report today."

Folding both arms, Whiskey waited for Tyger to reveal the results. "So, what did he say?"

"To make a long story short, Spencer didn't die from Nina hitting him with the crystal statue, the cause of death was drowning. He was still alive when I threw him in the lake."

Whiskey's mouth dropped, "What the Hell! He drowned."

"Yes Whiskey, Spencer drowned. Apparently, when he lunged at me he was having a heart attack. When we fell to the floor Nina thought he was hurting me and she hit him with the statue. Thinking that Nina killed him, I dragged Spencer to the lake and threw him in alive."

"Damn"

"Damn is right! The good thing is Nina did not kill her father. The bad news is Detective Arias is going to come with vengeance. If I would not have tied Spencer's hands and feet, it still could have been ruled an accident. At least it would look like he walked out to the lake and had a heart attack and fell in, but now…"

Whiskey stopped Tyger, "Look, you can't change what happened. You thought you were protecting Nina. Now we have to figure out the next move. You can't fall apart now, it's just you in this. You know Picasso and Ace can't get caught up in anything right now; they're being watched heavy."

Tyger lowered her head, "I know, I've kept them out of this as much as I can, but I don't even think Aiden cares if I killed Spencer or not, he just wants to pin this on Ace by any means necessary."

Whiskey sat back on the desk, "What's with this detective and Ace? Why does he want to get to Ace so bad?"

Tyger sat down in the chair across from the desk, "Ace and Aiden are brothers. They have the same mother. It's a crazy and twisted story that I don't have time to explain; all I know is that they hate each other to the point of death."

Whiskey smirked, "You're in a dangerous situation; you're caught up in a family feud. As far as Aiden is concerned, this investigation has nothing to do with justice and everything to do with revenge."

Looking away from Whiskey, Tyger tightened her lips and turned toward the wall. Trying to swallow the lump in her throat and fight back tears, she cleared her throat. Trying to manage her emotions, Tyger turned back toward her father. Catching his eye as she turned, Whiskey noticed the sadness in Tyger's eyes.

"Tyger, you can't keep going like this, you haven't given yourself time to grieve." Looking away from her father, Tyger focused on a photo across the room of her and her siblings. Taking a deep breath, Tyger stared at an imperfection on the tile. Reluctantly answering her father, she turned and looked at him with the same doe eyes she looked at him with when she was a child.

"You're right, my heart is broken, but I don't have the luxury of grieving right now."

"What you don't have, is the luxury of tucking the memory of your son away for another time that's more convenient for you. Look at you, you're falling apart before my eyes. I can't keep watching you pretend like you're not hurting."

Tyger snapped, "I wish I could pretend that it doesn't hurt that my son died inside me. Spencer is not the only person that died that night; a part of me died too. Every time I hear a baby cry in the grocery store, I lose my mind. Don't you think that I feel guilty? Instead of calling an ambulance to save my baby's life, I was too busy dragging Spencer's ass across my backyard."

Whiskey walked toward Tyger, "You thought you were protecting Nina. You can't punish yourself; you did what you had to do."

Tyger lowered her head, "Lately, it seems like that's all I do. I'm doing what I have to do to survive. When I was a little girl living down there at the end of nowhere, smelling that funky ass air every day, I promised myself that one day I'd make out. I'd live in a big house, drive a nice car, have a respectable career and have a husband who was legit. Well, I have the house, the car, I had the career, but I married a mutha-fucka who wasn't shit and I'm in love with a man that would kill for me, but no matter how he dresses it up, Ace will always be a street thug in tailored suits and handmade shoes. Now, I have to add murderer to my laundry list of issues. The sad thing is it's just the beginning. Before it's over, I'll have more blood on my hands and I can't blame anyone but myself."

Raising his brow, Whiskey questioned Tyger, "Why would you say that? What are you not telling me Tyger?"

Tyger took a deep breath and walked over to a vacant chair sitting in front of Whiskey's desk. Whiskey followed behind her and sat on the edge of the desk. Slowly sitting down in the chair, Tyger looked up at her father, "Gigi was there the night Spencer died. She was looking in the window and she saw the whole thing. She's been blackmailing me and now she wants more money. Earlier today, she threatened to go to the police if I don't give her more money. Gigi has no idea I'm the one that killed Spencer and not Nina. Dr. Milan is going to handle the autopsy report, but if Gigi decides to go to the police there is no way I can explain tying Spencer up, weighing him down and throwing him in the lake. There's not enough money on earth to keep me from prison. Even with all my connections and the fact that everyone hated Spencer, S.B. will make sure I rot in prison for Spencer's murder."

Tyger's mouth was moving so fast she started to lose her breath. Without batting an eye, Whiskey looked down and Tyger, "Stop right now and breathe."

Tyger took a deep breath and ran her fingers through her hair. Rising from the chair and walking toward the back of the office, Tyger felt anxious. Whiskey reached out and gently grabbed Tyger's hand. Guiding her back toward him, he took her hands in his and looked into her eyes, "Everything is going to be fine. I'm going to give you three minutes to take a few deep breaths, calm down and pull it together."

Whiskey stood with Tyger for a few moments then released her hand. Walking back toward his desk, Whiskey motioned for Tyger to take the seat next to him.

"Tyger, come over here and sit down. I need you to listen to me for a minute."

Tyger walked over and removed a seat resting on the wall. Whiskey pulled a chair next to her and sat down. "I need you to turn your chair this way, I need you to face me."

Without hesitation, Tyger positioned her chair in front of her father and sat down. Whiskey leaned in and looked Tyger in her eyes. As their eyes met, tears began to well in the corners of Tyger's eyes.

Clearing his throat Whiskey parted his lips to speak, "I need you to get yourself together right now. Don't let that tear leave the corner of your eye. Swallow that lump in your throat and focus on what I'm telling you right now."

Whiskey leaned back in his chair, "For the past six months, you've been walking around carrying the weight of a dead husband and baby. That's enough to send anyone over the edge. It's true, your life is pretty shitty right now. I'm sorry I couldn't be a better role model or provide a better environment for you. I'm sorry I raised you around hustlers, thieves, dope dealers and trash, but you're right, at this point in your life your fuck ups are strictly on you. When you had a chance to get out, you didn't. You chose to stay with Spencer and continue to have an affair with Ace. You weren't woman enough to admit that you were in love with a high-class street thug. So, now you have to deal with the consequences. That consequence is Aiden Arias who will do anything to pin this murder on Ace."

Whiskey leaned in closer to Tyger, "In the middle of all this, you need to remember that you are a Benedict by marriage, but you have Blackwell blood running through your veins. We are not white-collar criminals, the ugly truth is that we are cold hearted, get down and dirty put you in a body bag type of criminals; that is who we are. Behind that gate you live in, that Bentley you drive and that law degree that I paid damn good money for, you are and always will be Tyger Blackwell. You know I'm being watched right now. Things aren't like they used to be. You are the only one of us that no one suspects to do something gutter. You sittin around here worried about Gigi like you don't know what to do. Fuck her! You already know that Gigi can't make it through the night. And while you're worrying about Gigi, you need be worried about S.B."

Sitting in front of her father with her head buried in her chest,

Tyger looked up with puddles in her eyes, "I know what I need to do, but it's just too much. My job is to clean up the messes that you, Ace, Picasso and John Paul make. I'm not supposed to get my hands dirty; I clean the blood off your hands, not stain my own."

Whiskey laughed, "Baby, the men that throw dirt on graves get the same amount of dirt on them as the undertaker; it's all grimy. You are not exempt. You were strong and clever enough to tie your husband up, weigh his body down, drag him across the yard and throw him in the lake."

Tyger took a deep breath, "but that was to protect myself and my daughter."

Whiskey snapped back, "So, now that you know you're the one that actually killed Spencer, you need to protect yourself. Even if she doesn't tell the police, Gigi will tell S.B. what she saw, if she hasn't already."

With heightened curiosity, Tyger asked, "Why would Gigi tell S.B.?" Tyger already knew the answer, but she was curious to know if her father knew what was going on between Gigi and S.B. Tyger was more concerned that Whiskey knew about Delilah and S.B.

Whiskey took a deep breath, "Gigi's well has run dry, whatever that shit is she's snortin and smoking has her mind messed up. Spencer was the only one that was gonna take care of her. She has to keep up her lifestyle or the lifestyle she thinks she has. She's going to need money and she'll sell you out to S.B. She's an old hoe and her looks are fading day by day."

Tyger sat in front of her father breathing in the same air. She knew he was right; there was no way she could let Gigi live. Her mind was racing a thousand miles a minute. Images of every fight that she ever had with Spencer danced through her head. Tyger could still feel the pain of Spencer's kicking her in the small of her back the night he died. She remembered the moment she could no longer feel her son moving.

Seeing the pain in his daughter's eyes, Whiskey pushed his chair back and left his seat. He walked toward the door and grabbed the handle. Looking back at Tyger with her back turned away from him, he left her to battle the storm that was raging inside her; "I need to check on a few things at the bar, I'll be out here if you need me."

Without waiting for a response, Whiskey closed the door behind him. With the sound of her father's footsteps hitting the hard wood floor echoing through the building, Tyger felt a hollow emptiness weighing her down. She felt defeated before she'd even begun to fight. Throwing Spencer's body into the lake should have been the happy ending to the tragic life that she led with him, but it was just the beginning.

Taking a few deep breaths and wiping her tear-stained face, Tyger pulled her compact from her purse and checked her makeup. Looking at her reflection, she realized underneath her flawless makeup, perfect teeth and beautiful eyes she was slowly dying inside. Living with Spencer, loving Ace, missing Piper, worrying over Bella and John Paul and all the other bullshit that came with being Tyger Benedict was wearing thin. Sickened by her on image, Tyger closed the compact and placed it back in her purse. Startled by her hand brushing against her vibrating cell phone, her heart began to race. Taking a deep breath, she retrieved the phone from her purse. Pursing her lips together and squinting her eyes, she wondered why S.B. was calling. Hesitating to answer the call, her finger hovered over the green button. Selecting answer, she put on a big fake, "Hello…"

"Tyger, my gorgeous daughter-in-law, how are you this evening?"

"I'm fine S.B., and you?"

"Couldn't be better. Have you received a call from the coroner's office?"

Tyger's heart dropped to her knees, "No, I have not received a call. Why, do you ask?"

"I just wanted to make sure that you knew the cause of death has been determined. Of course, we knew it was a homicide, but we didn't know how Spencer was killed. Now we know for sure that it was blunt force trauma to the base of his skull." S.B. paused for a moment. Hearing the hidden innuendo in S.B.'s voice, Tyger knew something was wrong. S.B. knows something that he's not going to come out right and say to Tyger over the phone.

Swallowing the lump in her throat, Tyger broke her silence, "Well, that's what we've all been waiting for. Hopefully, now this investigation can move forward, we'll find out who killed my husband."

"Yes, I think it will. I'm certain of that."

Reeling from Dr. Milan's false coroner's report, Tyger felt a small sigh of relief. But there was still something bizarre happening. There was an awkward silence between S.B. and Tyger. Finally, Tyger took a deep breath, "Thanks for calling S.B., I will stop by the house later."

With a hint of sarcasm in his voice, S.B. interrupted "Tyger, before you go, there is one item I recently ran across I think you'll be interested in. I'm texting you a photo now."

The sound of the notification of an incoming text was in sync with the sound of S.B.'s dropped call. Retrieving the text message, Tyger's temples began to throb. Staring her in the face was a photograph of the small statue Nina used to hit Spencer with.

Staring at the photo with her bottom lip hanging at her chin, Tyger became enraged. How did S.B. get his hand on the murder weapon? No one was home the night Spencer was killed. Only Nina and Tyger knew what weapon was used to kill Spencer. Before the ambulance arrived Tyger instructed Nina to hide the statue in her toy chest. After returning from the hospital, Tyger hid the statue in the basement of the old house she grew up in. Genoa and Bella walked into the house as the ambulance was pulling into the driveway for Tyger. Not knowing what occurred between Nina and her father, also without knowledge that Tyger dragged Spencer's body across the floor and into the backyard thinking it was Tyger's blood instead of Spencer's, Bella and Genoa cleaned the house without question. Tyger did not tell Genoa what happened until she returned home from the hospital and had a professional team wipe the house of any traces of the murder. No one knew what the murder weapon was or where it was hidden, so how did S.B. get his hands on it?

Staring at an inanimate object on a nearby shelf, Tyger tried to focus. Gathering herself, Tyger placed her phone back in her purse. Fumbling around inside her purse for her tissue, she felt the envelope that contained the photos. Pulling the envelope from the bag, she smiled. Tyger realized her father was right, she was a Blackwell by blood and Benedict by marriage only. She would not use the photos to blackmail her father-in-law that was too predictable, too easy. She had something else in mind for S.B., something more fatal.

Chapter Eleven

After pulling herself together, Tyger gathered her things and walked out of her father's office. On her way out of the club, she stopped and stood in front of the bar. Standing on the other side of the bar holding a glass of Cognac in his hand, Whiskey smiled, "You look refreshed."

Nodding her head in agreement, but not revealing her conversation with S.B., Tyger reached across the bar and grabbed her father's hand. "You always know how to make me feel better. I love you Daddy."

"I love you too Baby Girl. You know I've always got your back."

Stepping up on the bar rail, Tyger leaned in and kissed Whiskey on his forehead. "I'll see you soon."

Stepping down, Tyger tucked her clutch under her arm and marched out of the bar. Whiskey watched Tyger as she disappeared on the other side of the door. Waiting for the door to close, he walked over and grabbed his cell phone from the end of the counter. Once the door slammed, he scrolled through his phone and selected a number. Waiting for the answer on the other end, he tapped his fingertips on the countertop. Finally, Whiskey heard, "Hey, what's up?"

"Hey man, my baby just left the club and I think she is going to need a shadow later tonight. I'm not sure what time she's going out, but I'd be posted up after seven p.m. just in case."

"Cool, I got it."

"I'm pretty sure she has a meeting out in Troy tonight. After she leaves, I need you go in and make sure everything is good."

"I got you. I'll clean up just like I always do."

"Thanks man, we'll settle at the end of the week and remember, don't let her see you."

"She never does."

Whiskey and his contact ended the call. Placing his phone back on the bar, he picked up his glass of cognac and finished the last drop. When Whiskey found out Spencer had been physically abusing Tyger, he sent one of his associates to talk with Spencer while dangling him over the Ambassador Bridge. Whiskey's associate warned Spencer to never tell Tyger of their encounter and keep his hands off of her. Spencer managed to keep his hands off Tyger until the night he died. When Aiden Arias showed up in town ogling Tyger at Ace's trial, Whiskey's associate started following Tyger to ensure she was well protected. Out of all of his girls, Whiskey knew Tyger could handle her own, but he also wanted to make sure she was safe at all times.

After leaving the club, Tyger replayed the events of the day over and over again. She felt uneasy about deceiving her father. She'd failed to mention the naked photos of her mother. Delilah and Whiskey had not been together in quite some time, but Tyger knew her father was still pining over her mother. She didn't want to see her father hurt by her mother again, so she kept the photo a secret.

Once Tyger exited the club, she spared no time getting home to report the events of the day to Genoa. When she reached her house, Tyger entered through the kitchen. Genoa, Nina and Lillian, the housekeeper, were sitting at the kitchen table. Nina was sitting at the table with crayons drawing one of her magnificent works of art.

Not wanting to disturb Nina's routine, Tyger motioned for Genoa to follow her. As she prepared to leave the room, Tyger leaned down and kissed the top of Nina's forehead. Tyger shuttered at the thought of Gigi Palmer having the power to single handedly take her precious child away from her. Tyger looked over at Lillian, "I need to speak with Genoa for a few moments alone. When I return you can take the rest of the day off." Lillian replied "Take your time Mrs. Benedict, I love taking care of Nina. I have no plans for the evening." Tyger smiled at Lillian and exited the room.

Genoa and Tyger reached the office and closed the door behind them. As soon as the door was closed, Tyger sneered, "We've got a problem."

"What's the problem now?"

Tyger folded her arms, turned her back to Genoa and abruptly turned back toward her, "While I was at Spencer's office, Gigi Palmer paid me an unpleasant visit."

Genoa wore a bewildering look, "What the hell did that little tramp want?"

"Initially she came to claim her portion of what she thought Spencer left her in his will. The night Spencer went missing she drove him here to the house. Once Spencer was inside, she decided she wanted to see how I was living. While peeking through my windows she saw every- thing. She had the nerve to try and extort one million dollars from me, but of course I told her I wouldn't give her a dime."

Genoa reached in her pocket and grabbed her pack of cigarettes. Tyger immediately snapped "Genoa don't light that in here. You know better."

Genoa snapped back "And you know better than to stand there and tell me about this Gigi whore as if you're waiting on me to give you the right answer. You already know what to do. You know damn well you can't let her walk around holding on to the truth. You have to kill her and you have to do it soon."

Tyger threw up her hands "Whoa Genoa calm down, just hold on, you know I have a plan." Tyger reached in the inside pocket of her jacket and pulled out the envelope and handed it to Genoa.

Genoa shrugged, "What's this?"

Tyger smiled, "Just open it, but brace yourself first. I think we've found a get out of jail free card." Without any consideration for Genoa's feelings, Tyger waited for her reaction.

Genoa anxiously opened the envelope, reached inside and pulled out the photos. As Genoa held the photos in her hand her eyes grew wide and her mouth fell open like an unhinged door, "Well I'll be damned. Look at this son-of-a-bitch." Tyger stared at Genoa waiting for her take everything in.

Finally, Tyger broke her silence, "I know what I have to do. I know I can't let Gigi Palmer walk away from this, but I need to figure out how to take care of her without tracing it back to me."

Tyger sat on the side of her desk staring into space. Finally, she looked up at Genoa, "Genoa, are you ready to be a widow?"

Without hesitation Genoa looked into Tyger's eyes, "Hasn't that always been our plan?"

"Well, all right then!"

Genoa smirked, "Then this is a better time than any."

Tyger took a seat behind the desk and Genoa took the seat in front of her. "I haven't told you everything, there is more." Tyger retrieved her phone from her pocket, found the photo S.B. sent earlier and showed it to Genoa.

Curling her lip, Genoa questioned, "What is this?"

Tyger leaned back in her chair, "That's what Nina used to hit Spencer."

Genoa stared at the phone for a while until the photo disappeared. "How did S.B. get this?"

Tyger shrugged her shoulders, "That's the million-dollar question. I hid the statue in the basement of our old house. I didn't tell anyone what Nina hit Spencer with or where I hid it. There are only two people that know what happened that night; you and me, but I never told you where I hid the weapon. I can't figure out for the life of me how you found it."

Genoa jumped to her feet and started yelling, "I know damn well you don't think I gave this to S.B. How could you even suggest that I would betray you? I can't believe you would…"

Tyger calmly motioned for Genoa to sit down, "Genoa sit your ass down and relax. I don't know who to trust. S.B. is your husband and Spencer was your son. No matter how much you despised your own son or how long you've been oppressed by your husband, you've been drinking the Benedict crazy juice for so long, I don't know what's going through your head. I hope you wouldn't betray me, but I can't afford to trust anyone. As far as I'm concerned everyone is guilty until proven innocent."

Genoa sat in front of Tyger with a sullen look on her face. Tyger tilted her head, "please stop looking like I just slapped you in the face. This is real, this is not a game we're playing. I need to know I can trust you."

Genoa started to cry, "You're like a daughter to me, I know Spencer was my son and S.B. is my husband. But neither of them has ever given a damn about me. The bottom line is I would do anything to protect Nina."

Tyger narrowed her eyes, "Save your tears for you husband's funeral. I'll give you a chance to prove it, but may hell help you if I find out you're setting me up."

Genoa wiped her face, "I'll do whatever you need me to do."

Tyger leaned back in her chair, rested her neck on the head rest and looked over at Genoa, "You need to call Gigi…" Genoa started to shake her head, no. Tyger pointed her finger at Genoa, "Yes, you will. Call Gigi tell her you want to meet her at Whiskey's in thirty minutes. When she arrives, you tell her you need her to have S.B. come to her house tonight and have sex him. I need for him to be in her house. I need there to be evidence that he was there."

Genoa interrupted Tyger, "So, you just expect Gigi to just do what I ask. What if S.B. won't go to her house?"

Tyger raised from her seat and walked over to the picture on the wall. She pulled the picture from the wall and revealed a safe. Tyger opened the safe and pulled out a stack of cash. Tyger locked the safe and replaced the picture on the wall. Walking beside Genoa, she threw the money on the desk, "That's ten thousand dollars, you give that to Gigi and she'll do anything you want. As for S.B. he's a nasty old man…enough said."

Genoa smiled wickedly, "I knew you wouldn't let me down."

With a stern look, Tyger leaned in toward Genoa, "You just try not to let me down."

Genoa took a deep breath, "Wait a minute, so how will this make me a widow? The way I see it S.B. will get his rocks off once again and none of us will be satisfied."

Feeling annoyed Tyger shrieked, "Just trust me. Gigi should have him out of there by midnight. Once he leaves, I will go in and take care of Gigi and S.B. I will make sure that someone witnesses S.B. leaving Gigi's house. You tell Gigi that you are planning to divorce S.B. and you need evidence of infidelity. Tell her once she completes the job, you will give her an extra twenty-five thousand dollars. If she asks for more, agree to whatever she wants. For now, you don't need to know any more details. Just get this done and I will do the rest."

Genoa shook her head in agreement. Tyger instructed Genoa, "After you meet with Gigi you come right back here. I need you to sit with Nina while I go out."

Genoa nodded her head, "ok." She took the money, tucked it in her pants and pulled her blouse over the stacks. She headed for the door to complete her assignment. Suddenly Genoa stopped and turned toward Tyger, "Are you sure you know what you're doing?"

"Don't worry, everything is gonna work out!"

Genoa pulled her lips in, turned and walked away without uttering a word. Just before, she disappeared, Tyger called her name, "Genoa, please be careful and do what you need to do, all eyes will be on you." Genoa lowered her head and walked out of the office. Once Genoa was gone, Tyger telephoned Whiskey and instructed him to have Genoa and Gigi sit at one of the private tables, yet visible enough for someone to see them meeting. She had to make sure that if anything went down, she had evidence of Gigi and Genoa's meeting. If need be, she would quickly flip on Genoa.

After giving Whiskey his instructions, Tyger called Picasso, "Hey Tyger, what's up!"

"I'll be coming to the club tonight. I'll be there around nine."

Picasso laughed, "Sure, I'll have your usual waiting for you."

Tyger's conversation with Picasso was short and sweet; they had been playing that game for years. Tyger would go to the club and sneak out the back. Picasso would have a car waiting for her and she'd drive off to meet Ace. Tyger could always count on someone seeing her at the club and report to Spencer that she was there and there were no signs of Ace in sight. Tyger knew Spencer would never come to the club and make a scene; he'd wait until she got home and they'd fight all night.

Picasso knew something was up, but he also knew whatever it was couldn't be discussed over the phone. Once Tyger arrived at the club she would fill Picasso in on the events of the evening. From that point on Tyger would have to be extremely careful.

Tyger felt a bit uneasy about not revealing to Genoa that she was the one who killed Spencer. As far as Genoa knew, she was protecting her granddaughter. No matter how much of a snake Spencer was, he was still Genoa's flesh and blood, finding out that Tyger killed Spencer by throwing him in the lake alive could drastically change the game.

Chapter Twelve

After Genoa sent a cryptic text message to Tyger confirming her meeting with Gigi went well, she hopped in the car and drove to the club to meet Picasso. She then waited for the follow-up text to let her know that S.B. left his house; Tyger left the club and headed to Gigi's house. Genoa knew S.B. was meeting a woman. He always took a long shower, shaved his genital hair, shaved under his arms and plastered himself in offensively loud cologne that made the sinuses tingle. Genoa and S.B. were rarely intimate. On the desperate occasion they did have sex he didn't bother to shower or shave. He was like a wild reckless dog that gave four or five humps and fell asleep. Besides the huge imprint his flabby flesh made on her body, Genoa wouldn't even know they'd just had sex. Ironically, Genoa wasn't jealous of other women, she was grateful that S.B. wasn't at home pouncing up and down dripping sweat on her. After receiving Gigi's text that S.B. was on his way to her house, Genoa gave Tyger the green light.

Tyger waited to see S.B. enter Gigi's house. Approximately forty-seven minutes later, she saw him leave. The two-minute man had struck again; S.B. was quick like a woodpecker, pecking his nasty wood a mile a minute. Waiting for S.B.'s light to disappear in the distance, Tyger darted behind Gigi's house. She reached into her pocket and retrieved the set of keys to the condo Spencer left behind. Once Tyger reached the back door, she carefully placed the key in the lock and turned her wrist until she heard the lock click. She eased into the door carefully closing it behind her.

As she stood in front of the washing machine dressed in all black wearing soft sole shoes, a skullcap and leather gloves she heard Gigi bumping about. Not making a sound, Tyger eased down the hall carefully. She tiptoed down the hall as if she were walking a tight rope. Finally, she reached the living room and saw Gigi's back turned to her. Gigi was preparing to take the wine glasses into the kitchen she and S.B. had used earlier.

As the hair on the back of her neck stood up, Gigi carefully placed the bottle of wine and the glasses back on the coffee table. Still facing forward, her stomach boiled with fright. She knew someone was standing behind her waiting to make her a victim, but she had no idea who. She took in a deep breath of air and slowly exhaled. She turned slowly and stared into Tyger's eyes.

Gigi's heart began to beat rapidly, beads of sweat formed over her lip, her pulse quickened and her breath became shorter as the sight of Tyger standing in front of her in a skullcap and gloves scared the hell out of her. Tears streamed down Gigi's face as her legs began to quiver.

Finally, Tyger broke her silence, "Before you go, I just wanted you to know why Spencer didn't leave you anything in his will." Tyger threw Gigi the pictures, "pick them up." Kneeling scrambling to retrieve the photos, her mouth dropped at the sight of the photos. Gigi peered up at Tyger. Tyger had been very careful in handling the photographs. She made copies of the originals. The pictures that were found in Spencer's office earlier had her fingerprints on them, so Tyger made copies from home and only touched them with gloves.

As Gigi thumbed through the pictures her eyes grew wide. Gigi explained, "I promise you I would never ever tell what I saw. I was just trying to get more money, I just needed money…"

Tyger tilted her head, "Speaking of money, where is the ten thousand that Genoa gave you earlier."

Putting two and two together, Gigi realized that she'd been played, "Damn, I should have known…"

Gigi swallowed hard, "I'll give it to you and then we can talk about this."

Tyger sternly yelled, "Where is my money?"

Gigi nervously answered, "It's in my purse." Gigi pointed to her purse resting in the chair.

Holding the gun in her hand, Tyger backed up toward Gigi's purse and pulled the stack of money out. As she watched Tyger, Gigi stood still trying not to pass out from the shock of knowing that she was about to die.

Tyger waived the money in front of Gigi, "I told you I wasn't giving you a dime of my money."

Gigi nervously waived her hands, "Tyger please, wait, I have something I think you want!"

Tyger narrowed her eyes, "What could you possibly have that I need."

Gigi pleaded, "If you just let me go for one minute, I'll get it."

Tyger laughed, "Really Gigi, what are you smoking? Do you really think I'm gonna let you go find something to kill me with? Please, shut up before you really piss me off."

Trembling, Gigi yelled out, "I have the statue that Nina hit Spencer with. S.B. asked me to hide it."

Tyger took a deep breath, "Where is it?"

Gigi pointed down the hall, "It's in my bedroom."

Tyger raised her gun, "Turn around slowly and walk toward the bedroom. If you make any sudden moves, I will shoot you."

Gigi, slowly turned and walked toward her bedroom, "Spencer paid me to keep it here, he didn't want to risk Genoa finding it."

Tyger took the opportunity to find out how S.B. got the statue.

"Did he tell you how he got the statue?"

"No, he just told me what it was and asked me to hide it."

"What did he promise you for hiding the statue?"

"S.B. was going to blackmail you for the property that you own in the Hole. He said the Salt company was buying up all those houses to expand the underground salt mine. He said you wouldn't sell the old house. Before he died Spencer and his business partners were working on a way to take the land from you. S.B. said that once Spencer took the property from you the two of them were going to make millions. Now that Spencer is dead, S.B. still needs the property, but you own it. He'll do anything to get it."

Tyger interrupted Gigi, "Who are these business partners?"

"I don't know, before he died Spencer wouldn't tell me and S.B. claims he doesn't know who they are. All I know is Spencer mentioned a company that he started with two other people. The company was called BAS Industries…"

"Wow Gigi aren't you just a little **songbird tonight**. You're singing all the Benedict family secrets. I just don't understand how you had all of this in the palm of your hands and ended up with nothing, but an eviction notice and a closet full of bargain basement rags. I almost feel sorry for you."

Gigi buried her head in her chest, "Please Tyger, I'm sorry. I can work with you and get S.B. to tell me who gave him the statue…"

Tyger laughed, "Do you really think, I can trust you? Nothing can help you now."

Glancing over at a bag on the bed, Tyger could see the statue peeking out of a felt bag. Tyger motioned for Gigi to pick it up,

"Slowly, pick up the statue from the bed and hand it to me." Gigi gingerly walked toward the bed and picked the statue up. She turned around and handed it to Tyger. Tyger raised her gun, "Put the statute on the dresser." Gigi leaned over and placed the statue on her dresser. Tyger instructed Gigi to strip naked, "Take off your robe, pull back the sheet and lie in the bed."

Perplexed, Gigi questioned Tyger, "Do what?"

"If I have to repeat myself, I'm going to be pissed."

Gigi, walked toward the left side of the bed and dropped her robe on the floor, she pulled the sheets back and lay in her bed." Tyger walked toward the center of the room in front of Gigi's bed, "Pull the sheet up to your neck." Gigi pulled the sheet up and Tyger raised her gun.

Gigi started pleading with Tyger, "But I gave you the statue, now S.B. has nothing on you. I promise I won't say a word."

Tyger laughed, "Gigi, you are a whore to your core. You whored yourself out to Spencer and S.B. for money. You whored yourself out to Genoa and took her money to betray S.B. and you whored yourself out to me to betray S.B. You ain't loyal, but worst of all you're a snitch."

Tyger pulled the trigger and listened to Gigi take her last breath. With the photos in her hand, Tyger opened the drawer of the nightstand next to Gigi's bed. Leaving the drawer ajar Tyger took one last look around the room. Tyger walked past the dresser and grabbed the statue and exited the condo the same way she entered.

Trying to gather herself, Tyger ran to the car. She sat in the passenger seat staring into space, taking in one deep breath after the other until she felt faint. With her chin hung in her chest, Tyger felt sick to her stomach. Fighting back the urge to hurl in her lap. She took a deep breath, cleared her throat and wiped the sweat from her face. Gripping the statue in her hand, she reached over on the seat and stuffed it into her bag. Trying to catch her breath she finally called Vincent to inform him that everything had been taken care of. Pushing "END" on her phone, Tyger put the key in the ignition started up the old box Chevy, she'd borrowed from Picasso and drove off with her heart racing and the lights turned off. Driving down the street in a daze, Tyger grabbed the bag and pulled it next to her. She refused to let the statue out of her sight. This time she knew just where hide it.

Once Tyger made it back to the club, she took a shower in the office suite, dressed in her best drag, fixed her face and strutted through the crowd. She mingled just to make sure she'd been seen. She wasn't worried about an alibi, because everyone who was anyone would make sure Tyger was taken care of, she was just that type of lady.

Tyger knew Ace would be arriving at the club soon and she didn't want him to catch her there. She'd been ignoring his calls all day. She knew he wanted to see her, but she just couldn't fit him into her schedule and now it was time for her to get to her restaurant before closing time. Since Spencer went missing, Tyger had poured much of her energy into her restaurant.

Tyger owned Brown Shuga, a gourmet soul food restaurant. You could eat collard greens and fried chicken while listening to live blues, R&B and jazz. Brown Shuga was open from 4pm until midnight during the week and 2am on Friday and Saturday. There was always a line outside the door at Brown Shuga. people begged Tyger to stay open just a few more minutes after closing so they could continue to enjoy a good time. Brown Shuga was the one place where Tyger could lock out the rest of the world and relax. Every once and a while when the mood hit, Tyger would sing a song or two. Music was in Tyger's blood, she could play the piano and belt out a sultry soul-stirring tune. That was a talent Whiskey and Dee Dee both passed onto their children.

Exiting the club, she hopped in her car and headed to Brown Shuga. It was eleven o' clock and her heart was heavy. Tonight would be the night she would grace her patrons with a song. Tyger had become overwhelmed by something she could not explain. As she pondered the events of the last few weeks and what was yet to come, Tyger began to feel mentally and physically exhausted.

Driving down the freeway at top speed weaving in and out of traffic, she became lightheaded and her stomach grew increasingly uneasy. The image of the terrified look that Gigi wore before she took her last breath began to weigh heavily on Tyger. She knew she couldn't trust Gigi to keep her mouth shut. Tyger knew she had to protect her family. It was too late to turn back. The next move had to be made; She had to get rid of S.B. soon. Knowing someone close to her had given S.B. the statue wore a hole deep in her soul. Who could it be? Someone had to be following her, tracking her every move. Whoever it was, when found she would show no mercy.

Suddenly, Tyger felt her stomach rumble and her mouth began to taste sour. She turned on her hazard lights and pulled over on the shoulder of the highway. Before she could get her door completely open, she leaned her head out of the car window and vomited. She began to sweat profusely, a wave of warm air swept through her body. With her hands trembling, she opened the door to the car and breathed in the night air. Hanging her head out of the side of the car she felt the wind of the passing cars whip through her hair. Frightened by the piercing sounds of the horns passing bellowing in her ear and the vibration for the cars passing by, Tyger quickly grabbed a hold of the door. She pulled the door shut and reached out for the button to recline her seat. Waiting for her stomach to settle, she lie on her back staring at the stars through the moon roof wondering when the madness would come to an end.

Chapter Thirteen

W hen Tyger arrived at the restaurant, she hurried to her office to change her clothes, yet again. She slipped into a slinky black dress that hugged her curves like wet paint. Feeling like a stuffed pig she discovered the dress that she'd purchased only a month ago was just a tad too tight. As she sucked in her stomach and arched her back, she noticed her reflection in the mirror. Spencer's murder had taken a toll on her. Her cheeks had become round, her neck was a bit puffy and her skin was becoming haggard. Curling her lip in disgust, Tyger screeched, "Oh, hell naw. You will not break down." Making a mental note to call the doctor and schedule a routine exam, she shook her head and took a deep breath and flashed a fake smile.

Holding her head high she walked out of the office silently praying the dress would not rip in half. Floating on air she entered the dining room. She elegantly moved across the room greeting each table. If only for just a few moments Tyger had put GiGi out of her mind. After working the room, she stepped on stage and prepared to sing. Singing was her own personal therapeutic escape. Turning toward the band she instructed them to play, "At Last." The band smiled with excitement; this was as much of a treat for them as it was to the audience. As the band began to play, Tyger introduced herself, "Good evening, my name is Tyger Benedict, I am your host and I just felt like singing tonight." The crowd erupted in clapping, catcalls and whistles as they waited with bated breath to hear her sing.

Tyger closed her eyes and crooned a soulful tune that bellowed through the building. Tyger's true calling was singing. It made her feel free and alive. At her core she had the soul of a blues singer. She knew enough about the blues to have a catalog of music to last a lifetime. Tyger used the stage to confess her love for Ace and disdain for Spencer through song. Desperately regretting the life she chose, she often got lost as her mind wandered to places she would never go as she took the audience with her. When Tyger sang people hung on every note with an awe struck gaze.

With a surge of adrenalin flowing through her veins, Tyger was electrifying. Standing in front of the microphone with the light from the street shining through her eyes sparkled like exquisite diamonds. Walking through the door Aiden was arrested by the statuesque vision of perfection standing before him. With his eyes glued to her silhouette his breath quickened at the sound of Tyger's voice rolling through his body like thunder. Standing against the wall with his hands by his side Aiden became hypnotized as Tyger sang, "At last my love has come along…" The words stung his soul leaving remnants of regret. Aiden knew she was singing about Ace, but for one moment in time he imagined she was signing to him. Piercing Tyger's soul with an intrusive, yet admiring gaze, Aiden could not take his eyes off her.

Disconnected from reality, Aiden vowed he would have Tyger by any means necessary. Remembering the last time she and Ace were together, Tyger displayed a sensuous smile. She had become lost in a world where only she and Ace existed. Slowly opening her eyes, she looked out over the dining room and noticed Aiden invading her space. Knowing who he was and how much Ace loathed him Tyger felt she was betraying Ace by allowing Aiden to gawk at her with lust in his eyes. Scanning the room to figure out an escape route that would take her from the stage to a place where Aiden could not easily get to her the tone of her song changed. Her fire had been extinguished. Watching him walk over and take a seat at the bar, her heart sank to her feet, now she would have to pass Aiden to get to her office. There was no way to avoid him. Tyger would have to play his game.

After she finished, Tyger exited the stage as gracefully as she had arrived. Standing to their feet the crowd begged for more. Inhaling the energy from the crowd she strolled over to the bar and took a seat next to Aiden.

Helping her onto the stool, Aiden flashed his perfectly beautiful white teeth and shook his head. Tyger sneered, "Is there something wrong detective?" Tyger knew good and well Aiden was officially sprung and she hadn't even breathed on him yet. Depending on Aiden's tenacity to get what he wanted, Tyger knew she was playing with fire.

Tilting her head to request a glass of water from the bartender, Aiden became lost. Her flawless coca skin, beautiful eyes and plump lips made him drunk with the thought of tasting her. Turning to ask Aiden his drink preference, she caught him glaring at her. Aiden didn't blink or flinch; he continued to concentrate on making sure she knew he wanted her. Tyger looked into his eyes, "What would you like..." Tyger paused, "...to drink."

Aiden smiled, "Your best Scotch on the rocks with water on the side." Tyger nodded her head for the bartender to honor Aiden's request. She requested a glass of wine.

She turned her back to the bar and crossed her legs. Aiden continued to face the bar. Tyger took a sip of water and cleared her throat, "I thought I made it clear that if you had any questions for me you would contact my attorney."

Aiden raised his brow, "This visit is definitely not business."

Tyger laughed, "Really, then why are you here?"

"I'm here to see you."

"So, this is personal?"

"Yes, but I think you already knew that. I don't think I've done a good job of hiding the fact that I'm quite taken with you."

"You're taken with me, my how gentile of you." Tyger took a deep breath, "Look, Aiden there is nothing I can do for you. You're the lead detective in my husband's murder investigation and I'm one of the prime suspects. Outside of this investigation, we have nothing else to discuss."

Taking a sip of Scotch, "You have interesting taste in men. You married Spencer Benedict, but you won't hold a conversation with me. I don't understand, why Spencer? What was it about him?"

Tyger laughed, "I admit Spencer never made me melt. But, he was charming in his own way, everyone has some sort of appeal."

"Really, so what is my appeal?"

"It's wisdom, the wisdom to know when you're treading on dangerous ground."

"When it comes to you, my judgment is a bit impaired."

Turning toward Aiden, Tyger's eyes widened, "A man loses his charm when he's no longer breathing."

Resting his arm on the bar, Aiden smiled in defiance, "Is that a threat."

"Of course not, it's just a little advice."

As Aiden's spirit grew dim, he watched Tyger's eyes tell the story of her contempt for him. He knew Ace had shared their family secret and Ace's enemy had become Tyger's nemesis as well. Still parked on the barstools, both Aiden and Tyger sat at the bar all night engaged in conversation about everything Aiden could think of to monopolize her attention.

The night began to draw near to closing time. Tyger and Aiden had spent two hours engaging in mindless chatter. She soon realized the restaurant was empty and the staff was almost done cleaning and closing down. Tyger, glanced at the clock on the wall, "Damn, it's late I should have been home by now. Now I have to drive home with this pounding headache."

Aiden flashed a coy smile, "I can drive you home."

"Nice try detective, I'll drive myself."

"Alright I get it, my rap is weak."

They both shared a laugh followed by an awkward silence. Tyger turned her attention away from Aiden and asked the bartender to hand her the medication bottle behind the bar. The bartender placed the bottle on the counter and resumed counting down the register. Before she could open the bottle, the manager of the restaurant pulled Tyger away for a moment to discuss a few housekeeping items. Leaving Aiden seated at the bar, Tyger stepped to the back. After her brief meeting with her manager, she rushed back to get Aiden out of the restaurant. Walking back to the bar with a pounding headache, she noticed the pill bottle was missing,

"Where are my pills?"

"I gave them back to the bartender. You shouldn't mix medication with all that wine you've been drinking tonight."

Without responding to Aiden, Tyger thanked the staff for another amazing night. She instructed everyone to come in two hours later the next day. Finally bidding Aiden a good night, she hoped he would get the hint and leave, "Aiden, thanks for keeping me company tonight, but I must get home to Nina. So, I'm going to gather my things and head out. I'm sure we'll see each other soon."

With excitement in his voice Aiden offered, "I'll wait around to make sure you get to your car safely."

Tyger smirked, "I don't think that's necessary. Someone is always watching after me, but thanks for the offer."

Guarding her personal space, Tyger stood between the bar and the hallway leading to the back of the restaurant to make sure Aiden left the restaurant. Aiden sluggishly slid off the barstool, "I guess I'll take a hint. Be careful going home Mrs. Benedict."

Tyger watched as Aiden walked out the front door. She motioned for one of the servers to lock the door behind him. Everything had been shut down and everyone was ready to head out. Tyger's manager asked, "Do you want us to wait for you?"

She smiled, "No go on home, I'll be fine."

Before the manager exited the building Tyger asked, "Karli, if you see the man I was talking to earlier, will you text me, please?"

"Yes of course, if he's still outside I'll text you and wait for you."

"Thank you so much, you know I'll take care of you."

"Come on Tyger, you already take good care of me. Good night."

"Good night Karli."

Feeling uneasy, Tyger waited to hear the doors lock and hurried to collect her things. Entering her office, she ripped her dress off, pulled her t-shirt over her head and reached for her jeans. Trying to gather her breath the room began spinning. Falling against the wall, she slid to the floor. Crawling toward the couch she felt an overwhelming sense of euphoria; like she was floating on air. Her vision grew hazy as she placed her hands in front of her to feel her way to the coach. Reaching out to grab one of the cushions on the couch, she felt a human hand touch her hand. Before she could scream, she felt a hand cover her mouth. Hearing a voice warn her, "Don't scream," she felt helpless, but tranquil. Suddenly, the hand was removed from her mouth and she came face to face with Aiden Arias.

Like a helpless rag doll, she lay in his arms. Trying to lift her hands in protest, they became heavy and weak. Aiden whispered, "It's obvious you've had too much to drink. You need to relax and wait until you feel better."

Still fairly lucid, Tyger asked, "How did you get in here?"

Aiden laughed, "I'm a cop, I have uninhibited access to everything I need."

Batting her eyes and rubbing her face her body grew warm, "I'm not drunk, I know what drunk is, this ain't it."

With cynical reassurance, Aiden caressed Tyger's face, "You'll be fine, don't worry it will wear off soon."

Feeling confused, Tyger tried to scream, "What the fuck! Did you drug me?"

"No, it's an herbal supplement. You needed something to help you relax."

Helping Tyger to her feet, the two of them stood within inches of each other. Tyger could feel Aiden's massive hand resting in the small of her back tighten. Trying to free herself from Aiden's grasp, she became exhausted; she was too weak.

"Aiden please let me go, I need to call Ace to pick me up."

Aiden tightened his grip and placed his full juicy lips on the side of Tyger's neck, "No, I am the brother you need, not Ace."

As his plump tongue brushed against her neck, Tyger struggled, "Aiden Stop!"

He whispered, "Just relax."

Resisting, Tyger's voice grew loud and strong, "No, Aiden please stop…" Aiden ignored Tyger's pleading, he could hear her mouth saying no, but he could feel her body relax.

As Aiden parted Tyger's lips with his tongue, he kissed her as if she would be the last woman he'd ever kiss. This time everything was real. This was far from one of Aiden's fantasies. Pulling Tyger closer to him, he palmed her bottom in his hands. Tyger was firm and perfectly rounds, she felt just like Aiden had imagined. As Aiden ran his hands up Tyger's spine, he continued to kiss her allowing her no room to deny what was happening. Aiden retreated from Tyger's lips and looked straight into her eyes. As their eyes met, Tyger thought about Ace.

Suddenly, Tyger slapped Aiden across his face and scratched his cheek. When Aiden grabbed his face Tyger tried to head for the door, but with little to no effort, Aiden reached out and grabbed her arm. Aiden pulled Tyger closer to him and grabbed her waist. As he spun Tyger around in his direction, their eyes met; All Tyger could see was Ace whooping her ass and throwing Aiden's body in the Detroit River.

As Tyger raised her hands to try and free herself from Aiden's hold once again, he grabbed her left arm leaned in and kissed her lips. His lips were so soft and Tyger almost succeeded at resisting until, he parted her lips with his tongue and entered her mouth. Aiden's tongue was sweet and juicy. As their tongues touched, Tyger felt her clit pulsate. There was a war going on inside her body. Tyger's mind kept telling her to stop. The voice inside her head was screaming, "Get this man off of you and get out of here." The voice between Tyger's legs was saying, "Please, just get a little taste of his fine ass."

As Aiden continued to kiss Tyger, the voice between her legs started to overshadow the voice in her head. As Tyger heard the phone ringing in her purse she started to come back to her senses. Feeling her body starting to resist him once again, Aiden placed his left hand on the small of Tyger's back picked her up and danced her over to the couch. Aiden softly laid Tyger down and ran his hand up her thigh. As the cool breeze from the air conditioning made her body shiver, Aiden's warm kiss shot through her body like a flame.

Feeling herself slip away, she whispered, "Aiden, I can't do this... please stop..."

In a low and commanding voice that moved through Tyger's body like warm water, Aiden whispered, "I wouldn't dream of having you do anything, this pleasure will be all mine."

Aiden slid Tyger's panties off and gently opened her legs. With the tip of his middle finger, he gently rubbed Tyger's clit. Tyger's lips became moist and her mind started to wander off to some place that was far from Brown Shuga. Aiden took his index finger and entered Tyger's flesh. As he searched for the spot that made Tyger let out a low and sensual moan, paralyzed, Tyger stared at the ceiling thinking she wanted him to stop, but she couldn't speak.

As Aiden caressed Tyger's clit, she lay on her back her head continued to spin. How could she ruin a lifetime with Ace because her flesh had surrendered to the man he hated most? At that moment, Tyger's fear of Ace and what he might do was stronger than what Aiden was putting down. Just as Tyger looked toward the ceiling to gather her strength, she felt the tip of Aiden's tongue and the warmth from his breath tickle her. She knew she had been defeated; she couldn't do a damn thing but lay there.

Feeling Aiden's wet tongue slowly and gently flickering against her clit, warm waves of ecstasy mixed with the effects of whatever Aiden had given her sent Tyger out of her mind. Like a succulent slice of fruit Aiden sucked Tyger's clit. Tyger could feel her juices flowing as he licked her with long slow strokes outlining her lips with his tongue. Still trying to fight the inevitable, Tyger's mind was trying to figure out how to get away from Aiden, but she could only howl, "Damn..." In an instant Tyger was calling the Lord's name in vain as her body shook. She couldn't control what was happening. Just when Tyger thought she couldn't take anymore; Aiden placed his plump tongue inside of her rolling it around. With his tongue still inside her, he placed his lips full against her lips and French kissed the inside of Tyger's warm flesh. With every stroke of his tongue Tyger's started to quiver and her voice climbed an octave. Tyger had fought the good fight, but she ultimately lost control.

Tyger couldn't hold on any longer, she relaxed her body and gave in. Hearing the sounds of Maxwell playing in the restaurant Aiden hummed the tune to the song while the vibrations from his mouth and the rolling of his tongue made Tyger explode like a geyser Reaching a climax, Tyger's eyes rolled in the top of her head and a tear strolled down the side of her cheeks. As her body twitched uncontrollably, Tyger's flesh was weak and tender. She could feel the warm eruption of excitement streaming through her body. Tyger lay there with her mouth wide open staring at the ceiling wondering, *"what the fuck was that."*

Aiden stood over her with a huge grin, "Sometimes in my business we get caught up when certain technicalities are involved. Now you never have to admit that you had sex with me…It was all *my* pleasure!"

Hearing Aiden's voice echo in her ear, Tyger's head started to spin. She felt like she had just gone on a long trip through a tunnel. Regaining her senses, she felt like cold shit on a kitchen floor, nasty and out of place. While rubbing her temples and trying to focus, Tyger could see Aiden standing over her. Tyger tried to get up abruptly, but she still felt weak and woozy. As Tyger, feel back on the couch, she said, "I need you to leave, now."

"Come on Tyger, you're hurting my feelings, I know I wasn't that bad…as a matter of fact, I felt you enjoying yourself. No matter how hard you tried to resist me, there was something inside of you that at some point you were happy as hell to let me enjoy a feast fit for a king."

"You are a sick son-of-a-bitch, you will pay…" Walking toward the bathroom, Aiden interrupted her.

"Who's gonna make me pay for anything? I know you're not gonna tell Ace about this and it's not quite time for me to tell him yet, so I'm not worried."

"I don't always rely on Ace to fight my battles. You forget one thing, this is my city, and the only reason you're not dead yet is because no one has said that it should be so, just yet. Don't let my pretty face and sweet juice fool you. A man that I slept with for ten years ended up at the bottom of a lake. Don't think that badge makes you exempt from getting buried in concrete..."

For a brief moment, there was an awkward silence. Finally, Aiden reappeared. Walking close to Tyger, Aiden handed her a warm towel and whispered, "I don't know what my brother told you about me, but it seems you have both underestimated me. I would love to keep you out of our little family feud, but if you wanna play with the big boys then that's fine with me...It's such a shame though, I sure was looking forward to hearing you call my name again..."

Just as the words escaped his lips, Aiden turned to walk out the door. He stopped and turned toward Tyger, "Oh, I guess I should ask the question again."

Tyger squinted, "Huh, what are you talking about?"

With a haughty grin Aiden asked, "What do you find appealing about me now?"

Chapter Fourteen

Feeling like she was walking barefoot on hot glass, Tyger grabbed her shirt and pulled it over her head. Squeezing into her jeans she headed toward the back door. Securing the door, she watched as he sped through the alley. Tyger locked down Brown Shuga and sat in the dark trying figure out how the hell she was going to get out of this. Tyger knew eventually Aiden was going to tell Ace. Tyger knew Aiden had to go, but she didn't know how. Growing weary of plotting and scheming she retired to the bathroom, took a shower, dressed in loose fitting sweats and headed home. Still feeling woozy, she drove slow and careful stopping along the way to rest. What should have been a twenty-minute drive home turned in to an hour-long ride.

Arriving home, she entered the back of the house from the garage. Opening the door to the kitchen, Tyger fumbled for the light switch. As the light popped on Tyger almost peed on herself. Ace was standing in front of her like a big ass bear breathing fire from his nose. As her heart fluttered with fear, she knew Ace must have known she'd been with Aiden. Ace moved in close to Tyger and pinned her against the wall. He leaned in and pressed his body against hers. Faintly whispering in her ear, he made his demands clear, "This is the last time that I am going to tell you to stay away from Aiden. I am trying hard to respect you because I love you with every fucking breath that I breathe...please don't take my love for granted..." Ace stepped back and pointed his finger at Tyger, "Please, don't make me whoop your ass!"

Ace didn't wait for a response; he walked through the house and exited through the front door. Dazed and shaken, she couldn't figure out how she could kill another woman but be shaken by the words of one man. Ace had never put his hands on Tyger, but she knew if it came down to it he would carry out his threat. Tyger stood in the middle of the floor holding her chest wondering how much Ace knew about her encounter with Aiden. She figured he didn't know the whole story because she was still breathing. With her head still woozy and guilt weighing heavy on her, Tyger slowly felt her way through the house. Finally arriving in her bedroom, she collapsed on the bed fell asleep.

The day after her encounter with Aiden, he called relentlessly, but Tyger continued to ignore his phone calls. Aiden was clearly on some other shit that wasn't at all normal. It seemed that in Aiden's mind he thought he had a chance with Tyger.

Still recovering from the effects of Aiden's drug and Ace's threat, the morning after was riddled with sickness and remorse. She traveled to the kitchen and made a cup of peppermint tea. Eating half a box of antacids, she was anxious to find out who Spencer's partners were. She called one of her old colleagues Tanner Hicks to do some digging. Tanner was a very shrewd private investigator who knew how to squeeze blood from a turnip. Tanner knew how to wiggle his way out of trouble, but Tanner was most useful in the area of elimination. He could make you disappear without a trace as if you'd never even existed. Tyger hoped Tanner would come through quickly and she would know who or what was trying to destroy her.

Sitting at the kitchen counter letting her thoughts wander and clutter her mind, Tyger failed to see her sister Bella standing in the doorway on the other side of the room. Startling Tyger, Bella asked, "A penny for your thoughts."

Tyger laughed, "My thoughts aren't even worth a penny."

Bella walked over and sat down next to Tyger. "What's going on with you, you've been acting strange lately. I mean stranger than usual."

"With everything that's going on, don't you think I have the right to act a little strange?"

"Yes, but this is different. For the last two days you've been really anxious and I haven't seen Ace around."

Tyger nervously poured Bella a cup of tea and took a breath. Hesitating before she spoke, "I had a weird encounter with Detective Arias last night that left me a....well...for lack of a better word concerned."

Bella shrugged her shoulders "Concerned...concerned about what?"

"Since Aiden showed up on my doorstep the day Spencer's body was found, he has made it clear that he wants to pin this murder on Ace and have a little piece of me in the process. He has been relentless, showing up here at the house, at the restaurant and any place else he can find me."

Bella laughed, "Damn sis you've got the detective sprung... Did you give him some?"

Guilt ridden, Tyger lied through her teeth. She regretted mentioning Aiden's name. Tyger backpedaled, "No, of course not. He is investigating Spencer's murder...did you forget that?"

"No, I didn't. That's an even better reason than any to give him some of your cookies. He'll get so caught up in you that he'll forget about the case."

"Bella, please. Aiden will never give up. He doesn't really want me, he thinks being with me will hurt Ace..."

Bella looked confused, "What does he have against Ace. He's only been in Detroit a few months."

Tyger took a sip of tea, "Aiden and Ace are brothers. They haven't seen each other in years. They absolutely hate each other to the point of death; one would kill the other if given the chance."

Almost choking on her tea, Bella shrieked, "Damn...are you serious. No wonder Aiden is so damn fine, he's related to Ace...and here you are caught in some steamy love triangle shit as usual. My dear sister, how do you do it?"

"Do what?"

"How do you get these men to fall all over you? I mean you're cute, but damn."

Bella could see how tense Tyger was, so she tried to ease the tension. "Come on sissy lighten up? You're really scaring me right now, what's going through your head right now?"

Tyger looked up at Bella with a somber gaze and in a cold-blooded tone said, "I'm thinking of how to kill Detective Aiden Arias and get away with it."

Bella looked at Tyger with deviant sincerity, "I'll do it."

"You'll do what?"

"I will kill Aiden. He will never expect me to be the one."

"Hell…NO…you sound crazy!"

"I'm serious Tyger, let me do this. I mean, if he can't have you then he can have the next best thing. Hell, he's a man, he can't refuse. I'll give him the speech about how much I hate Ace and I wish that you would leave him routine. I'll get him drunk, fuck him good and put a bullet in his head."

"Bella, are you high?"

"No, I'm just tired. I'm tired of feeling helpless. I see what's about to happen to this family and you're all I got. I can't have nobody comin' up in here taking you, Picasso, Ace, none of you, away from me. If it wasn't for Ace and Picasso coming to get me the night Shake died I would be dead. I was so helpless that night. I couldn't save him, and I couldn't help myself. I just watched…I watched as Shake died and a part of me died with him. I just can't sit back and watch now. I promise you I can do this. I know I can…please let me help you."

Pondering the thought of including Bella in her plans to get rid of Aiden, Tyger knew Bella could charm anyone, but she was unstable. She couldn't be around drugs or alcohol for more than two minutes without getting wasted. Bella's addiction seemed to be getting worse; she'd become more distant and unstable.

Bella had been trying to forget Shakes murder half her life. As Tyger's world spun out of control, Bella was a nervous wreck now more than ever.

Listening to Bella beg, Tyger shouted, "No, I can't risk something happening to you. I'm sorry, but it's out of the question."

"Don't worry about me Tyger, I can handle myself. I'll be fine."

"Bella…I said no. You're not thinking rationally right now. You can't stop snortin' powder long enough to get yourself together. What you need to do is help yourself and let go of that shit…it's got you messed up. Look at you, you're shaking right now…"

Belle jumped from her seat, "I can't stop because I don't want to. If I stop, then I will remember. Don't you understand, every time I go to sleep I see Shakes face and I see his head exploding? I can't get that out of my head. I can never get it out of my head…Do you know how hard I've tried to erase the memory of that night and forget that I ever knew him…So, yes, I am a drug addict, I'm a junkie and yes…You don't know how it feels because Ace is alive…Picasso, John Paul, they are all alive. They played the game and won. All of them are running around like they own every damn thing in the world. Look at you, living this lavish life, what about me. When is my turn to live like this? I want to live like you, not mooch off of you. Picasso, Ace even John Paul, they all deserve to be dead, but Shakespeare is the one who died. It's not fair…"

Things had gotten real quickly. At top speed, Tyger stepped toward Bella reared her hand back and slapped her across the face. "Don't you stand in my house and wish death on our family; the people that take care of you. The people that keep your crackhead ass off the streets. I've let you live with your little story about why you're on drugs because you saw Shakespeare get his head blown off and that would fuck anybody up. But I will snatch the life right out of your body if you ever say that bullshit again."

With their pulse racing and hearts beating out of their chests, Tyger and Bella stood toe to toe like two wild lions ready to tear one another apart. Staring at the hatred in her sister's eyes, Tyger realized she was staring into the eyes of the one who betrayed her. Feeling Tyger's anger burning through her skin, Bella took a deep breath and slowly backed away from Tyger. Tyger swallowed the lump in her throat and narrowed her eyes, "I hope this little melt down is the result of one of your drug induced rants, because if this is fueled by something else you will wish you were out there in Wood Acre Cemetery next to Shakespeare." Feeling her fist ball, Tyger carefully stepped away from Bella. Hoping she was wrong about her sister, Tyger whispered, "Whatever you've done, fix it, now."

After Tyger exited the kitchen, Bella grabbed her chest and inhaled a few deep breaths. She ran to the sink and filled a glass with water. Her hands were shaking, she couldn't move. Standing in front of the sink, she was startled by a sputtering noise. She looked over and noticed Tyger's phone vibrating on the kitchen island. Recognizing the caller, she pondered whether or not to answer. Bella picked up the phone and touched "accept." Anxiously waiting to hear the voice on the other end of the phone, she finally heard him say, "Hello…"

Pausing for a moment, Bella reluctantly said, "Yes, hello."

The voice on the other end seemed puzzled, "I'm sorry, I must have the wrong number."

Bella raised her voice, "No, please don't hang up. This is Bella." "Bella?"

"Yes, Bella."

"Why are you answering Tyger's phone. Are you crazy?"

"No! We need to talk, now. I'm on my way to see you."

Before she gave the caller a chance to respond Bella disconnected the call. She ran upstairs and changed into the most legally skanky ensemble she could find. Half-dressed she ran out the front door and hopped in her car. Heading across town, Bella was manic. She knew she'd pissed Tyger off and she was afraid of what would come next. Bella hoped for the sake of sisterhood and blood relation Tyger wouldn't honor her threat. She needed to put things in reverse and figure out what to do next.

Arriving at a less than desirable apartment community, Bella checked herself in the mirror before exiting the car. Opening the door, she stood next to the car and pulled her skirt down. Adjusting her blouse, she pushed her sunglasses close to her face with her index finger. Checking her surroundings to make sure she had not been followed, she headed toward the stairway leading to a second-floor apartment. Arriving at the door, Bella reached in her purse, grabbed her compact and checked her face once more. After running her fingers through her hair, she closed the compact placed it in her purse and took a deep breath. Extending her reach, she balled her hand and knocked rapidly on the door.

Holding in her stomach and arching her back, Bella stood in front of the door waiting with her head held high. Finally, the lock clicked, the doorknob turned and the door opened. Aiden Arias stood behind the door welcoming her with open arms, "Come on in." Bella walked through the door of Aiden's apartment and closed the door behind them.

Chapter Fifteen

Watching Bella walk past him and into the living room, Aiden asked, "What's so urgent you had to show up at my house?"

"Don't act like I've never been in this house; in your bed before."

"Bella, you know the rules. We can't risk being seen together."

"Oh really, can you risk trying to screw my sister? What's up with you Aiden, are you trying to sleep with my sister?"

Aiden laughed, "Sleep is the last thing I want to do with your sister."

Bella raised her hand to slap Aiden. Aiden grabbed her hand and spun her around throwing her on the couch. Standing over her he sneered, "You better control yourself and stop acting like you don't know what this is. Don't let your emotions get you in trouble. I need you to stay focused. This is not the time to catch feelings worrying about who I may or may not be screwing."

Aiden walked over to the kitchen and retrieved a bottle of water from the refrigerator. He grabbed a few ice cubes from the freezer and dropped them into a glass. Walking toward Bella, he poured the water into the glass. Handing her the glass, he questioned, "Now, why are you here?"

Bella took the glass from Aiden and placed it on the table in front of her. Shaking her head she said, "I can't do this Aiden. I think Tyger suspects something."

"Why would you say that?"

"We had a bad episode today just before you called and it didn't end well. Tyger slapped me and threatened me."

Aiden gasped, "What? What the hell did you do?"

"I ran my mouth a too much and told her I wish Ace, Picasso and even my brother were dead."

Aiden ran his fingers through his hair and grabbed a hand full from the top, he spun around the room, "Why would you say that? I ought to slap you my damn self for saying stupid shit."

Realizing Bella was more unstable than usual, he couldn't afford to rattle her, "I'm sorry, I didn't mean to yell at you, but you can't piss Tyger off. I need you."

Bella smiled like a naïve little girl, "You need me?"

"Yes Bella, I need you. You're close to Tyger. I need to know her every move."

"So, all this is really about you falling for my sister."

"No, that's not all. Although she is worth risking my life, I need to destroy my brother. I want to take away everything he has, his freedom, his woman, his city…"

Bella laughed, "You might take his freedom, but you will never be Ace Del Toro. You're too weak. My sister will chew you up and spit you out and the city will never be yours. You're a dirty junkie cop, you'll be dead before the bars on Ace's cell close."

Aiden walked over to Bella and took a seat in front of her, "Junkie, huh? Did you forget we met in that rehab in upstate New York? I was ordered by my job to get clean and you, well you were just on a little vacation. We're both junkies Bella, we always will be. The difference between you and I is, my hatred for my brother is stronger than my addiction. I know who and what I want. I can't let this shit throw me off my game. Can you say the same?"

Taking a small glass vile from his pocket he threw it on the table that sat between he and Bella. He watched her mouth water and her eyes dance as the glass bottle filled with her best friend, rolled toward her in slow motion. Bella's pulse raced as she looked at the crystal rocks that filled the tiny tube of temptation. In an instant her body started tingling with pleasure.

Trying not to break…. Bella looked down at the bottle then up at Aiden. The two didn't speak one word to each other. There was nothing left to say. Aiden was speaking a language that she clearly understood. He sat back in the chair with his right foot positioned on his left knee and stared into Bella's eyes. Like a panther waiting to attack his helpless prey, Aiden revealed a disparaging smile and winked at Bella. Bella inhaled in a swig of air, "What's this?"

"Just a little something to help you relax."

Leaning forward Belle smiled, "I know what I need to relax and that's not it."

On the surface, Bella appeared to handle temptation like a champ, but she was dying inside. The rocks were calling her name, they were screaming to be released and taken on a trip; a trip that Bella knew would take her into another world. Sliding to the edge of her seat she rolled the glass vile back to Aiden. With a furrowed brow Aiden watched as Bella stood to her feet and glided toward him. Reaching around her back, she carefully unzipped her dress. Falling to the floor like a delicate rag she stood before him in a black lace bra and panties.

Bella has failed his test. Unhooking the clasp in front of her bra, her firm perfectly round breast popped out like two savory melons. Her body was perfect. Tyger's body had been a pleasing sight, but there was someone real standing in front of him that actually wanted to feel his touch. What man could resist a sensuously delectable gift neatly wrapped in such an exquisite package?

Without uttering a word, Bella stepped between Aiden's legs resting her knee between his crotch. Placing both hands on his shoulders, she leaned in and softly kissed his lips. Grabbing the back of her neck,

Aiden pulled Bella close to him passionately suckling her tongue. No words were spoken between the two; only sounds of pure lust were released as Aiden unbuttoned his pants and lifted Bella's thighs. Bella opened her legs and straddled Aiden, slowly and carefully easing her way down as he entered her. As Bella carefully moved her hips to the rhythm of his motions, she stared into Aiden's eyes and watched his bottom lip drop as his eyes closed. Aiden began to lie back in the chair like he was royalty gripping the arms of the chair trying not to lose control. It was too late, Bella was taking him to a place that he wished he could escape with Tyger. With each stroke, Bella sent waves of ecstasy through Aiden's body. Bella's warm flesh tightened each time she stroked him. Opening his eyes and staring at the ceiling Aiden moaned letting out a slow and faint "Damn…"

Feeling Aiden's muscles tighten Bella leaned in toward Aiden, arched her back and took him deeper into her world. Grabbing hold to the back of the chair to brace herself for Aiden's energy, Bella, looked into his eyes as they rolled toward the ceiling and he yelled "Oh… Oh…Oh shit!" With his heart racing a million miles a minute, Aiden pulled Bella close to him as he erupted with ecstasy. Squinting his eyes to gain control of his sight, sweat poured from Aiden's forehead dripping. Still straddling Aiden feeling his heart beating against her chest and listening to his labored breathing all she could think of was that little glass lifeline sitting on the table.

Her animalistic display of lust was not motivated by the fact that Aiden was irresistibly handsome, she needed a distraction from the overwhelming urge to feel the euphoric orgasm that only smoking rocks could deliver. Hoping Aiden's energy was depleted; Bella knew she needed to get out of that apartment. She couldn't go through with her original plan. She could not deliver on her promise to reveal the identity of Spencer's killer, as she knew it to Aiden.

Pulling away from Aiden she stood to her feet. Reaching down to pick up her clothes from the floor she quickly dressed herself. Before she could zip her dress, Aiden grabbed her hand.

"Whoa, where do you think you're going? We've got some unfinished business."

"I'm sorry, I have to go…"

Aiden pulled Bella close to him, "Just relax, we don't have to talk about the case right now. You're shaking; I can't let you leave like this. Sit down, let me get you some more water."

Hurrying to the kitchen Aiden left the room. Standing in front of the table Bella couldn't take her eyes off the little bottle. She felt like she was paralyzed, she couldn't move. Aiden peeked around the corner to watch Bella battle the demon that she could not shake. Growing tired of waiting for her to break, Aiden walked out of the kitchen and handed the glass of water to Bella.

"Why don't you sit down and relax. You don't have to stay, but just sit here for a while until you feel better. I know you're not ashamed about what just happened. We're grown, it's not like it's the first time."

"But it certainly is our last."

"What's wrong with you? I don't understand you. We've been having sex since we met at rehab. Did you all of sudden grow a conscience? What the fuck?" Searching for her shoes, Bella became enraged.

"Before you came here you said you loved me. You convinced me to tell you my sister's secrets. I kept tabs on Ace for you. I've done everything you asked me to do and all this time, all you really want is Tyger."

Sensing that he needed to change his tune before he lost Bella's trust completely, Aiden turned up the bullshit.

"Bella, I admit I got caught up and I let my hatred for my brother cloud my judgment. I thought making Tyger fall in love with me would destroy my brother. Seeing how I've hurt you makes me feel like shit. I'm sorry, you have everything I need. I fucked up in New York, so I desperately need to prove I belong here in Detroit. I can't afford to fuck up this job. Spencer's murder is my chance to redeem myself. I don't want Tyger, I just need a win. Unfortunately, I have to sacrifice your sister and brother to secure our future. Solving this case would set us up to live the life you and I deserve to live. I'm doing this for us. It's time you became the sister with everything."

Bella's voice cracked, "I understand, but I'm having second thoughts about setting Ace and Tyger up. Spencer's death was not in the plan, now look he's gone and we're scrambling trying to figure this shit out. When we started this I was in a dark place, I wasn't lucid, I was all over the place. You are so wrong about Ace, he has always been there for me and everyone else he loves. Tyger and Ace are just trying to save the family. Ace has a good heart and he'll do anything to protect all of us. I don't know what happened between you and Ace, but he's your brother and you have to know that he's not this terrible person you think he is…"

Hearing Bella sing praises about his brother, Aiden exploded, "What makes you so sure he's the saint that you say he is? I know he killed Spencer in cold blood, just like he's killed other men and showed no remorse. Everyone thinks Ace is such a good man despite the fact that he's just a street thug, hustler and killer. Even when people see him holding a smoking gun in his hand, *he* can do no wrong. I know who he really is and he comes from a bad seed…"

Bella nervously yelled out "Ace didn't kill Spencer Nina did…" Trying to swallow her words, Bella held her breath.

"What did you say?"

"I can't believe I said that. I…I…"

"Liar! You can't make me believe that an eight-year-old special needs child killed her father. What is it about Ace that you would lie like this to protect him…"

"It's not a lie, it's the truth. Nina didn't mean to kill Spencer; she was trying to protect Tyger."

Pacing across the floor, Aiden was a nervous wreck. Bella stood in front of him trying to smooth things over, "Earlier in that day before he died Spencer and Tyger had an argument. Spencer was ranting and raving about the baby being Ace's. Spencer and Tyger started fighting and Spencer kicked Tyger in her back and drug her across the floor in front of Nina. Nina was scared and upset, she started screaming. Leaving my sister lying on the floor, Spencer, just ran out of the house to see his mistress GiGi Palmer. Later that night, when Spencer came back to the house he was still erratic. He came in ranting and raving about not being able to trust people and how much he hated his father. He was out of control, he ran toward Tyger like he was going to choke her. They fell to the floor and Nina grabbed a small statue from the table and hit her father in the head. She didn't mean to kill him. Nina was trying to stop Spencer from hurting Tyger."

Bella pleaded, "You see, Ace didn't kill Spencer. An innocent little girl who was trying to save her mother accidentally killed her father. You can't let Ace go to jail over an accident and you can't take Nina away from her mother. Please Aiden, let this go!"

Aiden stared into Bella's eyes trying to decipher fact from fiction. In his heart he knew she was telling the truth, but he didn't care. The stakes had changed, everyone was protecting someone that was much more valuable than Ace. His plans would have to change now. Five minutes prior to Bella's shocking reveal, he was certain that Ace had killed Spencer. He was certain that he would find the missing piece that would tie Ace directly to Spencer's murder. Aiden also knew he could not let Bella leave his place alive, she was sure to run and confess to Tyger what she revealed to Aiden. He needed time to figure out how this would work for him. He wanted Bella dead, but he couldn't get his hands dirty.

Like a chameleon Aiden changed from red-hot to lukewarm. Kneeling in front of Bella he gently touched Bella's face, "It's ok Bella, I'm not going to take Nina away from her mother. Don't worry, I know what I need to do to make this right. I just need to clear my head."

Still on his knees he reached across the table and grabbed a small storage box. Opening the lid, he reached in and pulled out a glass tube. Extending his reach, he grabbed the tiny bottle of temptation. Looking over at Bella he held the tube and the rocks in his hand, "I need to relax and figure out how I'm going to help Tyger without compromising my job. I just need something to take the edge off. Please don't make me smoke alone. I need you Bella!"

Bella's body tingled, her heart raced, and her eyes grew wide. Falling to her knees preparing to pray to her glass idol, she rushed to Aiden's side. Sly as a fox, Aiden loaded the pipe with the candy-coated crystal dynamite and handed it to Bella, "I love watching you enjoy yourself, let me make you happy."

With her hands trembling she grabbed a hold and placed the glass rod into her mouth. Startled by the sound of the glass hitting her teeth, she snickered. Coaxing Bella with a reassuring smile, Aiden lit the torch and waited for Bella to give him a nod of approval. Nodding her head, Bella welcomed Aiden's assistance. Bella's eyes danced as she watched Aiden light up her world. Mesmerized by the tiny melting rock, Aiden's mouth began to water. Ready to take a trip to paradise, Bella took the pipe in her hand and forcefully rotated it. Taking a slow robust drag, she held the smoke in her mouth and released filling the air with the retched smell of burnt plastic. As Bella's body buzzed with orgasmic butterflies fluttering through her soul, Aiden grinned like a satisfied beast as his partner in corruption became his prey.

Chapter Sixteen

W hile her sister was being delivered to the belly of a beast she could not defeat, Tyger and Nina were having dinner with the in-laws. Like clockwork, Genoa invited Tyger and Nina over for dinner one night a week. Although, Tyger had no interest in sitting across from S.B. watching him devour his food like a wilderbeast, she had to stick to the plan.

As soon as she entered her in-laws' home Tyger announced she was going to put Nina's backpack and other items in Nina's room. She prompted Nina to go into the den with her grandfather. Genoa had fixed a special room for Nina filled with beautiful frilly pink little girl novelties. As Tyger ascended the staircase, Genoa ran up the back staircase located in the kitchen. The two met in the hallway on the second floor. Quietly Genoa asked,

"Did you bring it?

"Yes" Pulling the small statue from Nina's backpack wrapped in a cloth, Tyger handed it to Genoa. Genoa held the statue close to her chest and tiptoed off to S.B.'s office. Arriving inside the office Genoa scurried over to the left-hand wall as Tyger stood guard in the hallway. Pulling the painting to the side, Genoa began keying in the combination to the wall safe. Opening the safe Genoa shoved the statue inside the safe, closed the door and straightened the painting. Without a word or a wink, the two women walked down opposite sides of the hallway feeling confident their mission had been successfully executed.

After settling in for a long uncomfortable visit, Tyger was on pins and needles waiting to hear the news of Gigi's body being discovered. It had almost been 48 hours since Tyger killed Gigi; time was winding down. Gigi's housekeeper was set to clean the condo earlier in the day and she was sure to find Gigi's body. It seemed everything was hanging in limbo by an ultra-thin thread.

Things were oddly pleasant between S.B. and Tyger. Genoa was the one fidgeting and stumbling over her words for most of the evening. S.B. was snooty as usual; he walked around like he was the king of the castle telling stale jokes at Genoa's expense while shooting Tyger the side eye. The poor son-of-a-bitch had no idea that Gigi was dead and he was the prime suspect. He was oblivious to the fact the highly coveted statue that he was using to Blackmail Tyger was upstairs in his own house.

As the evening progressed and there were no signs of dinner hitting the table any time soon, Tyger ran out of small talk. On the verge of suggesting they boil some hotdogs and call it a night, she offered her assistance, "Genoa, please let me give you a hand in the kitchen." Genoa quickly responded, "No, no you just relax. I started a little late, but dinner will be ready in fifteen minutes."

Despite, having a full course meal already prepared by a profes-sional chef S.B. insisted Genoa cook his favorite meal for the evening. S.B. bragged to Tyger about making Genoa prepare a separate meal at his request. Sitting across from him with his belly lapping over his pants, a cigar hanging from his fingertips and drink number five resting in his left hand, Tyger wished S.B. would spontaneously combust. He reminded her so much of Spencer; it took every ounce of restraint she had not to leap over and strangle the life out of him. Listening to S.B.'s speech lapse into an embarrassing incoherent slur, Tyger struggled to stay awake. Looking across the room, Tyger discovered Nina had already been bored to sleep by her grandfather's incessant banter. Rising from her seat to go and cover Nina, Tyger was startled by S.B. yelling her entire name. The hair on the back of her neck stood at attention. The damn of idiocy had just broken, what would he say next. S.B. had drank his way into confronting her about the statue and she was ready for whatever came next.

"Tyger Blackwell – Benedict! Don't think I've forgotten about you. We have some unfinished business to discuss." Walking over to Nina and grabbing the afghan, Tyger covered her and turned toward S.B.

"Don't worry S.B. I haven't forgotten about you either. In fact, pretty soon you'll have everything you deserve."

Removing the cigar from his mouth and resting his drink on the table, S.B. struggled to wiggle from his seat. Once he'd freed his fat ass from the bondage of the chair, he met Tyger in the middle of the room. Standing just a few feet away from her, S.B. smiled.

"Little Miss Tyger, did you really think you could kill my son and get away with it?"

"How can you be so sure I killed your son? The list of suspects is a mile long and if I'm not mistaken, you were questioned as well."

"Don't play games with me little girl, you know damn well I have your get out of jail free card. I hold your freedom in the palm of my hands. I know what happened the night my son was killed. I know Nina was the one that hit Spencer. But, we both know she will be drug through a long investigation, you'll be charged with accessory to murder and disposing of the body. So, it doesn't matter who killed Spencer, Nina will still end up without a mother because I will make sure you will go to prison. So, the way I see it, you should be much nicer to your dear old father-in-law, if you want your freedom."

"S.B. and I sincerely mean son-of-a-bitch, do you really think I need you to save me. The way I see it, you need me. I'm sure your concern for my freedom and the welfare of my child has nothing to do with parental concern or justice for your son. So, let's just cut the shit, because it's getting real stank in here. You want to trade your silence and the statue for your raunchy little sick photos that you know I found in Spencer's office." S.B. laughed,

"For someone whose about to lose her freedom, you're pretty

cocky. Since the day my son brought you into our lives, you have been one cocky bitch. Did you think becoming a Benedict would wash the stench of the hole off your low-class ass?"

"As low class as I might be, I'm still smarter than you and your phony pedigree." Still standing a few feet away from Tyger, S.B. held his cigar by his side. A clump of ash fell from the cigar landing on the rug. Tyger stepped closer to S.B. and smashed the ashes into the carpet with the ball of her shoe, "Listen to me very carefully. The next time you decide you want to blackmail me, pick a more astute accomplice…"

With his eyebrows raised, S.B. asked, "What the hell is that supposed to mean?"

Tyger revealed a smirk, "You'll find out real soon."

While S.B. and Tyger eyeballed each other, Genoa gently walked into the room, "Dinner is ready." Trying to swallow the lump in her throat, Genoa was startled by the sound of the doorbell. Paralyzed by the sight of Tyger and S.B. engaged in a willful battle of mind games, Genoa could not take her eyes off the two. Once again, the sound of the doorbell rang through the house like a warning siren.

Frustrated, S.B. turned and yelled in her direction, "Don't just stand there, answer the damn door." Genoa quickly turned and shuffled toward the front door. Opening the door, she felt an overwhelming wave of relief as the police stood on the other side. Recognizing the officers she greeted them with a smile, "Hello."

"Hello Mrs. Benedict, Is Judge Benedict home?"

"Yes, he is. We were just about to have dinner with our grand-daughter and daughter-in-law. You're just in time to join us."

"I'm sorry, but unfortunately this is not a social call."

Genoa opened the door and invited the officers inside the house, "Please come in, I'll get my husband."

The officers followed Genoa down the hall and into the dining room. Waiting for Genoa to come in and serve him, S.B. had taken his place at the head of the table. As the officers entered the room, S.B. slid his chair back and raised himself from the table. With a huge smile on his face, he greeted the officers, "Hey, you're just in time for dinner. Come on in, there's enough for everyone."

With Nina by her side, Tyger entered the dining room, "Detective Leonard and Officer Beale, will you be joining us for dinner?"

Detective Leonard, shook his head "No, ma'am I'm sorry but this is not a friendly visit."

S.B. took a deep breath, "Is this about the investigation of my son's murder?" Detective Leonard looked straight into S.B.'s eyes, "No sir. Gigi, I mean Gabrielle Hunter was found dead in her condo earlier this morning. We have a few questions to ask and we think it would be best if you come down to the station."

S.B. belted out a robust laugh, "Come down to the station? It sounds like you're trying to blow smoke up my ass. Who do you think you're talking to? Why do I need to go to the station? Anything you need to know you can ask me now in my own house."

"Judge, I understand how you feel, but I think it would be best if you would just come with us. I'm sure this will be cleared up soon."

Turning a shade darker S.B. exclaimed, "Maybe you didn't hear me, I'm not going anywhere." Turning in Genoa's direction, S.B. yelled "Genoa, get Paul Gentry on the phone…"

Just as S.B. finished his sentence, Captain Gentry walked into the dining room. S.B. walked over to Captain Gentry like a raging bull. "Paul, you must be crazy…"

Captain Gentry held out his hand and stopped S.B. He leaned in to S.B. and whispered, "You need to calm your ass down. Gigi's house has your fingerprints all over it. Witnesses saw you leaving her house last night and we found a photo of you and Gigi in her nightstand. So, you need to cooperate and do what they tell you. Now out of respect for your position, I'm trying to do this the easy way. If I have to I will handcuff your ornery ass and throw you into the squad car." Captain Gentry stepped back, "Are we clear?"

S.B. took a hard swallow, put one hand on his hip and ran his other hand through his hair. Surveying the room, all eyes were on him, but he focused his attention on one person, Tyger. As their eyes met, he finally understood what she meant by getting what he deserved. Staring into Tyger's eyes his blood boiled. Knowing she had the statue back in her possession and he was sure she planted the photo he knew he'd lost his bargaining chip.

Breaking the silence in the room, Tyger stepped forward "S.B. don't worry, I'll call your attorney and we'll meet you at the station. In the meantime, don't say a word, I will act as your attorney until yours arrives."

Feeling like the wind had been punched from his lungs, S.B. turned toward Captain Gentry and walked through the dining room on into the hall. Walking down the hall toward the front door, S.B.'s heart dropped as he heard Captain Gentry inform Genoa they had a warrant to search the house. He knew that statue was somewhere in the house, but what could he do; he didn't have time to think of one of his clever schemes to get out of the mess he was in. With Nina and Genoa following behind, Tyger walked outside watching as S.B. walked toward the patrol car. Tyger called out to Captain Gentry, "Paul, may I speak with S.B. for a moment?" Captain Gentry nodded "yes." Tyger strolled over to S.B. and whispered, "Just in case you're thinking of throwing my name anywhere in this investigation, I want you to remember one thing, I know Spencer and Gigi were blackmailing you, I have boxes of tapes and photos that will destroy you. So, right now you need to start kissing my **low-class** ass or you will go down for the murder of your son and your whore."

Void of any tangible emotion, S.B. conceded, "Well, I guess you're a real Benedict after all." Revealing a smile, Tyger curled her lip and widened her eyes.

"No S.B., I am a stone-cold Blackwell."

Genoa stood on the steps of the house holding Nina's hand. With a forced gesture of goodwill, she called out to her husband, "S.B., don't worry I'll be there soon!" Before entering the patrol car, S.B. looked over his shoulder and peered into his wife's eyes. For the first time since they were young and truly in love, he noticed a spark gleaming in her eyes, a light that he had extinguished decades prior. S.B. finally realized that it was not his daughter-in-law who had hammered the final nail in his coffin, but his good and faithful wife that he had foolishly underestimated.

Chapter Seventeen

Standing in front of the house alone Tyger watched the patrol car's taillights disappear in the distance, she looked back over her shoulder to make sure Genoa and Nina were back in the house.

Tyger quickly called Judge Gray. Thumbing through her contacts and selecting, J.G. Tyger waited for him to answer.

"Hello"

"Hello, Judge Gray. This is Tyger Benedict. I need to see you as soon as possible." Sensing his reluctance to respond, Tyger didn't give him the opportunity decline her request. Breaking the silence Tyger took a short breath, "Judge Gray, please don't mistake this for an option to decline. I found a lovely photo of you in my husband's private collection that I think you would appreciate being returned to you...or maybe not?"

There was a brash silence that loomed in the air. Inhaling a deep breath, Judge Gray responded, "Yes, of course. I will be hanging around the house all evening, when would you like to stop by?"

"I'm leaving my in-laws house now, I should be arriving in fifteen minutes. See you then."

Judge Gray was sure to handle Tyger with kid gloves. He knew the wounds were still fresh from his fling with her mother that had taken place years ago. Although she never openly proclaimed her disdain for Judge Gray, he knew she blamed him for breaking up her family and leaving town with her mother in tow.

Approaching Judge Gray's estate, the gate opened. Tyger wheeled her car through the driveway. She had been instructed by Judge Gray to enter through the back entrance where his home office was located. When she rang the bell he greeted her with a Cheshire cat grin, like they were old friends. The two exchanged superficial pleasantries and walked toward the office. Judge Gray took a seat behind his desk and offered Tyger the seat in front of him.

He retrieved a cigar from his humidor and asked, "Do you mind?"

"No not at all."

After lighting his cigar Judge Gray extended his manufactured condolence to Tyger, "Please forgive me for not calling to offer my sympathies sooner in regard to Spencer. Taking a drag from his cigar, the Judge leaned back in his chair, "His death was such a tragedy and a major blow to this state's judicial structure." Propping his foot on top of his knee, he crudely reminded, "You know it doesn't seem to be a good time for the Benedict men, after you called I heard about S.B.'s misfortune…"

Tired of playing the cat and mouse game, Tyger laughed, "Ok Kyle, time is of the essence so, let's cut to the chase. We both know you're not the least bit concerned about Spencer's death or S.B.'s recent run in with the law, frankly neither am I. The bottom line is, I have something that you want and you have something I need. I know my husband was blackmailing you. I'm sure you've been wondering where your rather compromising photographs landed after his unfortunate demise."

Turning beet red, the judge opened his mouth to address Tyger. Raising her hand she shut him down, "Don't worry, I am the only one with access to the pictures of you, my father-in-law and Gigi Hunter, engaged in an unsettling ménage â trios. I had enough trouble keeping my lunch down after the sight of the three of you, but the photo of you and S.B. now that really made me gag. I never pegged you for a man's man. Honestly, I really could give a damn what or who you do. But, the way I see it you are in a shit load of trouble if any of these pictures fall into the wrong hands. Hell, blackmail really isn't my thing. So, all I need is for you to make sure S.B. is detained for twenty-four hours for the murder of Gigi Hunter. I need him to spend the night in jail. I don't care how you do it, but it has to be done…" Watching Kyle Gray's sour countenance, she needed to be sure he was still coherent, "Just in case you don't understand, I brought along a few things to help you out…"

Inhaling a hearty pull of his cigar; he nodded his head and instructed Tyger to continue, "It seems that while I was searching through my husband's personal effects I found more than just pictures, I found a box of recordings. There is a shitload of evidence that S.B. and some of your colleagues accepted bribes, engaged in other illegal activity and were caught in compromising positions. I'm sure I don't have to tell you your voice is on some of the recordings. But, like I said blackmail takes up too much of my time, so it's simple. If you get me what I need, I will give you everything I have. This will give you the leverage you need to charge S.B. with murder, bribery and whatever else falls into the category of keeping him in jail…"

Judge Gray rested his cigar in the ashtray on his desk and leaned forward, "Why should I trust you? How do I know that you haven't made copies of everything? Why did you just show up today with this info? You could walk through that same door months from now needing another favor…"

Tyger repositioned herself in her chair "Look Kyle, timing is everything and it's really not about you and your fucked up little perverted escapades with S.B.'s funky ass. Finding the photos of you and S.B. was just pure luck. For the record, as far as what happened between you and my mother, I really don't give a shit. Spencer is gone and now S.B. is the person standing in the way of my happiness. If I didn't need to get this Son-of-a-Bitch S.B. out of my life I would just give you the damn tapes and the pictures, but I need insurance. I'm just doing whatever I need to get rid of S.B."

Concerned, the Judge asked," What if S.B. is charged with the list you named, what am I supposed to do when he starts dropping names. If he implicates me or my colleagues, we're all up shit's creek."

Tyger leaned forward," I don't think you understand, S.B. won't make it through the night." Judge Gray starred at Tyger trying to process the words she spoke.

"I want S.B. gone just as much as you. Between me and my colleagues, I won't have a problem getting you what you need."

Tyger smiled, "Good then. I need access to S.B.'s holding cell. I need to get in and out without being noticed."

Judge Gray pursed his lip and inhaled a deep breath, "Tyger, getting you inside the jail without being detected is going to be difficult, but I will try my best. I hope you have a plan B."

"No plan B. Kyle, this has to be handled delicately. There will be bloodshed and a fatality…"

Shaking his head, he wore a stone face, "I wouldn't have it any other way."

Tyger reassured the judge, "If you get me access to S.B. I'll give you everything that belongs to you…"

Kyle questioned, "And if I can't get you inside?"

Tyger smirked, "Let's just say, if you want me out of your life, you'll help me get S.B. out of mine…So, you have him processed and make a way for me to get inside his cell and this little partnership will be over within twenty-four hours."

Just as Tyger turned to exit the judge's office she turned toward him, "Oh and, if by chance you're trying to figure out a way to run me off the road or put a bullet in my head to get what you need from me, I promise you that I will literally bury you alive…So be very careful and get me what I need, Kyle."

Bug eyed and speechless., Judge Grey nodded. Tyger tilted her head, "Are we clear?" Judge Grey took in a gulp of air and nodded in agreement.

Chapter Eighteen

Tyger left Judge Gray and went home to await her next move. Feeling worn out, Tyler stretched out on the couch and took a well-deserved nap. Startled by the sound of the bell, Tyger sprang from the couch like a frightened doe. Gathering her thoughts Tyger walked to the door, staring at her through the stained glass were a pair of blue eyes under a black baseball cap. Hoping the package she'd been waiting on had arrived, she opened the door. Before she could greet her guest, the man on her doorstep acknowledged her, "Mrs. Benedict?"

"Yes?"

Extending his hand forward like a programmed robot, he handed Tyger a blue duffle bag. "This is a package from Judge Gray, your instructions are inside."

Tyger grabbed the bag, before she could say thank you, the blue-eyed man turned and walked toward his car.

Slamming the door behind her, like a kid on Christmas day, Tyger ran up the stairs to her bedroom. Dumping the contents of the bag onto her bed, she curled her lip and displayed a sinister grin. Laid out like a priceless gift was a police uniform, a badge, handcuffs and a service revolver. At the bottom of the pile was a white envelope with a handwritten note inside. With her hands trembling in anticipation, Tyger read the note outlining her instructions to access the jail and cell where S.B. was being held. The instructions included an exact time to arrive at the station and the person to report to.

Preparing for the next stop on her journey, Tyger called Vincent and instructed him to meet her in exactly one hour with a car. Preparing to leave, Tyger stuffed the uniform into the duffle bag, dressed in her club attire and headed out the door.

Arriving at the club, she fell into her same old routine. Tyger mixed, mingled and made her way up the steps to the office. Still keeping her plans a secret from Picasso and Ace, Picasso had no idea what Tyger was up to, but he knew whatever was going down he needed to have her back. Picasso didn't follow her upstairs for an explanation; he stayed downstairs just in case Detective Arias came snooping around.

Against his better judgment, Picasso continued to stand down and let Tyger to handle her business without interference. With all eyes on Ace and Picasso and the emergence of Aiden Arias, they had to be extremely cautious. Both Ace and Picasso agreed to let Tyger do what she needed to do, but if anything went down they'd be on standby waiting for action. They accepted the bits and pieces of information Tyger provided. Neither Picasso nor Ace could honestly conclude that Tyger had anything to do with GiGi's death or S.B.'s arrest.

Vincent was loyal to Tyger; he loved her like she was his sister and committed to protect her at any cost even if that meant protecting her from herself. He kept Picasso and Ace abreast on Tyger's activity without revealing too much incriminating information. There was no question whether Tyger was capable of taking care of herself, but it never hurt to have Picasso, Vincent and Ace waiting to catch her should she happen to fall.

Picasso wasn't at all worried about Tyger. He had a few cops on the payroll that he knew would do whatever he needed. Detective Arias didn't realize that although he was a damn good detective from "the big apple" Detroit belonged to Ace Del Toro and Picasso Kennard and Tyger Blackwell-Benedict was their Queen.

Tyger changed her clothes and slipped into the police uniform. Checking her drag before heading out, she admired her reflection in the mirror. She found it ironic as much as she tried to do the right thing, she always found herself on the other side of the law, but the law would always come to her rescue in the nick of time.

Hurrying down the back steps, she hopped into the car Vincent left for her and headed downtown. With a rush of adrenalin flowing, Tyger rode through the city feeling confident she was one step closer to ridding her life of S.B. More than anything Tyger was driven by love. She was driven by her love for Nina, the one person that could never get caught up in this mess. Tyger was determined to do whatever it took to protect the ones that she loved. Once S.B. was out of the way she would have to get Aiden off her trail.

Arriving at the police station Tyger parked in the spot where she was instructed to park. Taking a moment to gather her thoughts, Tyger inhaled a few a deep breaths. Putting her hair in a ponytail and tucking it under her cap, she took one last glance in the mirror. Without one stitch of makeup, she stared at her bare face and placed the cap on her head. Pulling the cap over her eyes, she exited the vehicle in her regulation blue uniform. Her belt weighed a ton, she wasn't in the best shape. Fatigue was getting the best of her and a nasty cold seemed to be trying to invade her body.

Entering the doors to her destination, everyone greeted her without reservation. As the letter instructed, Tyger strolled straight to the back to Chief Wyatt's office. Approaching the door, Chief Wyatt removed himself from behind his desk. Extending his hand with a firm shake, he welcomed her, "Good evening Officer Black, come on let me show you to where you'll be working tonight." Tyger's mind was so twisted in knots; she didn't realize the name "Black" was stitched on her shirt.

There was something distinctly familiar about the Chief's voice. He was articulate and spoke with a dark husky tone. A hint of Southern drawl danced off his lips. There was nominal banter between Tyger and Chief Wyatt. Chief Wyatt maintained his cool as if he were inten- tionally trying not to engage Tyger in conversation.

As they walked down the hall with Tyger following close behind,

Chief Wyatt thanked Tyger, "Thanks for working in "Officer Peters place." Officer Wyatt turned and looked at Tyger, "I'm going to assign you to Officer Denton."

Tyger graciously agreed, "Yes Sir." As they entered the last security checkpoint, there was a tall white officer standing on the other side of a wall that was made entirely of glass. Tyger stepped on the other side of the wall carefully avoiding physical contact with anything.

After introducing Tyger and Officer Denton, Chief Wyatt looked over at Officer Denton and then back at Tyger. The Chief narrowed his eye, "I'm sure you will be provided with whatever you need, Officer Denton will take good care of you."

As the words escaped the Chief's lips, Tyger recognized his voice. Chief Wyatt was the anonymous caller who informed her about evidence tampering in Ace's criminal case. As Tyger starred into the Chief's eyes, she smiled thanking him for what he'd done to help Ace The chief's nod acknowledged the acceptance of Tyger's gratitude. As, she walked back down the corridor, Tyger wondered why Chief Wyatt was willing to help her.

Once the chief was out of sight, Tyger and officer Denton walked into the office. As the door closed, she glided through the opening not touching a thing. He told her he'd sent the other correctional officers to do their nightly rounds. He advised her that it takes the officers approximately one hour to do the rounds. Officer Denton told her where S.B. was housed three cells down on the right. Tyger would be able to walk in and out. Officer Denton told Tyger this was the last check before lights out, so S.B. would not be found until the next morning. Officer Denton advised the policy and procedure was to make sure the cameras were on a timer and stayed on the officer's as they did their rounds. Everything was precisely timed, so rounds had to occur at the same time every night. Officer Denton advised to ensure the safety of the guards and inmates, each week the time and routine changed to avoid predictability. Since S.B.'s section had already been covered the cameras would not record Tyger.

As Tyger slid her fingers into her gloves, Officer Denton handed her a set of keys took a seat behind the desk and resumed monitoring the cameras. As he leaned back in his chair he said, "Our prisoner became angry when he heard he'd have to stay the night. He had to be restrained. We gave him a mild sedative. So, you shouldn't have any trouble with him."

Tyger smiled, "Damn you are making this so easy."

Officer Denton smirked, "Hell I would have killed the son-of-a-bitch for free." Just as Tyger was preparing to walk away the officer said, "Mrs. Benedict, tell me why would you do this yourself, I'm sure someone can do this for you? There are plenty of people standing in line just waiting for this chance."

With her eyes dancing with excitement, Tyger said, "Do you remember when we were kids, we used an instant camera that shot out the pictures as soon as they were taken..." Officer Denton nodded in agreement. Tyger continued, "Do you remember how excited you were at the anticipation of waiting for a picture to develop. I'd sit and wait as each little fleck of color came through. I remember even loving the sound the camera made when the picture shot out..." Tyger looked down at the officer, "That's how I feel about watching S.B. die. I want to see it with my own eyes. I want to feel life drain from his body as he takes his last breath and I want to be the last picture that his mind ever sees..." The officer took a deep breath and nodded in agreement.

Tyger slowly walked down to S.B.'s cell and placed the key in the lock. S.B. struggled to sit up. Realizing he was a bit disoriented, Tyger walked over and bent over in front of him. She reached out and grabbed his hand to help him sit up. Focusing his eyes, he sat up straight he noticed she was no ordinary guard. There was a shapely figure in an ill-fitting uniform standing before him.

As Tyger moved in closer to him he squinted, "Tyger, what the hell are you doing here?"

Without hesitation Tyger whispered, "I'm fulfilling a promise that you made to me years ago."

Rubbing his head S.B. questioned, "And what would that be?" Staring into S.B.'s eyes, Tyger rested her hands on her knees, "You once promised me the only way I would leave this family was in death, but you didn't say whose death.

S.B. laughed, "Do you really think, I'm gonna let you come up in my jail and let you kill me."

Tyger laughed, "Your jail, Mutha-Fucka please, do you really think that these people give a damn about you? How do you think I got in here? Your so-called people didn't hesitate to help me walk up in here and make your ass extinct."

As S.B. slowly rose from his seat Tyger stood up and stepped back. Wobbling over to Tyger they now stood an inch from each other. Without flinching Tyger said, "Back the fuck up."

S.B. took in a gulp of air, "So, you did it. You actually pulled it off. You set me up. This murder, bribery everything!"

Tyger laughed, "Murder, yes. But you set yourself up for all that other dumb shit. How long did you think people were gonna let you walk around here acting like king of the fools? How long did you think grown men and women would let you control them? How long did you think your little nasty ass secrets would stay hidden?" The look on S.B.'s face told Tyger he knew she'd discovered the picture of S.B. and Judge Gray.

Trying to intimidate Tyger, S.B. moved in closer to her, "You may have been able to get rid of my weak ass son, but I'm a different breed and the little ole sedative they shot me up with can't take me down."

As he snarled threats, Tyger didn't move one inch. Standing her ground Tyger snarled at S.B. "I told you to back up off me."

With a sarcastic grin S.B. showed all his pearly whites, "Why, because you're scared or cause you're getting turned on."

Tyger smirked, "Neither, I just don't want to get blood on this suit!" With one flip of her wrist, Tyger cut S.B. from ear to ear with a shank included in the package given to her by Judge Gray. It was quick and clean just like Picasso taught her. She left S.B. just enough life to feel the pain for a few seconds.

S.B. grabbed his neck and fell to his knees. As his body traveled to the ground he reached out for Tyger, but she was nowhere near his grasp. Finally, his body hit the floor like a bag of rocks.

Tyger knelt down and wiped the blood from the blade on S.B.'s shirt. She rose up, straightened her hat, and stood erect as she grabbed the door handle and opened the door. Tyger walked out of the door and looked straight over at Officer Denton. He nodded in her direction and pushed the button to open the door for her release. This time as Tyger walked down the corridor, no one asked her to stop at the security checkpoints, they just nodded her on through. It was as if everyone she passed was in on the plan. Before exiting the building, Tyger stopped by Chief Wyatt's office. She stuck her head in the door and bid him goodbye, "Have a good night Chief."

The chief responded, "You too Officer Black."

Tyger walked out of the station as freely as she'd entered. Once she was inside the car, she took a deep breath turned the key and sped off into the night. As Tyger drove back to the club she kept telling herself that it was almost over. Once again Tyger's stomach started to churn. She talked herself out of becoming sick. She told herself she had every right to protect her family. She had to convince herself what she'd done was necessary.

As she approached the club, she was running off pure hope and determination to stop the rollercoaster she was on. Tyger ran up the back steps and into Picasso's office. She quickly changed and called to tell Vincent she was done. As she exited the club, Tyger said a quick goodbye to Picasso. She walked out the front door with her bag in tow and got into her Jag. When Tyger arrived home, she went into the basement and threw the suit, latex gloves, shoes, belt, hat and everything else she had worn to carry out the deed into the incinerator. Tyger had given the gun to Vincent to dispose of. Although, Tyger had taken care of S.B., she was more worried about Bella. Bella had not been home; she hadn't heard a word from her. It wasn't at all strange for Bella to stay away from home, but Tyger was particularly worried about Bella's mental state during their last conversation. Feeling mentally and physically fatigued Tyger settled in for a catnap and tried to forget the events of the night.

Chapter Nineteen

Night had passed and daybreak made its way in gleaming with the promise of a better day than before. Lying on her back Tyger rolled over and reached toward the nightstand. Checking her phone to see if she missed a call informing her of S.B.'s death, Tyger realized she'd forgotten to put her phone on its charger. Frantically placing the phone on the docking station, she waited for the battery icon to light up. Glancing at the clock she realized it was 6:13 a.m. County Jail isn't a five-star hotel, so she knew the inmates must've been up. Trying to remain calm, she sat on the side of the bed and inhaled a few deep breaths. Staring down at her feet, she wondered if murdering S.B. in cold blood had been one colossal dream. Enjoying a moment of peace, everything in the house was quiet. For a moment her world stopped spinning with chaos.

Preparing to check on Nina and see if Bella returned home last night, Tyger pushed herself up from the bed. Feeling a sharp pain shoot through her abdomen Tyger fell to the floor, the room began to spin. Feeling her stomach gurgle, she crawled to the bathroom and vomited into the toilet. Breathing like a wounded bear, she wrapped her arms around the commode as she hurled until there was nothing left. Hearing the toilet flush automatically, she held her hands in front of her and watched as they began to shake. Her skin felt cold and sticky as sweat spewed from her pores. Crawling around on all fours, she collapsed onto the floor. Trying to find relief on the cool granite, she struggled to catch her breath. In a low agonizing tone, she whispered, "Please, help me!"

Weak and unable to move Tyger lie on the floor for what seemed like an eternity. Peeling herself from the surface, she grabbed a hold of the toilet and pushed herself from the floor. Walking to the sink, she brushed her teeth and washed her face. Exhausted, Tyger brushed her hair and pulled it up in a ponytail. Feeling like a truck had hit her, she walked back into her bedroom and set a reminder on her phone to call her doctor for an emergency appointment.

Needing a breath of fresh air, Tyger opened the French doors and stepped out onto the terrace. Feeling the cool wind sweep across her face, she gazed at the sky. She prayed this would all blow over soon. The lying, the murders, and the sneaking around had taken its toll on her. S.B., Spencer and Gigi were all gone; Aiden was her only threat. A part of her wanted to lure him to the woods and put a bullet in his head, but she knew that wasn't possible. Tyger had grown weary; she was tired of the cat and mouse game she had been playing with Aiden for the last few months. It was finally time to end the game.

Feeling anxious, she returned to her bedroom and entered the bathroom. Disrobing she walked over to the shower turned on the water and stood under the waterfall. After showering, she threw on a pair of jeans, a tank top and a jacket. She slipped her foot into a pair of sneakers, grabbed her purse, and headed out the door. She checked her cellphone and discovered miscellaneous text messages but nothing concerning S.B. Tyger was restless and she needed to take a little ride.

Before leaving Tyger looked in on Nina. Nina was fast asleep. She stood in the doorway and watched her baby girl sleep peacefully. Oblivious to what was happening around her, Nina slept without a care. Everything Tyger had done to keep her safe played in her head like a moving picture; how could she ever think twice about protecting her family.

With her heart resting at her feet, she backed against the wall and looked toward the ceiling searching for answers. She knew it had to end and it had to end soon. She'd danced around Spencer and his family and ducked punches for ten long hellacious years. During their marriage Tyger had cleaned Spencer's messes and kept him alive. The more Tyger replayed the last ten years with Spencer the angrier she became.

Just as she was getting ready to morph back into her uncaring vengeful wrath, Nina let out a faint cough. Tyger snapped back and wiped the tears and carefully backed out of Nina's room.

Tyger stood outside of Nina's door with her back pressed against the doorknob. She reached inside her purse and called Vincent to pick her up. She needed to go someplace where she could release all of her negative and confused energy. Just to make sure someone was home with Nina she walked down the hall to check Dee Dee's room. As she approached the door, she heard laughter on the other side. Of course, Dee Dee was up gossiping on the phone with one of her friends. Shaking her head and rolling her eyes Tyger headed toward the stairs.

As the car drove around and stopped in front of the house, Vincent hopped out and opened the door for Tyger. Once she was inside Vincent said, "We going to see Whiskey or Picasso?"

Tyger responded, "Neither, we're going to see Ace." Vincent and Tyger didn't speak a word. Vincent knew Tyger like the back of his hand. Vincent knew Tyger was nothing to be trifled with, he also knew she had a heart and a conscience. Vincent knew Tyger loved deeply. He knew the uncertainty of her future with Ace and protecting Nina was weighing heavy on her. No matter how hard she was, Ace was her soft spot.

Vincent drove straight to Ace's place at top speed. As he pulled in front of the house, Ace opened the door and stood on the porch waiting for Tyger to exit the car. Without saying a word to Vincent Tyger stepped out of the car and walked toward Ace's door.

As she approached the door, Tyger glanced over and saw Ace's bodyguard Nico standing in the window peeking through the curtains studying Vincent. Tyger's heart sank to the floor. She was so tired and disgusted with sharing Ace. Tyger and Ace had not been completely alone in ten years. Someone was always in another room or close by just in case something jumped off.

Nico nodded hello in Tyger's direction. Tyger gave him a strained smile. She didn't dislike Nico, but he made her uncomfortable. Ace greeted her at the door with a kiss on her forehead. Clutching her hand, Ace led Tyger up the stairs.

Entering his bedroom Tyger smiled as she noticed the fire in the fireplace. The fire was a reprieve from the dampness of the cold rain falling outside. As the flames from the fireplace danced in Tyger's beautiful brown eyes, Ace blushed with admiration. He watched as she fluttered her thick lush lashes. Gazing at Tyger he realized just how exquisite and rare she was. Ace's heart ached at the thought of losing her. He knew if he didn't make some drastic changes he would lose her for good this time. Chattering away Tyger continued to speak, but Ace couldn't hear a sound escape her lips, he could only gaze at her with awe and remember the first time she told him she loved him. Ace watched as her lips curled and her dimples grew deeper when she laughed. He was in complete awe and yet he grew even more afraid that he'd finally lost his edge.

Ace had always known Tyger was the exception to the rule. No matter how tough and rigid he was there was always that unspoken "what if" between them. Both Tyger and Ace wondered just how far she could push him before he shook her, hit her fiercely or threatened her life. After all, he is Ace Del Toro. He was that man that wasn't supposed to express love or show remorse; he was rough, rugged and raw. For years Tyger had turned Ace to mush, she'd pushed close to the edge many times before, but she knew how far to go. Ace knew deep down an unsettling anxiety rested inside Tyger. They both knew that as deeply as they loved each other they were a horrible accident waiting to happen. Tyger and Ace worked diligently not to push each other's button that led to the point of no return. Ace worked hard not to show Tyger the side of him that the streets knew all too well. Tyger buried the secret tryst she shared with Aiden deep inside her mind. The knowledge of her encounter with Aiden would destroy her relationship with Ace.

Listening to Tyger babble about much of nothing, Ace's heart continued to flutter as he shouted, "Marry me!" Tyger's babbling halted instantly; the room was completely silent. Staring straight ahead Tyger fell on the bed.

Tyger sat on the edge of the bed glaring into space. This is the moment she'd waited for and yet she felt paralyzed. Breaking her silence Tyger slowly turned toward Ace. Suddenly her stomach grew uneasy and she began to sweat profusely. Her heart started to race and the room felt like a sauna. Clutching her stomach with her left hand and covering her mouth with her right, she sprang to her feet and ran to the bathroom where she vomited until she had nothing left.

Sitting on the cold bathroom floor Tyger was grossly embarrassed. She sat on the floor with her knees pulled close to her chest and her hands over her face. Ace walked into the bathroom and flipped the switch to warm the floor. Ace grabbed a towel from the linen closet and turned on the faucet. Moving in silence he carefully saturated the towel with warm water. Wringing the towel with his massive hands, he walked over to Tyger and placed the wet towel on her forehead. Ace opened the shower door and started the shower.

As the water ran Ace closed the shower door and took a seat next to Tyger on the floor. He leaned over and laid his head on her shoulder and laughed, "That wasn't the response I was hoping for. Should I be offended?"

Still holding the towel against her forehead, Tyger opened her eyes and looked at Ace "No, you shouldn't be offended. I have no idea what that was about. I think my nerves are shot. I've been having headaches and hot flashes for weeks. I'm just sick and tired of all this bullshit that's been going on. I want all this to just go away, I want Aiden to go away, I want S.B. to go away, hell I want to go away…" Tyger could tell by the look in Ace's eyes he was wondering if he was one of the things that she wanted to go away. "…And no baby, I don't want you to go away."

There was an awkward silence between Ace and Tyger. Ace was

waiting for a response to his question and Tyger was waiting for Ace to ask again. Ace looked over at the shower, "You better hop in before the water gets cold." Feeling awkward she pushed herself up from the floor and prepared to shower. Stepping into the shower she watched as Ace exited the room feeling defeated.

After Tyger finished her shower and brushed her teeth, she walked into the bedroom where Ace was nestled under the covers asleep. Tyger walked over, dropped the towel from her naked body and grabbed the t-shirt Ace was wearing when she arrived. She slipped the shirt over her head, walked over to the bed, pulled back the cover and sat on the side of the bed. Noticing a ring box on the nightstand, Tyger reached over, grabbed the box and opened it. Her eyes marveled at the exquisite seven-carat round pave cushion halo platinum diamond ring. Like an anxious child, she pulled the ring out of the box and slid it on her finger. With her heart pounding and her body fluttering like a love-struck teenager, Tyger looked over her shoulder and beamed as she watched the reflection of the flames dance off Ace's perfect bronze body. Settling in under the sheets, Tyger snuggled under Ace. Ace threw his arm around her body and pulled her close to him. Feeling her body release the burden of carrying the weight of her family's future, Tyger closed her eyes and enjoyed the security of Ace's touch.

Sleeping like she hadn't slept in months, Tyger lie in Ace's arms snoring like she was sawing logs at a lumber mill. Jolted by the sound of the phone ringing, with one eye open she reached across the bed and grabbed her phone from the nightstand. Genoa's name flashed across the screen. Tyger scurried to get out of bed to answer the call, but Ace pulled her back toward him. Answering the call, Tyger seemed winded.

"Tyger, are you alright?"

"Hey, yes, I'm fine. I was lying down, the phone startled me."

Careful, not to sound too excited, Genoa masked her amusement with a sympathetic tone. Tyger and Genoa had to play the role of a grieving family just in case their phones were bugged, "I'm sorry for waking you, but I have bad news."

"What's wrong?"

"S.B. is dead."

"What! What happened?"

"All I know is when the guard checked on him this morning, he was found on the floor of his cell with his throat cut. They have no leads. Apparently, he was killed after lockdown."

"I'm just stunned, I don't know what to say."

"There is nothing you can say. Unfortunately, my husband was public enemy number one. I'm on my way to the station now to find out more details."

"Ok, I will call you later or stop by the house. The coroner finally released Spencer's body, so I have an appointment at the funeral home today. It looks like we might have to have a joint memorial service for S.B. and Spencer."

"That is definitely something to consider. We'll talk later."

Tyger ended the call with Genoa. Sitting on the side of the bed Tyger faced the wall and felt relaxed as a Cheshire cat grin covered her face. Feeling a burst of freedom sweep through her body, her heart skipped a beat as she heard Ace call out to her, "Baby, what's wrong? Who was that on the phone?"

Slowly turning her head to the right, Tyger looked over her shoulder, "It was Genoa, S.B. is dead. They found him this morning in his jail cell with his throat cut."

Feeling the bed move, she looked down at Ace's face staring up at her. Kissing her on her thigh, he looked at her with his beautiful brown eyes, breathed deeply and asked, "So, how did you get inside his cell?"

Evading his gaze, she looked forward, "What?"

"Don't what me, answer the question."

Acting as if she were offended, Tyger threw her hands in the air, "Why do you think I did it?" Tyger watched as Ace's abs danced when he laughed, "What's so funny, the man is dead."

Ace rolled his head toward Tyger, "Really Tyger, this is me you're talking to. You don't have to answer my questions and I don't have to know the details, but I know you did it or had something to do with S.B. being killed."

Curious, Tyger moved in closer to Ace. Reaching up to move the hair that covered her face, Ace displayed an amorous smile. "I'd need to know why you automatically think I killed S.B.?"

Ace sat up straight and swung his legs around Tyger. Sitting behind her he cuffed her body between his legs and kissed her neck, "Don't worry, I'm sure no one else suspects you. The reason I know it was you because it sounds like it was quick and clean. There has been no chatter in the streets, the police department or inside county lockup about a hit on S.B. Picasso and I both know how much you've risked your life to protect us all. You should know the night you killed Gigi, I knew you'd stopped by the club and exchanged cars. A few days later she was dead and S.B. was arrested for her murder…"

Tyger moved his hands from around her waist, "So you're saying I'm predictable."

"Not at all, I'm saying you're diabolical and it's a little sexy and scary at the same time."

"So why didn't you say anything? And hold up, how do you know the cut was quick and clean? Please don't say it sounds like it. There is no way you got that info from my two-minute conversation."

"What did you want me to say? You are an exceptionally intelligent woman. You're not impulsive. Poor impulse control is the enemy of the wicked. You either kill due to a severed emotional attachment or out of necessity. Emotions are dangerous; they cause you to be sloppy and irrationally impulsive making traceable mistakes. When your survival depends on the existence of another person who is trying to destroy you, your family and your livelihood, you have an obligation to protect what's yours, a job that must be handled with the utmost discretion and methodical provision. You are a cunning attorney by trade, a hustler by nature, and your environment has taught you how to survive. When Spencer's body washed up you told Picasso and I to let you handle the situation, that's what we did. But trust and believe, I'm always somewhere waiting to protect you." Listening to the sound of Ace's voice as he preached his street gospel made Tyger's body tingle.

His deep sensuous voice vibrated through her making her clit jump and throb with excitement. Feeling Ace slowly rising up her backside, Tyger trembled with the anticipation of his touch. Growing firm, Ace felt his body flutter as he gently brushed Tyger's hair away from the back of her neck. Suckling her soft skin with his full plump lips he stroked her neck with the tip of his tongue. Caressing her thighs with his warm palms, Ace slid her panties down to her knees. Wrapping his arm around her waist he picked her up and positioned her on top of him. Pulling her t-shirt over her head, Ace watched as her long black hair cascaded down her back. Placing the tips of her toes on the floor, Tyger opened her legs and stretched her back. Like a glove, Ace was a perfect fit. Slowly sliding downward, Tyger tightly griped him as she opened her legs. Ace rested his forehead on her spine as he caressed her breasts with his hands. His breath grew faint as his head swooned with excitement. Stifled with ecstasy, unable to make a sound Ace's mouth fell open as he breathed deeply. With her feet placed firmly on the floor Tyger placed her hands on Ace's knees and arched her back. Losing control Ace's body trembled as he lay staring at the ceiling with his eyes wide open. Feeling Ace penetrate the depths of her soul, Tyger tugged on her bottom lip with her teeth screaming "Fuck." Tyger gripped Ace's legs with the tips of her fingers. Feeling a surge of erotic bliss shoot up her spine Tyger wound her hips to the rhythm of her rapid heartbeat.

Hearing Ace call out, "Damn Tyger", she felt him tremble inside her. Feeling her warm flow, Ace screamed "Fuck!" Opening her legs and clinching her lips tightly around Ace, Tyger felt her clit tingle as she grew lightheaded. Rolling her head around she ran her fingers through her hair. Tugging on her bottom lip, Tyger felt an orgasmic wave shoot through her womb and vibrate through her entire body. Feeling the pressure release from her clit her body exploded as she quivered with pleasure. As her body grew limp still feeling Ace inside her, Tyger's body collapsed. Struggling to catch her breath, Tyger rested her hands on her knees. With Tears streaming down her cheeks an after-shock rolled through Tyger's body like an earthquake. Releasing a high-pitched moan, Tyger was comforted by the warmth of Ace's lips on her spine as he gently kissed her.

Chapter Twenty

Escorted by Ace holding an umbrella over her, Tyger exited Ace's condo and hoped in the car with Vincent. Feeling relaxed and ready to bid her final goodbye to her husband before his cremation, Tyger settled into the bucket seat and exhaled a slow deep breath. Admiring the smile covering Tyger's face, Vincent chuckled,

"I assume you're ready to go home." Tyger looked over at Vincent and laughed, "Yes, but can you stop by the pharmacy, I need to pick up something for this bug that's trying to take over my life. I can't afford to get sick right now."

"You probably need some rest. When was the last time you had a good night's sleep?" Tyger smirked

"Ten years ago, before I married Spencer."

Vincent laughed, "I don't doubt that."

Vincent drove a couple blocks up the road in silence. Finally, he turned to Tyger, "So, you know S.B.'s death is all over the news. According to the news as far as the police are concerned, they have no suspects in the murder. They think another inmate killed him, but there is no evidence to support that theory at all. Video surveillance shows nothing. The prosecutor made a statement that S.B. killed Spencer and Gigi."

Using air quotes Vincent continued to spill the tea on the Benedict saga, "The news mentioned compromising photos of Gigi, Spencer and S.B. When they searched S.B.'s house the police found the statue they think killed Spencer. The lab is running blood samples. The police also found recordings of S.B. taking money in exchange for lighter sentences or acquittals. They rattled off so many charges in that press conference I got tired and shut it down."

Running his fingers through his beard, Vincent asked, "So, how do you really feel. During the press conference, I heard a few names of some pretty high-profile people that you and Spencer used to break bread with."

Tyger looked over at Vincent, "It's like the poison apple the queen gave to Snow White, you can't take food from the hand of everyone who smiles in your face. I listened to all of the recordings I found to make sure I recognized certain voices. Every recording that was uncovered at S.B.'s house was there for a reason. When I was the District Attorney. I learned things about people I wish I could erase from my brain. All I know is there are sick and twisted people who hold people's future in the palm of their hands. I know the perverts, the racists, the abusers, the closet addicts, I know all the men and women that sit behind the bench, prosecutors and defense attorney's that knowingly and willfully incarcerate our black boys and girls and give a shit about them. Those are the names you heard in that press conference. I know a sin is a sin and a lie is a lie, but I made a choice who to sacrifice and I'm alright with it."

Vincent reached over and touched Tyger's hand, "Thanks to you, we should all get a good night's sleep."

Tyger shook her head, "I know I should be more excited than I am. S.B. and Spencer are gone, but something tells me we're not gonna get rid of Aiden Arias that easy. I still don't know where Bella is and I have to plan a memorial service for both Spencer and S.B. A real good night's sleep is definitely not in my future anytime soon."

Vincent dropped Tyger off in front of the store. Quickly making her way through the door, Tyger walked down the digestive health and nausea isle of the pharmacy and stopped in front of the antacids. Eyeballing the infinite options from laxatives to upset stomach relief, Tyger grabbed a box of antacids and a bottle of Bismuth to soothe her stomach. Turning to walk toward the front of the store Tyger stopped and stood in the middle of the isle. Taking a deep breath, the nagging reality that her problem could possibly be greater than a pesky stomach bug, Tyger took a few steps over to the feminine health isle and grabbed a pregnancy test from the shelf. Trying to appear inconspicuous Tyger tucked the test between the box of antacids and Bismuth. Grabbing a bag of chips on the way to the counter, she tried to camouflage the contents of her bag.

Walking out of the store with her bag suspiciously tucked by her side, Tyger took her seat next to Vincent and stuffed the bag underneath her legs. Vincent looked over at Tyger, raised his brow and stared straight ahead. Vincent was no fool. He'd been watching Tyger long enough to know the physical changes he'd noticed coupled with the symptoms she'd been displaying was something they all needed to lift the cloud of darkness that covered them.

Chapter Twenty-One

I t was still fairly early when Tyger arrived home. Noon was slowly creeping around the corner. Tyger needed to prepare for her appointment at Metcalf Funeral Home. Spencer's body had been delivered to the funeral home the night before. Tyger decided to have Spencer cremated, but she requested to personally flip the switch. The Metcalf's were a cherished staple in the community, for the right price they asked no questions and granted peculiar requests.

On her way up the stairs, Tyger called Lillian to check on Nina. Lillian and Nina were out enjoying the day.

"Hello!"

"Hey Lillian, I have an appointment at the funeral home today. I will be later than I planned…"

"… don't worry Nina is fine."

"I know she's in good hands, I didn't see her before I left this morning and I miss her. I have an appointment at noon; it should only take an hour. I can meet the two of you for a late lunch."

"That sounds good, I'm sure Nina will be hungry by then, we just had breakfast and we're on our way to see a matinée."

"Ok, call me when the movie is over. You pick the restaurant, anywhere you want, your choice." Tyger could hear Lillian smiling through the phone, "Lillian, I know I've been depending on you to take care of Nina these last few weeks. I want you to know I really appreciate you."

"Tyger, I love Nina. You and Nina are like family. You forget I've been around for a while. I know what you've been through. You deserve a break every now and then."

"Thank you Lillian. You know Nina and I love you. I'll see you later today."

Ending the call, Tyger threw her phone on the bed. Carrying the pharmacy bag into the bathroom, she poured the contents out onto the counter. Ripping open the pregnancy test box Tyger's hands began to shake. Trembling, Tyger pulled out the plastic package, grabbed a pair of scissors out of the drawer and cut the top of the plastic and pulled the stick out. With her heart pounding Tyger held the stick in her hand and walked over to the toilet pulled her sweatpants down and peed on the stick.

Feeling anxious Tyger inhaled a few deep breaths, flushed the toilet, closed the lid. She reached over and unrolled a few sheets of toilet paper, folding the tissue she stacked it on top of the toilet and placed the stick on the paper. Needing to settle her spirit, Tyger removed her clothes and stepped into the shower. Turning the handle, she felt the cool water shock her body as the water sprayed her face. Washing away the memory of throwing Spencer into the lake, losing her son, killing Gigi, and killing S.B. she smiled to herself at the thought of finally having a little Asa Del Toro running around. Why should she be apprehensive or ashamed about having a child with the man she loves? With all the death lingering in the air over the last few months the excitement of the possibility of a new life entering their world almost made Tyger forget Bella had not been seen in days.

Reality has once again invaded Tyger's safe place, that space inside her mind where everything is perfect and the last ten years of her life had all been a horrible nightmare. Annoyed, Tyger turned off the water stepped out of the shower and grabbed a towel. Wiping her face, Tyger walked over to the toilet and looked down at the plastic stick. Wrapping the towel around her body, Tyger walked into her bedroom and stood in the middle of the room. Struggling to organize her thoughts and manage her emotions tears began to well in the corners of her eyes. Unable to identify emotions as tears of joy or disappointment, Tyger was paralyzed by the thought of being the mother of two. In seconds her life changed. Tyger knew she couldn't raise this child the same way she raised Nina. She had exposed Nina to a hostile environment filled with mental and physical abuse between two people that should have never been married. As the reality of Ace being her baby's father sank deep into her soul, Tyger questioned the rationale of having a baby with a man who lived his life on the edge of death every moment of the day.

Tucking her feelings inside, Tyger turned her attention to Spencer. It was time for all physical reminders of him to be erased. Tyger pulled herself together removed the engagement ring from her finger and prepared for her journey to the city. With the excitement of the pregnancy, Tyger had forgotten to check in with Genoa. Watching the screen in the middle of the dashboard light up with Genoa name scrolling across, she quickly answered the call.

"Genoa, I'm so sorry. I should have called by now."

"Don't worry everything is fine, no need to apologize."

"So, what happened? Are they going to investigate S.B.'s murder?"

"No, as far as the police are concerned another inmate killed him. The camera footage didn't show anyone entering or leaving his cell. The night shift and inmates are being interviewed. So far, everyone's story is the same. They didn't see or hear anything. I'm sure somebody somewhere needs answers, but as far Spencer Benedict, Sr. is concerned due to routine procedure when an officer of the court is killed everything is expedited. The autopsy is being performed as we speak. His body should be released tomorrow." Trying to contain her excitement Tyger asked questions she already knew the answer to, "What about the pending murder charge?"

"Well, all the evidence including DNA found inside Gigi, on her and in her house connect S.B. to the murder. The statue they found at the house had tons of fingerprints on it because it came from your house, but Gigi and S.B.'s fingerprints were on it as well. The police asked me had I ever seen the statue before, I explained I saw it at my son's house. With the photos of Spencer, Gigi and S.B., the police can't figure out if Gigi killed Spencer and S.B. killed her as revenge or if S.B. killed Spencer and Gigi was blackmailing him…" Tyger interjected,

"…and with Spencer, Gigi and S.B. dead who knows what happened."

"Exactly!"

"Since the news broke this morning, I've heard different versions of what allegedly happened. The consensus is S.B., Gigi and Spencer are tied up in this together.

"Yep, that's what it looks like so far. I don't think the official finding will prove any different.

"This is a lot to handle, how are you feeling about all this." Tyger knew Genoa was over the moon and probably going home to dance all over the house, but confessions during phone calls was off limits; they had to appear oblivious to the fact that the dead had all seen the same face before they took their last breath.

Genoa took a deep breath then slowly released air through her teeth, "I'm just ready for this to be over. Now, I to bury my son and my husband. Not to mention hiding from the bloodsucking media leaches."

"Hopefully this will all be over soon. I'm on my way to Metcalf's now to finalize the arrangements for Spencer. With S.B.'s death I think I should wait and schedule after things settle."

"I think the life and legacy of my husband and son should be celebrated together. We should schedule a memorial service that will honor them both."

"That sounds wonderful. We'll talk later. I'm pulling up to the funeral home now."

"Ok, talk to you soon."

Checking her face in the mirror before exiting the car, Tyger starred at her reflection. Her eyes were red and puffy. Although, the look of exhaustion came from sneaking around the city in the middle of the night, coupled with the baby draining her energy, she could use it to play the grieving wife for the parasitic press waiting outside the funeral home. In all her careful planning Tyger didn't factor performing in front of the press into the equation. At this stage of the game the question on everyone's mind was did her father-in-law really kill her husband and his mistress.

Exiting the car, she walked through the flashes and tuned out the questions. To her delight Michael Metcalf ran out of the front door, fended off the reporters and escorted Tyger into the mortuary.

"Thank you, Mike. I'm sorry about the circus outside. My mind is moving in so many directions, I forgot the media might be camped outside your door."

"Tyger please, you know with all the different people we've had in and out of here over the years, we're used to this by now." Tyger laughed, "You're right, I forgot who I was talking to."

Michael reached out and embraced Tyger. "No matter how crazy Spencer was I know this can't be easy." Tyger pulled away and shook her head, "No it's not easy, but I just want to get this over with as quickly as possible."

"Well, he's ready, we've been waiting on you." As they walked toward the back, Tyger paused for a moment. "Mike, you know S.B. will be arriving in the next few days, if not sooner."

"Yes, will you need the same additional service?"

"No, I'm good, but I can't speak for Genoa."

"If she doesn't ask, I won't mention it." Tyger placed her hand on Michael's arm, "I know it sounds heartless, but I just need to see Spencer's remains destroyed. I need to make sure he is really gone." Michael grabbed Tyger's hand, "Don't worry my friend I've seen what being married to that man has done to you. Considering I'm the one allowing you to flip the switch, there is no room for judgement."

Michael and Tyger walked down the hall and entered the room where the crematory was housed. Seeing the casket on top of the cremation trolley Tyger turns to Michael, "May I look inside, I want to make sure he's in there." Michael nodded, "of course,"

Michael grabbed the handles of the trolley and pushed a button. When the trolley reached an accessible height, Michael unscrewed the lid of the coffin and pushed it to the side. Tyger leaned in, "Yep, that's Spencer. It's amazing how well preserved he is after floating in a lake for months…" With a sentimental smirk, Tyger tilted her head, "Lying there he actually looks peaceful. If I didn't know him, I would think he was a good husband, father, son, and human being. There was a time in my life when I actually thought he was prince charming, but he turned out to be the wolf that ate grandma!" Michael looked over at Tyger, "Are you sure you want to do this?" Tyger nodded, "Oh yes! I'm fine. Just being a little facetious. Come on, close it up. Let's do this."

Michael secured the lid on the casket, lifted the trolley and pushed another button. As the casket approached the crematory door, Michael handed Tyger a pair of safety glasses. Reaching out for the glasses, Michael advised, "When that door lifts the fire is extremely hot, you might want to stand back, we wear the glasses as a precaution."

Feeling the heat from the fire as the crematory door lifted, goose bumps covered her arms. With the remote control gripped tightly in her hand, Tyger lifted her thumb and pressed the button. Spencer's casket slowly rolled through the door and into the fiery furnace. Once the casket reached its destination the belt stopped and the door automatically closed shut. The force from the close of the crematory door caused Tyger to flinch. The instability of redemption and remorse swept through her like a two-edged sword. As Spencer became an inconvenient memory, Tyger closed her eyes and did as most hypocrites do, she prayed for forgiveness.

Chapter Twenty-Two

I t had been two weeks since Tyger's husband and father-in-law were memorialized in a grand affair fit for royalty. Droves of people gathered to see the great American tragedy of the Benedict family.

Both Tyger and Genoa wore plastic smiles as they listened to ordinary people force themselves to say something endearing about Spencer and S.B. It was the obnoxiously wealthy that exerted the privilege of candor. In the upper echelon of society there is nothing more embar- rassing than a careless crook. The rules for the gutter and boardroom were the same; don't get caught, don't be a snitch, and don't embarrass the family. Tyger and Genoa had become martyrs and they played their roles well.

After the dust settled and everything returned to some form of normalcy at the Benedict Compound, Tyger made a midnight run to Picasso's place. She pulled up to Picasso's loft overlooking the river. A few years ago, Picasso purchased an old warehouse and turned it into lofts, he had the entire top floor to himself.

Picasso greeted Tyger with with a glass of Pappy Van Winkle as she stepped off the elevator. She declined his offer.

Picasso flashed a confused look, "Something must be wrong, you have never turned down Ole Pappy."

Tyger walked past Picasso stood behind the bar and fixed herself a glass of water. Swirling the ice around in her glass she stood in front of the enormous window and watched as the lights from the dock dance on the water. Overcome by nostalgia, Tyger stared out the window, "You remember after your mom's funeral we were in the basement of your apartment feeling sorry for ourselves and we promised each other that we would get out of the hole by any means necessary?"

Picasso smirked "I sure do. How could I forget? We worked our asses off, sacrificed everything and got out, didn't we?"

Tyger took a sip of water, pursed her lips together and relaxed them, "I'm not quite sure we did. I mean we got out of that dead end street, but we're still stuck in a hole. You're living up here isolated from everyone. I almost drove myself crazy trying to protect my daughter and myself from being locked away somewhere. Ace doesn't sleep at night and we're all a half step away from prison. We've got more money than we can ever spend in this lifetime and we're all still miserable. I'm sick of looking at this pissy river and smelling rotten eggs. Don't you ever get tired of living like this?"

Picasso walked over to the window and took his place next to Tyger. They both stood in the moonlight staring across the river at Canada. Picasso smiled, "Can you believe there's another country right in our eyesight. Do you know how many times I've wished I could just sail over there and get lost? Hell yeah, I'm tired of this shit, but what else do I know?"

As the moonlight hit her face, he noticed the tears streaming down Tyger's cheek. He stood frozen, unable to respond to his friend's obvious anguish. Picasso had not seen Tyger shed tears since the day her mother left. Finally, he reached over and wiped her tears. As Tyger Looked into Picasso's eyes she knew he felt uncomfortable, but his eyes told her that he was genuinely concerned.

"You should feel relieved. Spencer and S.B. are dead. Nothing is standing in the way of you and Ace finally getting together. You're free to live your life the way you've always wanted."

"All that sounds wonderful, but there is something inside me, something that won't let my spirit rest."

Picasso laughed, "Unless I'm wrong, you killed two people in cold blood. You dragged your husband's body across your backyard and threw him in the lake. A normal person's mind and spirit would be jacked up right about now."

Tyger's voice elevated, "No! That's not what I'm talking about. Something is not right. It's been two weeks since Spencer and S.B.'s memorial service. Both cases have been closed. S.B. was posthumously responsible for Spencer and Gigi's murder and everything seems fine, but Ace and I haven't seen or heard from Aiden and Bella is still missing. She's not in the hospital; she's not in the morgue. No one in the old neighborhood has seen her. I'm worried, I can't sleep or rest…" Tyger paused and gazed out the window, "I feel like there's something horrible waiting for me."

Picasso laughed, "Come on you're Tyger…"

Tyger shot Picasso a stern look, "I'm serious Picasso, I'm scared that I'm not gonna see my kids grow up. I feel like there's a dark cloud hanging over me."

Tyger took a generous sip of water and leaned against the window, "My father has a house near Charleston. It's on one of the islands. He's been restoring it for a while. It's gorgeous. It's nothing like the cold mansion that I live in now. It's quaint and warm like a home should be. It's got a wraparound porch upstairs and down, hard wood floors, an enormous yard, plenty of trees, green grass and fresh air…" Tyger's eyes danced with excitement as if she were a little girl waiting for a treat. "I've got to get out of here soon and I want you to go with me. Me, you, Ace, all of us can just get the hell out of here."

Exhausted, Tyger stepped back and fell into the chair closest to the window. She sat on the edge of the seat and lowered her head. Picasso watched as Tyger's silhouette beamed in the moonlight. Tyger's iridescent tears sparkled like crystals as they fell from the corners of her eyes onto the hard wood floor. Picasso stood dazed in a fog of uncertainty. He had no idea how to feel or what to say.

"Tyger I know you're worried about Bella. You know she's trying to handle life the best way she knows how…"

Tyger jumped up, "I know that Picasso, I know what she's trying to forget, but it still doesn't change the fact that she is a crackhead. She's desperate and in so much pain. She thinks the only thing that can help is whatever poison she's using right now. My sister is sick… and… you, me, Ace, John Paul, Shakespeare, all of us…we made her that way. The only reason why my sister isn't living in some dilapidated crack house is because she has a home with me. The only difference between me and Bella is that by some miracle Ace is not dead; he didn't get his brains blown out like Shakespeare did, but he could have. I am tired of sitting by the window waiting on someone dressed in a blue uniform to come to my door and tell me that my sister, Ace or you are dead…"

Angry, Picasso snapped back at Tyger, "Don't you think that every time I look at Bella I see Beverly. Since the day I saw my mother zipped up in that body bag, I have felt like I'm suffocating. You're sitting here talking about Shakespeare as if he wasn't my brother; I'm the one that had to go into that room and see his brains splattered on the floor…I'm the one that sees my mother and brother's face every time I close my eyes…" Picasso beat his chest with his right arm "…I haven't had a good night sleep in God's knows when cause I don't want to see their faces in my nightmares."

Picasso raised his shirt and turned to the left and pointed to old bullet and knife wounds, "I have the scars to prove that this is my life too… I know you're tired and I'm sorry that you got caught up. I'm sorry that everyone that you love is so fucked up. I'm sorry that Nina was born into this family and that she was the one that knocked Spencer over the head. I am sorry that the last memory that I have of my mother is that she smelled like shit and day-old piss and it made me throw up..."

Picasso rubbed his head vigorously and looked back at Tyger, "I'm sorry Tyger… All I have to give you is an apology, I'm just sorry!"

Tyger reached over and placed her hand on Picasso's face. With the palm of her hand resting on his face Tyger caressed his cheek with her thumb.

"Picasso, I'm so sorry! I'd forgotten you've been in this with me all the time." Tyger removed her hand from Picasso's face and leaned back in the chair and peered out the window across the river.

Picasso turned back toward the window, "Ok, with or without Ace I'll get you there...you will have your island."

Fixing her gaze on the rippling current, Tyger softly whispered, "I'm pregnant..."

Not batting an eye or turning his head Picasso jerked his head back, "What?"

"I am Pregnant."

"Damn, Ace told me he popped the question, but he didn't tell me this."

"Because he doesn't know"

"What?

"You heard me. When I ask him about moving to South Carolina I want him to make an honest decision. If Ace makes a decision based on the baby, I'm afraid he might feel trapped."

Picasso took a deep breath, "Tyger you know I love you dearly, but I can't lie to a man about his child. Do you know how bad I wish I could have a son or daughter? A child is the one thing in life I regret not having. You know Ace wants so badly for Nina to be his flesh and blood. I'm sorry I can't lie to Ace. I won't, not about this."

Tyger knew there was no convincing Picasso to keep her secret from Ace, but she didn't care. "I'm tired of being in love with a man who loves the streets more than me..."

Picasso snapped back, "Please Tyger, cut the bullshit. You know Ace loves you with all his heart and soul. He's loved you since the first day you met. He's watched you marry another man that treated you like shit, he watched you have Spencer's child. On his wedding day, he let you waltz into the church and demand that he leave Maria at the altar. You know you're his weakness. If you think about the type of man that Ace really is and the way he has allowed you to basically carry his balls in your purse, you're lucky. Any other man like Ace would have whipped your ass by now and said fuck you..."

Tyger raised her hand to stop Picasso, "Yes Picasso, I know …"

Picasso raised his index finger, "I'm not done. Ace is different from us. This is who he is. Those streets are like the veins in his arms. I was a greedy bitter little boy that saw a way to make shit loads of money and get the hell out of the hole, but I'm tired now. You got caught up in being taken care of by everyone. You've tried so hard not to be miserable like your mother, but in so many ways you are just like her. Since you were a little girl you've had to prove yourself. You and your sisters were like beautiful flowers that grew from concrete. The girls hated you because of your looks and boys resented you because you didn't want them. When you moved to Detroit you had to prove that you were hard and somewhere along the way you actually became cold and ruthless. Even Whiskey let you get caught up in our world and he never should have done that. You were supposed to go off to college, start a new life and forget this place. We never should have let you marry Spencer. There are a lot of things that I blame myself for, but I will not let you stand here and question Ace's love for you. I have stood by and watched Ace look at you with a love so intense that it scares me. Have you ever thought that he is afraid of not being what you need him to be? I mean what if he does go to South Carolina, do you really expect him to sit on the bank and fish and cut grass in a straw hat and shorts…"

Tyger yelled at Picasso, "…And what's so wrong with that? What's so wrong with living a normal life with your wife and kids? What's wrong with sitting on the porch on a summer day sipping iced tea and enjoying each other's company? What's wrong with watching each other's hair turn gray? "

Picasso lowered his head, "There's nothing wrong with it, if that's what that person really wants. Tyger, you might have to accept that the part of Ace that you truly want may always be out of your reach."

Picasso's words cut through Tyger like a knife, but she knew he was right. She also knew she had to tell Ace about the baby. Tired of being beaten over the head with the truth, Tyger strolled over to the sink and placed her glass on the cold steel. Grabbing her purse, she turned toward Picasso, "I get the point Picasso, I hear you loud and clear."

Walking into the elevator, Tyger pushed the number one button. As the doors closed Tyger yelled, "Whether it's South Carolina or Ass-Backwards Alabama, I am leaving this place with or without you or Ace, soon." As she descended to the bottom floor, Tyger and Picasso watched each other until she disappeared.

Chapter Twenty-Three

fter leaving Picasso's place, Tyger felt twenty pounds lighter, but she was still carrying a heavy burden. Tyger had not seen her sister Bella in weeks and it was eating her alive. Tyger felt guilty she'd neglected Bella in the wake of Spencer's body being recovered and the possibility of being sent to prison. Tyger had run around town plotting and scheming and committing God-awful acts in an effort to protect Nina, but she left Bella on her own. Now it was time to find her sister.

Tyger exited the freeway onto Fort Street and headed down to the old neighborhood. Even though she'd searched there previously, she decided to try her luck once again. Tyger's block had been turned into a one way in an effort for police to control the drug traffic going in and out of the dead-end street. Tyger ignored the Do Not Enter sign and barreled down the street. Just as Tyger reached the old house a woman ran in front of the car and scurried to a house on the other side of the street. The woman was quick, she moved like a cat. She didn't stop after she was almost hit by the car. Tyger looked at the woman's backside as the door to the house closed behind her. As the woman looked back Tyger realized that the woman was her own sister.

Tyger put the car in park and grabbed her gun from her purse. She left her door wide open and jumped out of the car. Tyger ran across the street, entered through a tattered metal gate and leaped onto the porch of a raggedy old house. As Tyger's foot hit the concrete step she teetered backward. The step was broken and warped. As she gained her balance Tyger held onto a wooden post with her left hand and held the gun in her right.

Gathering her balance Tyger walked up to the door and pushed it open. Standing in the doorway she looked back at her car sitting in the middle of the street with the headlights illuminating the pavement. Tyger looked back into the dark house and saw flickers of light shining in random corners. She could hear the sound of crackheads inhaling their blissful poison. The house smelled like citrus, piss and vomit. Crack has a distinct smell; it smells like burning rubber with a hint of sweetness. Tyger crept through the grimy smoke-filled house. Carefully tiptoeing down the hall with her finger on the trigger she quietly called out, "Bella, Bella, Bella..." There was no response.

Tyger's upper lip started to sweat and her entire body became warm. She prayed she wouldn't vomit. She placed her hand over her mouth and let out a silent burp. Tyger's stomach was queasy and she felt weak. She called out to Bella once again, but there was still no answer.

The house was dark and Tyger couldn't make out images in the dark. Finally, she pulled her cell phone from her pocket and let the light guide her through the house. Suddenly Tyger felt someone on her heels; she turned abruptly to confront the person that was invading her space. It was Tim Stokes. Tyger and Tim grew up together; the house was his family's old house. Tim's brother Nardo was the one that killed Shakespeare. Shakespeare used to work for the Stokes brothers, but he was much too smart to stay small time. Tim and Nardo ended up working for Shakespeare. Nardo was Shakespeare's right-hand man that's how he was able to just walk in the house and kill him. After Shakespeare was killed Nardo didn't make it through the night. Tim disappeared for years and resurfaced about a year ago, but no one had been able to get to him since his return to the city.

Tyger looked into Tim's eyes and knew he wanted to kill her.

Tim smirked "Well, well Little Miss Tyger Blackwell...does Picasso and Ace know their little princess is down here slummin."

With her gun resting at her side and her finger still gripped tightly on the trigger, Tyger inhaled a breath of the funky air, "Look Tim I'm just here looking for my sister. I saw her come in here. Can you please get her so we can leave?"

Tim laughed and slowly shook his head, "Can I get her? Bitch this is a crack house ...you think this is the fuckin five-star hotel...am I your bellhop? You got a lotta nerve comin down here all by yoself in the middle of the night demanding that I get your sister. Yeah, Bella is in here with the rest of these hoes. When I'm finished with her, I'll send her home."

Boiling with Rage, Tyger kept poking the side of her leg with the barrel of her gun debating if she should just blow Tim's brains out. Tyger had no idea who else was in that house packin heat, so she stood down. Tyger remained calm and stared Tim dead in his eyes. Still staring at Tim she opened her mouth and yelled out Bella's name, "Bella, get the fuck out here right now." Suddenly a tall barefoot scraggly woman, with filthy torn clothes, and matted hair appeared in the hallway. Her eyes were glassy, her lips were crusty and white.

Tyger's voice cracked; "Bella?" She'd never seen her sister look like a vagrant.

Standing in there was a classic textbook crack head. Bella whispered, "Tyger, what are you doing here."

In an angry tone Tyger said, "I am here to get you. Come on, let's go right now."

Tim laughed, "Oh no, I don't think so. Your sister is paying off her debt to me any way I want. I been supplyin' her all week on credit. I wouldn't want her to catch something, so as a favor to the family, I let her fuck me so she won't have to trick in the streets for her fix."

Tyger took a deep breath as she felt her temples throbbing with disgust. She looked over at Bella shaking like she was about to pass out. Trying not to breathe in the air Tyger talked through her teeth, "Come here Bella." Bella slowly walked over and stood behind Tyger. As Tyger stared into Tim's eyes she realized he had no plans of neither she nor Bella making it out of that house alive.

181

Tim would love to serve her head on a platter to Picasso and Ace. Tyger realized she'd walked into a land mine that was waiting to explode.

In the midst of an awkward silence Tim looked over Tyger's shoulder and blew a kiss to Bella, "So you think I'm going to just let Ace Del Toro's main bitch just walk out the front door. Do you know how much you're worth to me now? This shit is like Christmas. You bitches don't appreciate shit. When I killed Shakespeare, I let Bella live and the night I shot Picasso I let you live…"

Tyger lowered her brow in shock. Tim said "Oh you thought my brother Nardo killed Shakespeare…" Tim displayed a robust almost disgusting laugh, "So Bella, you never told her what happened that night…" Tyger could hear Bella sobbing behind her. Tyger knew deep in her soul that she shouldn't turn around and face her sister.

Tyger said, "Obviously my sister is in no condition to talk so why don't you tell me the story."

Tim hunched his shoulders, "Ok then." Tim locked his knees and pulled his hands up to his face to light his cigarette. Tim took a puff and held the cigarette in the tips of his fingers. "You see Nardo and I put on a little show for Shakespeare before he died. Nardo and your sister had their own thang going on while Shakespeare watched his wife and my brother…"

Tyger yelled, "I don't need to know what your piece of shit brother did to my sister." Tim smiled, "Alright, I can respect that, but would you like to know who let us into the house?"

"I'm sure you let yourself in or Shakespeare opened the door because he trusted you."

"Nope, wrong! Your sister, the one standing behind us let us into the house. She thought we were only going to rob him; take some cash, a little jewelry, you know shit like that."

Tyger's hand started shaking, "Why would Bella do that?"

"Because we paid her. Your sister has been a basehead since high school. And we all know you can't trust a drug addict. I've had a hold on your sister for a long time. We have a bond that can't be broken; she will forever be in my debt."

Refusing to hear the rest of the story, Tyger reached back and grabbed Bella's hand and held it tight. Everything grew silent. The sounds of people inhaling poison through glass pipes filled the air. Nasty coughs and snorts rang through the air like a deafening bell. Feeling her skin crawl, a wave of anxiety shot through Tyger's body. She took a deep breath and swallowed hard, "Well the good news is that neither one of us have to worry about unsettled debt…as far as I'm concerned, we're even. Your life for Shakespeare's life."

Tyger lifted her gun and shot Tim right between the eyes. Tim's body hit the floor like a ton of bricks. Tim lay there on the floor with his cigarette held tightly between his fingers and his eyes wide open. Tyger yelled to Bella to run to the car. Bella took off at top speed. As Tim's men came running down the steps Tyger unloaded her clip tagging anything that moved. She didn't know if she popped crackheads or mad men and she didn't care. Tyger ran and jumped in the car and put the car in drive. She drove to the end of the street and spun around. Shifting gears, the car roared at top speed. Hearing bullets blazing in the distance, Tyger prayed for a safe escape.

Chapter Twenty-Four

After a long and awkward drive back out to Lakewood Hills, Tyger rolled into the gate of her home and pulled into an empty garage stall. Noticing Genoa car in the front of the house, Tyger called for Genoa and Dee Dee to come out and help with Bella. Tyger had just about reached her tolerance limit. Bella had become sick on the way home and vomited all over herself and the front seat of the car. Tyger was covered in Tim's dried blood, she felt grimy and sick to her stomach.

When Dee Dee's feet hit the garage floor she immediately gasped displaying her disdain for Bella's appearance. Dee Dee stood in front of Bella holding her shoulders. "Look at you, you look a mess, you should be ashamed of yourself...you're filthy and you smell like shit..."

Tyger grabbed her mother's hands and forcefully removed them from Bella's shoulders. Tyger looked into her mother's eyes with years' worth of contempt. Tyger stretched out the palm of her hand and slapped Dee Dee across the face, "Don't you ever talk to her like that again. Maybe, just maybe if you would have been a better mother and stayed here and helped raise us instead of whoring around with Judge

Gray until he was tired of you then maybe your kids wouldn't be so fucked up." Unable to look at Dee Dee, Tyger focused on Bella.

Dee Dee stood in the middle of the garage holding the side of her face with her hand. She looked down at Bella and then over at Tyger. The hate in her children's eyes stifled Dee Dee's breath. As her voice quivered with regret Dee Dee said, "I'm sorry...I..."

Tyger quickly snapped, "Dee Dee, why don't you just leave...why don't you just leave us all alone, you're just here so someone else can take care of you..."

Suddenly Tyger heard Bella gasping for air. Bella yelled out, "Tyger please help me, I can't breathe." Tyger grabbed a hold of Bella. Bella fell into Tyger's arms and they both fell to the ground. Genoa ran out of the house with a cold towel and placed it over Bella's forehead. Tyger held Bella close to her and yelled for Dee Dee to call the ambulance.

Dee Dee stood paralyzed as she watched both of her children sitting on the cold concrete helpless. Dee Dee's feet were frozen, she couldn't move. Tyger yelled at her, "Dee Dee, please call the ambulance now..." Dee Dee didn't move.

Suddenly, Ace came running from inside the house, "What's going on out here, Tyger where have you ..."

Ace stopped mid-sentence at the sight of Tyger and Bella sprawled out on the ground. Ace knew what was going on, he didn't hesitate; "Damn, Bella..." Ace ran to call an ambulance. Returning to the garage he reassured everyone, "The ambulance is on its way." Ace reached down and pulled Bella form Tyger's arms. He instructed Genoa to follow him to the bathroom and turn the cold water on. Once inside the bathroom Ace held Bella under the shower. Bella yelled in agony as the freezing water hit her delicate skin. Tyger stood in the doorway with tears covering her face.

Ace continued to hold Bella close to him like a delicate flower as the water stung her body. Ace continued to comfort her, "Come on Bella, come on...hold on...come on Bella...I'm here...I'm not gonna let you die..."

Ace looked up over at Tyger, for the first time everyone including Tyger noticed that there was blood spatter on her face and clothes.

Ace almost dropped Bella, but held on to her "Tyger what the hell happened, whose blood is that…"

Tyger put her hand to her face and wiped the blood from her cheek. In a faint voice she whispered, "Tim Stokes… I found her in Tim's old house. I saw her running across the street like got damn cat and I followed her in…"

Ace started yelling, "Are you fucking crazy, why didn't you call me, Nic or Picasso… Vincent… anybody… Tim could have killed you…"

In a stern and clear voice Tyger said, "I got him first."

Ace said, "What?"

"I blew his brains out."

With little to no emotion, Tyger walked out of the bathroom and headed outside to meet the ambulance. When the ambulance arrived they entered the house and secured Bella on the gurney. Tyger informed them that Bella was a drug addict, but she wasn't sure what her drug of choice was. The attendants strapped Bella down and rolled her into the ambulance. An attendant turned to Tyger and asked if she was going to ride to the hospital in the ambulance. Inside the ambulance Bella continued to yell for Tyger. Tyger turned to the attendant and then turned to Dee Dee and raised her eyebrows "I will follow in the car; her mother will ride with her in the ambulance."

Dee Dee did not attempt to argue. Tyger, climbed in the ambulance as Bella continued to scream, "Tyger please don't leave me… Tyger please help me… Tyger…"

As Tyger turned to enter her home Ace said, "Genoa, will you stay here with Nina? We're going to the hospital…"

Tyger slowly turned in Ace's direction, "I'm going to the hospital alone."

"Look Tyger we don't have time for this right now we need to get to the hospital."

Tyger snapped back, "You have done enough. That shit you peddle in the streets in what did this to my sister. You knew that Tim Stokes helped kill Shake. Tim has been walking around this city alive and you just let him go free. All this time I've been thinking that you were strong and in control, but you let me, a woman, take out Tim Stokes.

What kind of so called gansta are you? You keep talking about how you can't stop doin this shit cause it's in you. You're just a selfish weak little bitch and I fuckin hate you right now…"

Without batting an eye, Ace slapped Tyger across the face with his open left hand. Before he could say a word, Tyger reached up and punched him in the face with her fist. Things happened so fast it scared both of them. Ace and Tyger stood within an inch of each other with both their chests heaving with frightful anger. Tyger and Ace were both out of breath as a warm rush of adrenalin flushed through their bodies. Both Tyger and Ace were unable to speak. Ace felt sick to his stomach, he'd never hit her before, but he couldn't apologize; things had been off balance in their relationship for far too long.

Ace took a deep breath and looked Tyger straight in her eye, "Every single one of us is guilty of what has happened and what is happening to us, including you. We have all been grown men and women for longer than we should and every decision we've made we have made on our own. All these years you've never complained about any of this while you were riding in Bentleys and Jags, wearing shit you couldn't pronounce. All these years I have been taking care of you with my money…the money that I made in these streets. Did Spencer even know that I was the one that bought your restaurant? I have loved you in spite of the choices that you have made. I'm the one running around town looking like a fuckin punk following behind some other man's wife. Everything that I do, I do for a reason. Everything I do, I do for you, for us…" Ace grabbed Tyger by her arm and pulled her close to him and shook her, "A long time ago you forgot that I am the man in this relationship. Don't you ever question me again about the choices that I have made or will continue to make. You need to remember that if you were any other woman you would be picking your teeth up off the ground right now. Let's not cross that line…my business is to take care of what goes on in the streets the way that I need to, so stay the fuck out of my business."

Ace released Tyger arm. Like a rodeo bull, he turned to walk away. Almost ripping the door of the car Ace swung the door open and sat in the driver's seat. As he drove off spinning tires and burning rubber Tyger stood paralyzed staring at his taillights. She knew that they'd crossed that line and things would never be the same between them.

Chapter Twenty-Five

Tyger spent most of the night by Bella's bed side. Sitting across from her sister's bed, she was fascinated by how Bella slept peacefully. This was the first time she'd seen her sister rest since they were children. The room was extraordinarily quiet and sterile. Balled up in a chair next to the window with a thin hospital blanket covering her, Tyger watched drops of rain land on the window and slide down landing on the windowsill. It had been a long time since Tyger sat in silence. Unable to force herself to think about anything of importance, she waited patiently for Bella to wake up.

While staring at Bella wishing she'd wake up, Tyger's phone began to vibrate. Retrieving her phone from her purse, Tanner Hick's name lit up the screen. Tyger quickly ran outside into the hall and answered the call. Excited to hear from Tanner, Tyger pressed "Answer."

"Tanner, hey! I was about to give up on you."

"I know I'm sorry, I had a family emergency, I've been out of town. But I hear things have been pretty crazy for you. S.B. and Spencer, that was crazy."

"I know, it still seems like one long nightmare."

Tanner took a deep breath, "Well I'm sorry, but I'm not calling to make it easier. I found out who the partners are in BAS Industries."

"Well! Who is it?"

"Bella Blackwell, Aiden Arias, and Spencer Benedict."

Trying to process the bomb that just exploded in her mind, Tyger remained silent.

"Tyger, are you still there?"

"Yes, yes Tanner I'm still here." Still unable to snap out of her trance, Tyger struggled to find her voice.

Trying to ease her pain, Tanner followed up with additional information, "I know this has to be devastating and I wanted to make sure I was able to answer all your questions, plus I was curious to know how this union was formed so, I did extensive research."

Snapping back to reality Tyger responded, "Thank you Tanner, I need to know how these fools got together."

"Remember when you sent Bella to that Rehab in Connecticut?"

"Yes"

"Well, as mandated by the New York City Police Department Aiden Arias was ordered to undergo treatment for his alcohol and cocaine addiction. Aiden was treated at the same facility during the time Bella was there."

"How could Aiden afford that place? Bella's treatment cost more than my car."

"Spencer paid for Aiden's treatment."

"What tha fuck? Why would Spencer pay for Aiden's treatment? How did they know each other?"

Tanner released a sigh, "That connection is still unclear. I'm still investigating how they became acquainted. I will tell you that Aiden Arias was brought to Detroit by Spencer to kill you and Ace. I'm not sure what Bella's role in the plan was, but her name and signature are on the incorporation documents."

Tyger's blood curled and her heart raced with anguish, "I'm sure I will have the answer to that question in a few minutes. I have recently discovered my sister's loyalty is to whoever can support her habit. In other words, that bitch ain't loyal to nobody."

With a hint of concern in his voice Tanner questioned Tyger, "Tyger, you sound like you're going to do something you'll regret."

"No sir, I won't regret a moment of it."

Tyger disconnected the call, closed her eyes and slid down the hospital corridor. Covering her face with her palms, she balanced her weight on her knees. Trying not to scream, her body burned with rage. Tyger wanted to burst into her sister's hospital room, snatch her out of bed and beat the life out of her. Thinking of the baby she was carrying and the stress that had already taken a toll on her, she inhaled a few quick breaths, stood to her feet and walked to the end of the hall. Feeling her blood boil inside her veins, a heat wave rushed over Tyger's body. As a huge lump lodged in her throat, she held her hand over her mouth. To no avail, Tyger yelled out, "Fuck!" and hit her fist against the wall. Looking around to see if anyone was watching, she wiped her face and exhaled three slow breaths. Straightening her back and holding her head erect, Tyger looked back down the corridor at the door leading to Bella's room.

Slowly walking down the hall, Tyger approached Bella's door and pushed it open. She stood with her back against the door watching Bella sleep contemplating how to kill her without getting caught. Shaking the thought out of her head, Tyger watched Bella sleep peacefully. Growing agitated Tyger walked over to the bed and shook it. "Bella! Wake up!"

Bella's eyes popped open and rolled around trying to focus. Glancing to her left Bella saw Tyger standing next to her bedside. Displaying a strained smile, Bella greeted Tyger, "Hey, sissy. I'm so glad to see you." Bella extended her hand and beckoned for Tyger to come to her, "Thank you for saving me. You're always there to rescue me." Tyger folded her arms together and pulled her lips inward. Noticing the contempt in Tyger's eyes, Bella began to cry, "I'm sorry Tyger, I know I keep disappointing you. I'm sorry. I was trying to stay clean; I promise I was, but…"

Startling Bella, Tyger clapped her hands together, "Shut up! You lyin bitch."

Bella struggled to pull herself up. Tyger leaned over the bed, "If I were you, I'd lay back down before I knock you down!"

Bella's eyes popped and her jaw dropped, "Tyger, what's wrong with you. You're scaring me."

Tyger rested her back against the wall and folded her arms, "I stood over there against the door and watched you sleep. As I watched you lie there without a care in the world, I was trying to figure out how to kill you. I thought about smothering you with a pillow, or choking you with my bare hands, but it would be premeditated murder and up until now I've evaded the law and I'd like to keep it that way. I stood there watching you feel safe and I actually started hating myself for not leaving you in that crack house, I mean one more day and you would have OD'd and I wouldn't have to figure out how to kill your lying, thieving, snitching ass…"

Pressing the button to raise her bed, Bella slowly stared into Tyger's eyes. Sitting upright Bella's voice began to crack, "So, you know."

"If you mean your botched attempt to partner with Spencer and Aiden to destroy me, then yes, I know…" Tyger unfolded her arms, "Oh, you might be talking about giving the statue that Nina hit Spencer with to S.B. It's so much shit you've done, I really can't keep up."

Bella started crying, "Yes, it's true, I admit to everything you just said."

With her hands shoved in her pockets Tyger walked toward the end of Bella's bed, "I feel like I'm out of the loop. I know how you and Spencer hooked up, but how did you two find Aiden, or how did he find you?"

"Tyger you have to believe it wasn't my idea. Spencer and Aiden dragged me into it."

Enraged, Tyger grabbed the foot of Bella's bed and raised it and dropped it back down on the floor. Bella jumped to the head of the bed and pulled her knees to her chest. With her adrenalin flowing like a water faucet, Tyger yelled, "I don't give a fuck. Tell me how you met Aiden!"

Mumbling in the midst of tears Bella tried to explain, "Spencer found Aiden. He was digging into Ace's past trying to find a way to get rid of him. Spencer found out Ace had a brother, who was a cop in New York. Spencer contacted Aiden. When Spencer and Aiden finally met he realized Aiden was an alcoholic and dope head on the verge of being stripped of his badge. Spencer paid for Aiden's stay at rehab…"

As if a light bulb had gone off in her head, Tyger interrupted Bella, "Damn, so when I was searching for a rehab for you Spencer was so helpful and concerned that he found the place in Connecticut, the same place Aiden had been admitted."

"Yes, before I went to rehab I didn't know Aiden. One day Aiden approached me and we started talking. We started spending time together, started having sex, and he told me he had fallen in love with me. A month before we were discharged Spencer came to visit, that's when I found out he and Aiden knew each other. Aiden told me about he and Spencer's plan to destroy you and Ace. They said they were going to destroy you financially, take everything you had…"

Tyger looked toward the ceiling and back over at Bella, "So, you just agreed to this plan? What was in it for you?"

"I was finally going to have a man who loved me. Aiden said he wanted a family. He wanted to marry me. So yes, I agreed. It was my time to have everything. You've always had everything. Money, men, respect, kids. What do I have? Nothing! I live with you, you support me, everything I have belongs to you."

Tyger laughed, "Oh so it's my fault you ain't shit?"

"That's not what I said."

"But that's what you meant. From the story Tim Stokes told you made a decision a long time ago to be a junkie. The moment you chose that shit, you fucked your own life up. You setup Shakespeare, you were there when Piper was attacked and never said a word. You signed your name on a piece of paper and formed a business with Aiden and Spencer to destroy me because a man you hardly knew said he loved you. You still haven't told me what you were getting out of it besides some crack head, alcoholic dick?"

Bella crawled to the edge of the bed and yelled in Tyger's face, "I was going to finally get the pleasure of being the sister that had it all. I didn't know Spencer was planning to kill you until we discharged from rehab and he told me the only way he could acquire the houses you owned in the hole was to inherit them. The only way he could inherit them was to kill you."

Tyger narrowed her eyes and moved in close to Bella. They were within inches of each other. When Bella exhaled, Tyger inhaled her air. "Wow, murder. That's deep. You hate me enough to kill me. That is so funny. All these years I have tried my best to protect you. I've gone inside of disease infected drug dens to get you out several times. You wanted to go to college I sent you and you failed your first semester. I didn't want you to feel like a child so I got you your own apartment, furnished it, bought your clothes, car, because you can't and won't keep a job. You've lied, you've stolen, you've done so much shit I can't even list them all and yet you were plotting with my no good sorry as husband to kill me…" Trying to hold on to her sanity, Tyger folded her arms and backed away from Bella, "So Bella, tell me, how did that work out for you?" Tyger threw her head back and laughed, "So, when is the wedding? I want to make sure I send a gift."

Bella lowered her head, "There isn't going to be a wedding or anything else. Aiden is the one that hand delivered me to Tim Stokes doorstep. The day he called your phone and you told me not to go near him, I went to his apartment to see him; we had sex and got high. I was so high I didn't even realize what was happening to me until I woke up laying on the steps at the trap house. What else could I do but walk through the door and smoke, it's what I'm good at, it's what I do!"

Staring at the ugly hospital floor tiles, Tyger felt her heart sink to her feet. Looking back over at Bella with a stone face, Tyger removed her hands from her pockets, "I've always looked at you as a victim, a product of our environment. But it is painfully clear to me that every choice you've made in your life was made with the conscious decision that you were hurting other people. None of your actions were in self-defense or even for survival, you do what dope fiends do; they rob, steal and kill just so they can poison themselves. Any way you look at it, it's suicide…"

Tyger paused for a moment and took a deep breath as though she was trying to choose her words carefully. "…As I have stood here and listened to the details surrounding how you were planning to destroy me and take my life, I was still trying to figure out a way to forgive you. I'm sure one day I will, but today is not the day. You are no longer my sister, you are dead to me. The only reason I won't snatch the life from your body right now is because it would break Whiskey's heart to know that one of his daughters killed the other." Tyger reached in her pocket and pulled out a hundred-dollar bill and threw it on the bed, "When you leave this hospital, if you look across the street there's a bus stop. At some point in the day a bus will come that says Fort Street/SW Detroit. Hop your ass on that bus, get off on Fort and Schaeffer and walk back down to that crack house and smoke, shoot, snort, or whatever the fuck you do until your heart gives completely out. When they call to tell me you're dead, I will give you the same burial you wanted to give me."

Grabbing her purse and her jacket, Tyger walked toward the door. Hearing Bella's voice, she stopped abruptly.

"Tyger?"

"What?"

"Why me and not you?"

With agitated curiosity, Tyger narrowed her eyes and shook her head, "Damn, what are you talking about now."

Swinging her feet to the ground Bella stood on the side of the bed, with her voice cracking and tears streaming down her cheek, she sobbed, "Ace and Shakespeare led the same life, but Ace is still alive. You and I are from the same place, yet you're the one with every-thing. I mean how do you do it…you threw one husband in the lake and now you have another man waiting to marry you. We're not so different, I made one mistake twenty years ago that cost me everything, but it could have easily been you."

Tyger started laughing, "Well honey, if it will help you sleep at night my life ain't that grand either. Morally and lawfully, both my dead husband and the man that I love ain't worth shit. You want to know why me and not you…it's because every day I wake up, I choose to live. I don't sit around feeling sorry because I'm a horrible person. I know I'm fucked up, I own that."

Stopping mid-sentence, Tyger moved closer to Bella, "Do you know why I married Spencer?"

"No, I don't. I've never understood why you married him."

"I married him because I thought he was just an ordinary guy. I thought he was going to save me from being the wretched person I knew lived inside me. Unfortunately, my plan to lead a normal life backfired. Instead of marrying an ordinary man, I married a man that had no respect for me. A man that kicked me in my back and watched me fall down the steps when I was eight months pregnant with his child. I'm in love with another man that I'll never have because we are too much alike; we are both volatile and very dangerous. So, while you're standing here wondering why me and not you, figure out which part of my twisted life you really want. If you're so weak that the only way you can deal with reality is by smoking crack then honey you couldn't handle my life. You couldn't do what I've had to do to save my life and the life of my child. We have both chosen our own paths. The key word here is chosen. Just as I have chosen to spare your life…"

Allowing rage to overtake her, Tyger walked over to the side of Bella's bed, leaned in close and palmed her neck wrapping her finger around Bella's esophagus. Frightened Bella began to cough as pee ran down her legs. Tyger's eyes turned cold as her grip on Bella's neck grew tight, "Instead of asking me some silly shit like 'why not me' you need to be thanking me, because the longer I stand here and breathe in the foul stench of your soul the more I want feel your life fade away."

Watching the terror in Bella's eyes, Tyger released her and threw her down on the bed. Tyger pulled herself together, ran her fingers through her hair and prepared to walk out the door. Before exiting the room, Tyger looked back at Bella one last time, "Don't let me catch you on the street."

As the door slowly closed behind her Bella watched her sister disappear. Lying on her back staring at the ceiling Bella's body was riddled with anxiety. She had never seen that wicked look in her sister's eyes. She was sure Tyger's threats weren't superficial.

Rising from her bed, Bella staggered into the bathroom and stared at her reflection. There was an old, ragged women with wiry hair, ashy skin and crusty lips standing where a beautiful vibrant young woman with rich flawless sun kissed skin once stood. Faced with a choice to make amends or end it all for the first time in her tortured life, Bella felt remorse. Her stomach ached at the thought of what she'd done to her sister.

Gripping her stomach, Bella turned toward the bathroom door. Paralyzed by the sight of Detective Aiden Arias standing in the doorway, tears welled in Bella's eyes. Trembling with fear, Bella slowly whispered, "What are you doing here?"

With a cunning smile Aiden stepped toward Bella, "You know why I'm here…" Aiden reached his hand out for Bella, "I'm here for you."

Chapter Twenty-Six

Tyger was jolted out of bed by the piercing sound of her phone ringing. She glanced at the clock and was blinded by 3:37a.m. staring at her in neon green lights. Without looking at the caller ID, she cleared her throat and picked up her phone, "Hello"

"May I speak with Mrs. Benedict?"

"This is Mrs. Benedict."

"Mrs. Benedict this is Alice Monroe from St. Luke's Hospital. I'm sorry to inform you, but your sister Bella passed."

In a calm tone, Tyger asked, "Passed, you mean she's dead?

"Yes ma'am, she is dead."

"I don't understand. When I left her she was fine?"

"Bella was found by one our nurses…it appears that she went into the bathroom smashed the mirror and cut her wrist…"

Tyger took a deep breath and sat on the side of the bed holding the phone. She could hear the faint sound of the nurse calling her name, but she pushed the end icon on the phone without saying goodbye. Not able to get a handle on a complete feeling or thought, Tyger walked toward the bathroom. She stood against the wall staring in the mirror from across the room. She slid down the wall and landed flat on her bottom. Tyger hung her head in her chest and tried to cry. Unfortunately, she could not find tears; her eyes were dry. Her mind was racing as her whole life flashed before her eyes. She thought about the birth of her child, the day her mother left the family, the night Spencer was killed, the last time she saw Piper and the day she saw Beverly's body in a body bag.

Tyger wanted so badly to mourn her sister's death, but all she could do was sit on the floor and wrestle with her demons. Sitting on the floor trying to figure out how she arrived at this place in her life, she watched the sun rise. Everything seemed to be in shambles. For the last few months, she had been scurrying around town trying to cover up Spencer's murder and protect the people she loved.

She wondered when everything went wrong. When did they become that family of hustlers and junkies that were slowly destroying themselves? After sitting on the floor her backside became sore, she pushed herself up and walked into the bedroom. She walked toward the window overlooking the front of the house. She had a magnificent home that some can only dream of. She looked at the garage on each side of the house. There were six stalls; three on each side of the house and each one was full. She thought of her Olympic size swimming pool that looked as if it spilled over into the lake and the boat docked out back bearing Nina's name. Tyger owned everything; there was no mortgage or payment due. On the surface her life seemed perfect, but what price had she paid to live such a lavish lifestyle. Her house was the house that was built by greed. Every moment spent in that house excluding the day she brought Nina home from the hospital was hell.

She thought about how she had so much and yet she still had nothing. Tyger graduated top of her class from law school. She had been the Assistant District Attorney and never lost a case. She was beautiful, brilliant and street-smart, but she wondered what happened to her good old-fashioned common sense. Over the past nine months, she had thrown her husband's dead body into the lake, murdered two people and blackmailed a judge. Her crack head sister had just committed suicide and she was in love with a man that less than twenty-four hours ago hit her so hard that her face vibrated from the impact. From where she stood the house, the cars and the money seemed irrelevant. Her stacks of money could not fix her broken life. Her money could not bring her sister back and it couldn't repair her relationship with Ace.

She stared out the window trying to subdue stifling feelings of hopelessness. How could she bring another child into her world?

Tears began to well in her eyes as she realized how alone she felt at that moment. The room seemed to grow smaller and her breath became shorter. She wasn't concerned about going to prison for the things she'd done, she was concerned about her soul. Tyger was not what you would call a regular church going woman, but she showed up at least once a month. She believed in God and she believed that someday she would have to atone for her sins, but she wondered when that day would come.

There was a nagging uncomfortable, yet persistent feeling that dwelled in the pit of her stomach. Something wasn't right and it had nothing to do with Bella's death. This was feeling of sadness and despair. There was something inside her that was starting to blaze like a four-alarm fire. Something was about to happen that would change her life, but she had no idea what. Tyger felt there was a force she could not see that had a hold on her and it wouldn't let her move forward, backward or in any direction. Whatever it was, it would hinder her plans to leave Detroit.

Pressing her face against the glass she held her hand against the windowpane. Faintly whispering, "What is this hold on my life and how do I rid myself of it," she felt her eyes burn with tears and her heart tighten with anxiety. Begging for answers to a question she feared she would never be answered, the sound of the phone ringing snapped her back to reality. She glanced over at the nightstand and realized Ace was calling. Ignoring the call, her heart sank to her feet. In an instant she knew what had been suffocating her and leaving her breathless. It was Ace; the love she had for him was consuming her. How could she let him go after loving him for most of her life? Now she was carrying his child it seemed impossible to walk away.

Feeling the sunshine on her face as it kissed her good morning, Tyger wiped away her tears and cleared her throat. Tyger's face felt grimy from crying and sitting up half the night. She washed her face brushed her teeth and put on a pair of sweats. With a heavy heart, she sat on the side of the bed grabbed her phone and dialed her father.

"Good Morning, old man!"

"Hey Baby! You had a long night; I left you at the hospital. Why are you up with the roosters?"

Tyger paused for moment. "I have something to tell you."

"What's wrong Baby Girl?"

"Bella is dead. I received a call from the hospital around 3am. She's gone."

Whiskey and Tyger sat on the phone with a mountain of silence between them. Finally, Whiskey broke, "When I left the doctor said she would be fine."

"Apparently she committed suicide. She slit her wrists with a piece of the bathroom mirror she'd broken."

Whiskey cleared his throat, "Have you told your mother?"

"No, not yet. I'll tell her when I hang up with you."

"Ok, I'm going to get dressed. I should be at your house in forty-five minutes."

Before Whiskey disconnected the call, Tyger yelled out to him, "Whiskey!"

"Yes?"

"I'm not going to the hospital with you. I'll make sure Dee Dee is ready when you arrive."

"I understand. I'll be there soon." Whiskey drew a deep breath, "I love you."

"I love you too daddy!"

After hanging up from Whiskey, Tyger walked down the hall to tell Dee Dee that her daughter was dead. She forcefully knocked on the door and waited for Dee Dee to invite her in. The faint voice on the other end of the door said, "Come in." Tyger walked into Dee Dee's room and stood next to the bed. She took a deep breath and sat down next to her mother,

"Dee Dee, I need you to sit up. I have something to tell you."

With a furrowed brow, Dee Dee pulled herself up, tilted her head and looked at Tyger,

"What's wrong?"

"The hospital called, Bella slit her wrist…she committed suicide. She's dead."

Dee Dee stared at Tyger as if she were waiting on the punch line to a joke. Dee Dee took a deep breath and hung her head. She raised her head and looked at Tyger, "Damn, where did I go wrong with my kids? Bella's dead, John Paul is God knows where, Piper has isolated herself from the family, and well, you're you. Where did I go wrong?"

Tyger shook her head, "Dee Dee, I would love to blame you for our failures, but it is what it is. We all made our own choices. Right or wrong, we have to own who we are. You didn't put the crack pipe in Bella's hand, you didn't make John Paul sell drugs, you didn't send Piper off out yonder, you damn sure didn't make me who I am. I wish I had something more profound to say, but I don't."

Tyger lifted herself from the side of bed, "Whiskey will be here soon to pick you up. The two of you will need to go to the hospital and make arrangements for Bella." Without uttering a heartfelt word to her mother, Tyger exited the room.

Arriving at the hospital, Whiskey and Dee Dee headed toward the floor Bella was housed the night before. Once they had exited the elevator, the two walked toward the nurse's desk. There was no need to announce who they were; everyone on the floor knew they were Bella Blackwell's family. Ironically, Tyger had spent a few days on that same floor the night that she dragged Spencer's body down the hill and rolled him into the lake.

As Whiskey and Dee Dee approached the desk, the nurse stood to her feet and welcomed them. With an apologetic tone, she greeted the family, "I am so sorry for your loss…"

In a low solemn tone, Whiskey said, "Thank you. We appreciate that. Can you tell us where Bella is now? Is she still in the room?"

The nurse shook her head. "Bella has been transported downstairs. We tried to wait until you arrived, but unfortunately, we couldn't keep her in the room. The cleaning crew just went in to begin cleanup. I was just about to walk down to see if she had any personal items that need packing…"

Whiskey interrupted the nurse, "I'd like to go and see my daughter, please tell me how to get to her?" It seems that no one wanted to say the word "morgue." No one wanted to acknowledge that Bella was lying in the basement of this hospital on a cold table waiting to be violated once again.

Dee Dee interrupted, "Actually, I would like to go to my daughter's room. Her sister brought her pajamas and a few other items last night. I'd like to get those."

The nurse smiled, "Sure, you're welcome to go to the room and retrieve those items."

Dee Dee and Whiskey stood in the doorway watching the lady clean the room where their daughter laid less than twenty-four hours ago. Bella had not been in the hospital long enough to make an imprint in the bed or leave fingerprints. Dee Dee slowly walked into the room and touched the sweatpants Bella was wearing when she was brought into the emergency room. When she moved Bella's shirt she noticed a gold lighter resting underneath. She picked up the lighter and held it in front of her face. Reading the inscription "Shakespeare Kennard" Dee Dee realized it was Shakespeare's lighter. Bella always had it with her, but she did not have it when Tyger rescued her from the crack house.

Dee Dee called out to Whiskey, "Whiskey, this is Shakespeare's lighter."

Whiskey turned in Dee Dee's direction. Moving closer he grabbed the lighter from Dee Dee's hand, "I thought Bella lost this the last time she was in rehab."

Dee Dee smirked, "So did I. We even called the facility to see if they found it."

Whiskey shook his head, "Why would she lie about losing the lighter."

"I don't think she lied. She was genuinely upset about losing it. When Tyger brought her home night before last, she was half naked, her clothes were filthy and torn…" Dee Dee picked up the sweatpants, "…These pants don't have pockets. When Tyger brought her home night before last everything she was wearing had to be thrown away. Tyger put these clothes on her before the ambulance arrived. Between the time Tyger found her, brought her home and she ended up here, where could she have gotten this lighter that's been missing for months?"

Rolling the lighter around in his hand Whiskey narrowed his eyes, "Bella didn't bring this into this room. Someone else has been here. Whoever she gave this lighter to or stole it from her was the last person to see her alive."

While Dee Dee and Whiskey stared at each other trying to figure out where the lighter could have come from the cleaning lady cleared her throat, "Excuse me, but I found that behind the toilet while cleaning the bathroom."

With his mouth almost resting at his feet, Whiskey asked, "Did you tell anyone you found this behind the toilet?"

The lady shook her head, "No sir."

Whiskey reached into his pocket and pulled out two one-hundred-dollar bills, "Good, keep it to yourself. Don't tell anyone you found this lighter. Do you understand?" The lady snatched the money, shoved in it her bra and shook her head in agreement.

Whiskey turned back toward Dee Dee, "I'll be right back, I'm going to ask the nurse something."

Dee Dee waited in the room while Whiskey went to the nurse's desk. Approaching the desk, with a commanding voice, Whiskey bellowed, "Did anyone visit my daughter after her sister left last night?"

Startling the nurse standing behind the desk, she dropped the papers she was holding. "Yes, a detective came by after Mrs. Benedict left. Visiting hours were over and we usually don't let people in, but he said he needed to ask her a few questions, so I let him see her. Is there something wrong?"

As his chest heaved with anger, Whiskey tried to remain calm. Shaking his head, "No, everything is fine."

Like a rogue bear, Whiskey charged down the hall. Standing in the doorway of the hospital room he yelled, "Delilah, come on. We have to go, now!" Dee Dee reached down to grab Bella's personal belongings she'd packed in a small bag. Whiskey yelled again, "Please, hurry!"

Hurrying out the door, Dee Dee nervously questioned Whiskey, "What's wrong?"

"I'll tell you when we get on the elevator."

Whiskey and Dee Dee sped past the nurse's desk without saying a word. Reaching the elevator, Whiskey pushed the down button several times, finally hitting it with his fist. Dee Dee, pulled the bag she was holding close to her, "You're scaring me, what the hell is going on?"

Whiskey stepped toward Dee Dee, grabbed her by the arm and pulled her close to him. Whispering in her ear, "Detective Arias was here last night after Tyger left."

Whispering Dee Dee asked, "Why would he be visiting Bella?"

Finally, the elevator doors opened. Pushing Dee Dee onto the elevator, Whiskey sneered "That's what I wanna know."

Stepping onto the elevator, Whiskey and Dee Dee watched as the doors closed. Extending his finger, Whiskey pushed the "stop" button. As the elevator came to a screeching halt, Dee Dee fell against the back wall. Whiskey pulled his phone from his pocket and selected Tyger's name from his recent call log.

"Hello"

"Tyger, we've got a problem"

"What's wrong now?"

"I just found out Bella had a visitor after you left.'

"Who was it?"

"Detective Arias."

Tyger released big hard sigh, "I'm not surprised, among other things she told me they had been seeing each other."

Whiskey's voice became weak, "What?" Holding on to the truth about Bella's betrayal and alliance with Aiden and Spencer, Tyger told her father only what he needed to know.

"Bella and Aiden hooked up when they were both in the rehab facility in Connecticut. They've been seeing each other since they met. That's how he came to Detroit."

Reading between the lines, Whiskey revealed he was not an idiot, "Tyger, there is something you're not telling me. The lighter that Bella lost while she was in that place showed up in her hospital room. The cleaning lady said she found it behind the toilet. Bella's body was found in the bathroom. Two things I know for sure, Aiden Arias was the last person to see Bella alive, and he had to have that lighter all this time. If the lighter was found behind the toilet that means he dropped it by accident while he was in the bathroom with my daughter. Now are you gonna tell me what's really going on or do I need to find the detective myself and ask him."

Tyger yelled, "No, Whiskey! I will take care of this. Please just go and identify Bella's body. See what you can find out from Dr. Milan. Find out if there is a way someone else could have slit her wrist."

Tyger didn't wait for her father's response; she abruptly ended the call. Tyger knew she had to get to Aiden before Whiskey. When it came to vengeance Whiskey was like a psychotic mad man. When it came to his children he was deeply emotional and extremely irrational. Aiden's demise needed to be handled with discretion; he was a police detective and no matter how much clout Whiskey held among the chain of command, killing an officer of the law would carry a stiff penalty if the wrong prosecutor or politician looking to make a name for themselves got a hold of the case. With her heart beating slow exhausting beats, Tyger felt the weight of the world crushing her chest. Thumbing through her phone she found Aiden's number. The sound of the phone ringing moved through her body like a tornado. She was so wound up she almost forgot that Aiden was Ace's brother. She didn't have time to think that she should probably tell Ace what was going on before she killed his brother. Just as she started to think more rationally, Aiden answered the phone.

"Hello."

"I need you to meet me at Brown Sugar's in thirty minutes."

"Who is this?"

"Aiden, you know damn well who this is. Either you can meet at the restaurant or I can come and get you. Trust me, you don't want me to come and get you."

Tyger didn't wait for Aiden's response, she ended the call. With anger stinging her nostrils as she huffed like a dragon, Tyger felt her stomach flutter. Remembering she was pregnant, she inhaled a few deep breaths, closed her eyes and tried to hold on to the little sanity she had left.

Chapter Twenty-Seven

On her way to the restaurant, Tyger met Whiskey and Dee Dee to retrieve Shakespeare's gold lighter. Convincing Whiskey to give it up was like trying to pull a Silverback's teeth. But he finally conceded.

After waiting thirty minutes past Tyger's requested time, Aiden knocked on the door to the restaurant. Tyger walked toward the door and grabbed the handle with one hand and turned the key with the other. The lock popped and the door opened. Tyger stepped to the side and watched Aiden as he walked through the door. Once Aiden was inside, she locked the door.

"Please, stop right there."

Tyger walked toward Aiden and stood in front of him. "Spread your legs and stretch your arms out."

Aiden laughed, "Are you serious?"

Without cracking a smile, Tyger replied, "Yes!"

Tyger proceeded to pat Aiden down. She searched every inch of his body. Aiden shook his head, "Tyger, I'm the law, of course I'm carrying a gun."

Tyger stepped back, "I could care less about a gun. That's the least of my worries, I'm looking for a wire."

Aiden was taken aback, "A wire?"

"Yes, a wire. I don't trust yo slimy ass.'

After searching Aiden and coming up empty, Tyger held out her hand leading him toward a nearby table. Walking toward the available table, Aiden noticed a glass of water and a gun resting on the tabletop. Aiden stood in the middle of the restaurant trying to figure out what was going on. Tyger walked past Aiden and extended her arm toward the chair, "Please have a seat."

"Thank you."

Still standing in front of Aiden trying to remain calm, Tyger asked, "Can I get you something to drink."

"No, thank you. I'm fine." Aiden took a breath, "Tyger, I'm so sorry to hear about Bella. If there is anything that I can do, please don't hesitate to ask."

Trying to restrain herself, Tyger sat in the seat across the table from Aiden and took a few sips of the water. Sensing the rage that boiled inside, Aiden slowly lowered himself into the seat across from Tyger. Finally, Tyger raised her head and stared straight into Aiden's eyes. Without saying a word, she reached in her pocket and pulled out the lighter and threw it onto the table.

"I heard you visited my sister last night in the hospital. It looks like you left something behind."

Aiden shook his head, "Yeah, I heard that she was in the hospital, so I decided to stop by to see her."

Tyger tightened her lips and then relaxed them. She leaned back in the chair crossed her legs, tilted her head and narrowed her eyes, "Aiden, it's clear to me that you came to Detroit with blinders on. You had no idea what you were getting yourself into. I can't blame you because you had no idea you'd partnered with a colossal fuck-up and a crack head. Hell, from what I hear you're a little cracked out yourself so obviously your decision-making skills are flawed as well. My sister allegedly killed herself less than twenty-four hours ago, a few hours before that she was in a disease infested crack house smoking on a glass pipe. Now, of course this information is not new to you because you hand delivered her to that house."

Aiden opened his mouth to speak, but Tyger's tone grew more aggressive. She snapped back, "Please, shut up…" Tyger took a breath, "Perhaps, I began this conversation wrong and you've misunderstood why you're here. So, let me start over. Over the past few weeks, you have been investigating the murder of my husband. That case is now closed. As far as the justice system is concerned, my father-in-law murdered his son and his mistress because they were blackmailing him. But I think it's only fair that you know what really happened. I threw my husband in the lake that you found him in. I was eight months pregnant when I dragged his body through our backyard in the middle of a blizzard. For the past few weeks, I have been running around town trying to protect my family. To make sure that I protect myself as well as my daughter, I killed my dead husband's mistress and my father-in-law. I walked into your jailhouse and gutted S.B. like a hog. Oh yeah, I also blackmailed a judge to make sure there were no hiccups in my plan…"

Tyger paused and took a sip of water, "…You're probably wondering why I'm confessing all this to you. Well, I'm glad you asked. I've learned something about myself that I guess I've always known. There is a side of me that I've tried to keep hidden. I've always had Ace or Picasso to protect me, so I never really knew what I was capable of. But these last few weeks have taught me a very valuable lesson. I have learned that I am capable of cold-blooded premeditated murder. With that being said, don't fuck with me Aiden. I am being courteous by asking you nicely, did you kill my sister?"

Aiden sat in front of Tyger with a lump his throat. Rendered speechless by the unsolicited confession that had just fallen from Tyger's lips without hesitation, Aiden chose his words carefully. Tyger was no longer the sexy, irresistible little vixen he wanted to steal from his brother. Her beautiful doe eyes had turned cold and her infectious smile had turned into the kiss of death. The voice that he found mesmerizing now spat venom that burned his ears. This was not the woman he spent his days and nights fantasizing about. There would be no embarrassing premature excitement leaving him holding himself in shame. This time the only thing he was holding was his bladder. The look in Tyger's eyes and her affiliation with his brother told him that she would filet him without blinking. Aiden knew he had to be careful. Sensing his reluctance to come clean, Tyger continued to educate him on his own sins.

"While you're sitting there thinking of a lie, I should tell you that the last time I saw my sister alive, she told me everything. I know how you met; I know you were using her to get to me; I know you dropped her off at that crack house to die. It's amazing how you came to Detroit and found the lowest gutter trash you could. I'm sure you know by now your buddy Tim Stokes is dead. I popped him right between the eyes and watched his body fall like a sack of rancid potatoes." Tyger began beating on the table, "Do I need to go on or do you understand what the fuck I'm saying to you? Did you kill my sister?"

Deafening silence filled the air as Tyger and Aiden sat staring into each other's eyes not uttering a word. Aiden glanced down at Tyger's hand and was almost blinded by the ice resting on her ring finger. He looked around the restaurant and then looked through the glass doors at the Bentley parked in front of the door. Aiden looked back at Tyger, who never took her eyes off of him. Looking into his eyes she knew what he was thinking.

Suddenly Aiden relaxed his shoulders and leaned back in his chair, "I clearly understand what you're capable of and for a few moments, I have to admit that I was quite disturbed by your demeanor. I don't want you to ever think that I don't know who you really are. Any woman that can be with my brother knowing what kind of man he is, is just like him. With you being a businesswoman above anything else, you can respect my request for one million dollars in cash to keep my mouth closed about everything you just told me, get on a plane and never see you or my brother again.'

Tyger laughed, "What makes you think I won't just kill you right here?"

Aiden smiled, "Like I said, I'd never underestimate you. I asked Officer Cavanaugh to follow me and wait across the street. If I'm not out of here or I don't give him a sign that I'm fine in ten minutes, he's coming in. I don't think you can kill me and hide my body in ten minutes."

Aiden looked at Tyger as if to say *checkmate*. Tyger stood up, "Please, if you don't mind I'd like you to follow me to the door."

Confused Aiden asked, "Excuse me?"

"Please, indulge me a little.' Tyger extended her arm once again for Aiden to take the lead. Once they reached the door, Tyger stopped and looked out the glass and pointed across the street. "Is that Officer Cavanaugh over there talking to my friend Vincent?"

Aiden shook his head, "Yes." Staring out the glass he watched Vincent and Officer Cavanaugh carry on a conversation like they were old friends. Tyger cleared her throat, "I'm not sure what Vincent and Officer Cavanaugh are discussing right now. I can only imagine that they are talking about how he has two children and a wife who lost her job a few months ago and bill collectors that won't go away. Maybe they're talking about how they used to play on the same football team when they were in high school or how Vincent saved Officer Cavanaugh's life during a bar fight one night when they were young and dumb. Or perhaps they are discussing how my father pays Officer Cavanaugh to follow me around town to make sure I don't do something stupid. Of course my father doesn't know that I know that the officer is on his payroll, but as you can see nothing gets past me…"

Parting his lips to speak, Aiden turned toward Tyger, but she interrupted him "…to answer your question, I could kill you in ten minutes and not have to worry about hiding your body because Officer Cavanaugh will not come in here to save you, in fact he would help me dispose of your body parts." Pulling her lips in and breathing deeply, Tyger made one last plea, "I'm going to give you one last chance to tell me what happened in that hospital room between you and my sister…"

Aiden interrupted Tyger "It seems to me you already know what happened. Or you think you know. So, what you gon do, shoot me? Mess up your beautiful restaurant with my blood. Because you're not going to get me to move from this spot. If you're gonna kill me, you need to do it right here in this open window for the world to see."

Tyger smiled, "That's fine you don't have to admit you killed Bella. But, there is something I do know. I know why you left New York. I know there are people after you that are far worse than I. In fact, I know these people so well that I can just reach out and touch them. With one phone call you can disappear forever and still have some parts of you show up in all fifty states. Because you 're Ace's brother and I know in spite of how much hell you've put him through, he promised his mother he wouldn't kill you. So, I will give you twenty-four hours to leave this city and never return."

Trying to not show reprieve, Aiden asked, "Tell me one thing…"

"What is it?"

"How did you pull all of this off. How did you kill S.B., Gigi, and Spencer all by yourself? My brother had to have helped in some way."

"It's simple. I've lived my life in the shadows of the men in my life. People have always seen me as Picasso Kennard's best friend, Ace Del Toro's woman, Whiskey's daughter, John Paul's sister, and Spencer Benedict's wife. For different reasons these men, even my evil ass dead husband has always been seen as the men who protect me. For years I was cool with letting them take care of me, but this time there was more at stake that I could not trust anyone to handle but me. My daughter's future was in jeopardy. Of course, I knew that if it came down to it, Ace and Picasso would protect both of us…" Tyger paused for a second or two, "… To be honest, I could not have done any of this without you; you actually made this easy for me. You were so busy having the usual suspects followed and watched like hawks that you left me free to do what I needed to do to save all of us and for that I thank you."

Aiden tilted his head and looked into Tyger's eyes, "You know what Tyger, you are absolutely right. I dropped the ball; I forgot why I came here. I didn't come here to destroy a little girl's life or extort money from you. You just reminded me of something very important and for that I thank you."

Smiling like a hyena Aiden looked past Tyger, "At least I'll always have that one special night we shared to remember you by. Sometimes I can still taste your sweet…well I'm sure you remember." Walking toward the front of the restaurant Aiden opened the door. Grabbing the door and looking back, Aiden smiled, "Don't worry little brother, she wasn't a willing participant. This was entirely my pleasure." Shooting a sarcastic wink Aiden exited the restaurant.

Like a wild tornado, Ace sprinted past Tyger and bolted toward the door after Aiden. Shattering the glass as he pushed his way through, the metal frame dangled on the hinges. Officer Cavanaugh and Vincent ran toward Ace. Unable to move or speak, Tyger stood on the middle of the shattered frame holding her chest. Narrowly escaping Ace's grasp, Aiden grabbed the door handle to his SUV. With the door hanging open Ace reached in and tried to pull Aiden out. Hanging out of the truck, Aiden struggled to reach for the ignition button. Trying to pull Aiden closer to him, Ace grabbed a hold of Aiden's shirt. Stretching out his foot toward the break, Aiden pressed the break with the tips of his toes. Pushing the start button, Aiden shifted the car in reverse and stepped on the gas.

Shifting the gear to drive, Aiden sped off with Ace hanging on to the door. With guns blazing in Aiden's direction, Officer Cavanaugh and Vincent emptied their clips trying to stop him. Finally, Ace let go of the door and fell to the ground. Rolling over on all fours, Ace lifted himself from the ground. Vincent and Officer Cavanaugh ran toward him.

"Do you want us to follow-up."

"No, I'll find him."

Leaving the two men standing in the middle of the street Ace walked toward the restaurant. Tyger stood in the doorway afraid to move. Ace walked through the door frame past Tyger barely touching her. Turning in his direction she followed him inside the restaurant.

Ace stood across the room staring straight through Tyger. Trying to shake the image of Aiden and Tyger together, he inhaled a slow deep breath. Closing his eyes, he exhaled. Reaching over to a nearby table he ripped the tablecloth of the table and wiped his hands. Throwing the tablecloth on the floor, Ace reached up and rubbed his eye.

Trying to figure out what to say, Tyger parted her lips. With a faint whisper she joked, "Damn, your eye is fucked up."

Ace shot back, "Yeah, I know a woman with a nasty right hook."

There was an eerie tranquility that filled the air. The air was thick with uncertainty; would these two rip each other apart or would they kiss and makeup? Realizing Ace was actually standing in front of her with a shiner covering his eye, the reality of their demise hit her like a brick to the chest.

"How long have you been here?"

"Long enough."

"How did you know we were here?"

"You're not the only one that's paying Office Cavanaugh's bills. I needed someone to keep track of Aiden while he was keeping track of you. He called me and told me Aiden was meeting you here. I waited for you to let him in then I came in through the back."

Tyger and Ace simultaneously walked toward each other stopping in the middle of the restaurant. Ace reached over and pulled the chair out and waited for Tyger to take her seat.

"Sit down, please." After Tyger took a seat, Ace walked over to the opposite side of the table and pulled out a chair. Taking his seat, he slowly tapped his fingertips on the table. Wearing a look of anxious concern, he tried to choose his words carefully.

"Before we discuss the special night that you and Aiden shared let me express that I honestly have no words that will express how sorry I am about Bella. You know I loved her like she was my blood sister."

Tyger nodded her head, "Thank you. In spite of her demons, she loved you."

The two were once again embraced in an awkward silence. There were so many unanswered questions and issues that needed to be addressed that there wasn't enough time to cover them.

Needing to move past the elephant in the room, Tyger finally broke her silence, "The night you saw Aiden here at the restaurant, he'd been here for quite a while. He just showed up in the middle of my set. When I saw him, I ended my song, walked over and asked him to leave. He refused to leave. We walked over to the bar and sat there for the rest of the night. At some point in the evening, I left the bar, I don't remember where I went but, I left my drink unattended. I think that's when he put something in my drink. When we closed the restaurant, I finally convinced him to leave. Before, I went into the back I asked someone to make sure he was gone. I thought he'd finally left the restaurant, I went back into the office to change and get ready to go home. As soon as I headed to the office I felt sick. The room started spinning and I was disoriented, I could hardly walk or talk. I was here alone, the club was locked down, and everyone had gone home. While I was trying to get myself together, Aiden showed up in the office. Apparently, he'd hid until everyone was gone. I even asked him to help me find my phone so I could call you to pick me up, but…"

Ace raised his hand for her to stop, "Did Aiden force you to have sex with him?" Tyger swallowed hard, "Technically, no!"

Ace's eyes grew wide. "What the hell does that mean?"

"It means there was no penetration, if you want me to be crude and explain…"

Ace raised his hand, "Please, don't"

"It was not consensual. It's not something I wanted to happen. I had no control over what was going on. I could hear myself telling him to stop, but I couldn't fight him off. My arms and legs were so week. I couldn't focus. I'm sure he dropped something in my drink, but I can't figure out how…"

Ace narrowed his eyes, "I believe you. It sounds like something my brother would do. I wish you would have told me."

"I was afraid to tell you. I didn't know how you would react."

Ace shook his head, "I can't lie, the thought of you and him together, however it happened makes me sick." Tyger tried to plead her case.

"Ace, I was drugged. It's not like I wanted to be with Aiden."

"I know; I get it. I'm not blaming you, but that doesn't mean it doesn't hurt any less." Ace rested his head in the palms of his hands "You do understand my brother has to pay for what he did to you and for what he's done to Bella. I would have killed him out there in the middle of the street."

Tyger shook her head, "No Ace, I want to take care of Aiden myself."

In a frighteningly calm tone Ace tilted his head, "This is not going to be a tug-of-war between the two of us. This is my brother; he's my blood. This is something I should have done a long time ago."

Leaning back in the chair, Ace began to tap his fingers on the table once again, "I don't want to add fuel to the fire that is brewing between us right now, but killing my brother is deeper than you and me. What happened between you and I the other night does not change the fact that I love you. I will do anything for you; I hate him for what he did to you, but this is something that I have to do myself. I'm not asking for your permission. I am telling you to stay away from my brother."

Ace lowered his head and stared at a small stain on the white table-cloth, "Aside from my issues with Aiden, we have a huge mess that we need to decide how to clean up. A thread has been torn in the fabric of our relationship and we need to figure out how to repair it."

Tyger's voice became elevated, "Ace, you slapped me like I was thug in the street. You didn't hesitate or think twice about it. There is no torn thread, there is no fabric, and there is no relationship, there is nothing. When your hand connected with my face our relationship ended, period."

Reaching across the table toward Tyger Ace tried to plead his case, "If I could take it back I would. You know how much I love you. Hell, you're still wearing my ring." Tyger grabbed the ring with her index finger and thumb and twisted the ring off.

Standing to her feet, she threw the ring across the table. "Now, we have nothing else that ties us together." Tyger pushed her chair closer to the table; "I have loved you since I was fourteen years old. I always thought our love would get us through anything and in the past it has. Even after marrying another man, I still couldn't get enough of you. Now that you know what happened between your brother and me even though I could not control what happened, you'll never look at me the same. Sitting here looking at the disappointment in your eyes I finally realized all these years we've been living one big beautiful lie that I just can't live anymore." Tyger looked down and stared at the tablecloth, "It's always been about that right moment with us. We'll get together when the time is right. Honestly, I don't ever think there will be a right time. There's always going to be something that stands between us. I can't live like this. I don't want to share you with Nico and whoever else is around to protect and watch over us."

Tyger looked up and pointed toward the street, "Those men out there know when I take a piss. I'm constantly worried and looking over my shoulder, I'm never alone. This is what our life together will look like and I don't want it."

Ace rose from his seat and reached out to her. Taking a few steps back, Tyger raised her hands, "No Ace, it's over." With tears streaming down her cheek, Tyger felt as though she were suffocating. Grabbing her stomach, she walked past Ace and through the shattered glass on into the street. Heartbroken, Ace called out to her "Tyger!" As she kept moving forward, he called out twice more, "Tyger!" "Tyger Blackwell!!" Finally, watching her drive away Ace stood in the middle of the restaurant peering through the tattered door frame with his hand extended whispering her name, "Tyger, please don't leave me." Pulling his hand close to his chest Ace stood alone watching as his future disappeared in an instant. Although large in stature, as his heart shrank, Ace felt like the smallest man in the world.

Chapter Twenty-Eight

O
n the day of Bella's funeral Tyger still had not shed a tear for her sister. When Bella died, Tyger lost the ability to feel any concrete emotion. With every waking moment her mind continued to race. She became consumed with planning her exit from the city; she knew she'd had enough. Sitting in the back of the chauffeur driven Rolls Royce staring out the window taking snapshots of the cities' scenery in her mind, she felt at peace with her decision to leave. The city had become like an unfamiliar friend. She had spent most of her life running through the streets with her siblings, Picasso, Shakespeare and Ace. Even though she wanted to leave and escape to some faraway place that was so far removed from what she was used to, Tyger still felt a connection to the city that would always be apart of her.

Arriving at Bella's gravesite, Tyger stood by and watched as Picasso, Ace, Vincent and other friends carried Bella to her final resting place. Refusing to take a seat across from her sister's bed of eternal rest, like a foreign language she could not understand, Tyger stood over the grave and listened as the minister's words echoed in her ears. Lost in a sea of meaningless words and grief-stricken faces, she glanced over at Ace.

They were standing a few feet away from each other, their eyes hidden by tinted lenses locked in what felt like a never-ending embrace. As Tyger and Ace stood there speaking to each other heart to heart in a language only the two of them could understand, her heart broke into a million pieces.

Tyger could feel a thunderstorm brewing inside her. The rumbling had begun at the tips of her toes slowly moving through her body and there was nothing she could do to stop it. Hidden by the brim of the hat covering her eyes and the midnight black glasses shadowing her from the world, a tear escaped from her heart and rolled down her cheek. The tear was quiet, graceful and did not intrude on anyone else's heartache. Still staring at Ace, Tyger stood quietly sulking in her own misery.

Watching the tears roll down Tyger's face, Ace placed his hand on his chest as if he were trying to keep his heart from bursting. He wanted so badly to reach out to her, to hold her, to let her know everything would be fine. Even in the most hopeless situation, Tyger was still the most beautiful woman he'd ever seen. She was his ride or die chick. She was the one that always had his back through thick and thin, good or bad. Whether their relationship was right or wrong, he knew she would sacrifice her life for him and he would do the same for her.

Standing with his hand over his heart staring at the person who made his heartbeat, Ace felt his heart sink to his feet. With a tear stuck in his throat almost stifling his breath, Ace knew because he loved her, he had to let her go. He knew a line had been crossed and things between them would never be the same.

Startled by the sound of the attendants lowering Bella into the ground, Tyger looked down and threw a single red rose on top of the casket. Turning to take her leave of what was now about to turn into an excessive display of emotion by mourners, the crowd parted as she walked toward the car. The chauffer opened the door; Tyger entered the car and slowly rode away.

Tyger did not join the rest of the family at the repast. She wanted to get home to spend time with Nina. Picasso joined the two of them as they shared memories of Bella, Shakespeare, and the rest of the family.

Over the last few days people had been in and out making funeral arrangements and packing the house to be sold. Nina and Tyger's clothes were packed and they were all set to travel. The plane would leave the runway at midnight and the two of them would arrive in New York to rest for a couple of days and soon after they would begin an island-hopping adventure until they were ready to settle in their final destination. Tyger wanted to be free. She didn't want to live by deadlines, appointments or calendars. She wanted to spend uninterrupted time with her daughter and enjoy life.

Over the past few days leading to Bella's funeral, Detective Arias had disappeared. Resigning from his position with the police department it appeared he'd finally grew tired of fighting a losing battle. It was as if he'd never existed, no one questioned his absence or his decision to resign, Aiden Arias was gone without mention or concern.

Everything was falling into place. The house was up for sale, the cars were being sold, the furniture was being sold, and everything about her old life was being auctioned off to the highest bidder. Tyger had purchased Dee Dee her own condo and given her a few dollars to hold her until her luck changed. Whiskey had signed the bar over to Dee Dee and was preparing to retire to South Carolina, so if she played her cards right the bar would take care of Dee Dee for as long as she'd let it. Genoa put the house on the market and prepared to move to L.A. to be with her only sibling; everyone was moving on to bigger and better things.

Sitting at the kitchen table across from Picasso sipping a cup of tea, Tyger stopped and looked at him, "Can you watch Nina for an hour, I need to make a run."

Picasso wore a scowl on his face, "Tyger, it's eight-thirty-five, our plane leaves at midnight. Don't get left behind!"

"I won't. I promise I won't miss the plane. Nothing can make me miss that flight."

Tyger ran through the house and grabbed a set of keys and her purse. She hoped in Picasso's car and drove off into the night. With the engine roaring like she was competing in the Indie 500, she drove at top speed. The sound of the rain dancing on the roof like wild horses drowned out the voices in her head that told her she was making a mistake. Tyger kept thinking she should turn the car around and spin a U-turn back to the house, but she kept driving. Visibility was close to zero, but she knew the route to Ace's house like the back of her hand. With her heart pounding and her blood racing she turned the corner on to Ace's street. Her mind was spinning in a thousand different directions. Why had she left her house like a thief in the night to see a man that she was trying to forget? Why would she risk missing the flight of her life to spend one last moment with a man she had no future with? Had she learned anything?

Pulling in front of Ace's condo, Tyger shifted the gear into park and sat in silence staring straight through the windshield. She turned the engine off leaving the windshield wiper stuck in front of her. She continued to stare at that one wiper wondering why she couldn't get out of the car. She stared at the windshield wiper so long her eyes started to hurt. Growing weary of her cowardly attempt to see Ace one last time, she looked down and rubbed her stomach. She knew Ace had a right to know she was carrying his child, but she also understood a baby would bind them together forever. Taking a deep breath, Tyger put her foot on the brake and stretched her finger to push the button that started the car. Before her finger could connect to the button, she released a piercing scream and turned her head to find Ace standing at the driver's side window knocking.

Staring at Ace holding an umbrella in the middle of a rainstorm, Tyger knew she was going to have to either let him in the car or get out and go into the house. Finally, she opened the door. Ace held the umbrella and helped her out of the car. Surrounded by darkness the two of them stood by the car staring at each other. The sound of the rain was muffled by the strong flutter of Ace and Tyger's heartbeats. There were no longer two separate heartbeats, their hearts were now beating as one with a distinct rhythm that only the two of them could feel or hear.

As the umbrella slipped from Ace's hand, he grabbed Tyger's face with both hands and kissed her. Standing under the open sky with the rain falling like a waterfall, the two locked in a wet passionate embrace. Ace's wet juicy lips kissed Tyger like he'd never see her again. Their slippery tongues touching with fierce excitement sent shivers up Tyger's spine. Suddenly, Tyger felt her feet leave the ground. As Ace picked Tyger up, she wrapped her legs around his body. Straddling Ace with her feet locked behind his back, Tyger held on as he carried her into the house.

Entering the house, Ace gently released Tyger from his embrace. Ripping her blouse from her body the buttons fell to the ground hitting the floor like tiny pebbles. Not able to tear herself away from the sweet taste of Ace's lips, Tyger unbuckled his belt and unbuttoned his pants. Pulling his t-shirt over his head Ace took deep passionate breaths. Grabbing Tyger with one hand, Ace scooped her up leaping up the stairs like King Kong scaling the Empire State Building. Entering the bedroom, Ace threw Tyger on the bed and stood over her staring at her with hunger and passion. Still wet from the rain, his magnificent olive toned skin glistened in the moonlight that shined through the window. He reached down and around Tyger, unhooking her bra with one finger. Falling down the sides of her shoulder's Tyger grabbed her bra straps and ripped it from her body. With her nipples standing at attention inviting Ace to taste them, Tyger lie flat on her back.

Ace leaned over Tyger, suckling her neck with his tongue. Pulling Ace closer to her, Tyger felt his warm naked flesh against hers. With their wet naked bodies clinging to each other like wet paper, the heat from their flesh created an intoxicating scent. Tyger's hand rolled up Ace's back caressing his smooth tight skin. Lying on her back, Tyger spread her legs and waited to feel Ace inside her. Staring into Tyger's eyes, Ace entered Tyger's tight body. As the Thunder rolled across the sky Tyger moaned in ecstasy.

Like a wild animal staring into Tyger's soul, Ace delivered slow commanding strokes whispering, "I love you," in her ear. Tyger's body quivered at the sound of Ace's voice moving though her body like a storm. Opening her legs wider, Ace went deeper. As the muscles in her walls tightened, Ace exploded like a pressure filled pipe.

Feeling the weight of his body resting on top of her she called out to him, "Ace, I need to tell you something."

Unable to gather his thoughts with bated breath he panted, "Ok, just give me a minute, I can't think straight right now."

Laughing to herself, Tyger smirked "Ok, take your time." Ace's minute turned into ten minutes, which turned into him snoring like a hibernating bear.

Rolling Ace off of her, Tyger ran into the bathroom. After a shower, Tyger stood in the doorway of the bathroom wrapped in a towel staring at Ace sleeping peacefully. She was amazed at how fast he could fall asleep. For a moment she contemplated slipping under the covers and spending just one more night with him. Shaking foolish thoughts of staying in Detroit to be with Ace, Tyger walked across the room and gathered what was left of her clothing. After stuffing herself into her jeans, she grabbed Ace's sweatshirt from the chair. She pulled the shirt over her head and turned to look at Ace one last time. Picking her shoes up from the floor, she slowly tiptoed out of Ace's bedroom and walked down the stairs. Stepping into her shoes and locking the door behind her Tyger walked out of Ace's house and into the storm.

Tyger drove back to her house in complete silence. Pulling into the driveway, Tyger exited the car and entered the house through the servant's entrance. She walked up the back steps and entered her bedroom. Preparing to change into her traveling clothes, Tyger pulled Ace's sweatshirt over her head and held it close to her face. Inhaling Ace's scent, Tyger closed her eyes and remembered their rendezvous. Taking a deep breath, Tyger walked into the bathroom and threw the sweatshirt into the trashcan.

After dressing into something more comfortable, Tyger gathered the last of her bags and walked out of her bedroom. Before reaching the stairs, she ran back into the bathroom pulled the sweatshirt from the trash and shoved it into her carryon. Taking one last look around her bedroom she headed for the stairs to make her final exit. Once she reached downstairs, she walked into the den where Nina and Picasso were watching television. Before she could announce her presence, the sound of the doorbell startled her. Picasso turned around and smiled,

"Looks like you made it back just in time. Did you get what you needed?"

Tyger smiled, "Yes, I did. Thank you!"

"Good, Now let's get out of here."

Nina ran toward Tyger and wrapped her arms around her waist. Tyger leaned down and kissed Nina on her forehead.

"Are you ready to go on our adventure?"

"Yes, is Ace going?"

"No honey, Ace isn't going with us this time."

Nina dropped her head in disappointment. Tyger tweaked Nina's nose, "Don't be upset honey. Ace told me to tell his favorite girl he's going to miss you, but he wants you to have lots of fun. We can send him postcards from all around the world."

Nina clapped her hands together and jumped up and down. Tyger held out her hand and Nina grabbed a hold of her. Tyger grabbed the remote and turned off the television. Tyger and Nina walked out of the den through the house. Picasso helped Nina into the car and waited for Tyger. Tyger stood in front of the house taking one last look at what stood before her. She'd spent ten years of her life in that house. For a brief moment her life with Spencer flashed before her eyes and she knew leaving was the best thing she could do for her and Nina. Tyger turned and walked toward the car and sat next to Nina. Picasso slid in next to Tyger and closed the door. Riding down the driveway cloaked in a veil of trees, Tyger didn't look back. On the way to the airport, Tyger and Nina sang songs as Picasso stared out the window in silence. Tyger did not look at Picasso; she didn't want to invade his thoughts. She didn't want to intrude on his memories and regrets. Tyger knew as much as Picasso wanted to stop looking over his shoulder, he was just like Ace. He was made to live on the edge. Tyger knew leaving Detroit was one of the most difficult things Picasso had ever done. Tyger parted her lips to tell Picasso that it was ok to stay in the city. She wanted so badly to tell the driver to stop the car so Picasso could go wherever he wanted to be, but she could not find the words. Tyger sat back in the seat cradling Nina in her arms staring out the window.

Chapter Twenty-Nine

A ce woke up to find his bed cold and empty. The only sign of Tyger was the alluring scent of her perfume lingering on a nearby pillow. Rolling out of bed and planting both feet on the floor, he looked at the clock. It was 10:12pm; Tyger's plane would be taking off soon. Taking a deep breath Ace pulled himself up from the side of his bed. He grabbed his pants and reached for his sweatshirt, but the shirt was gone. Smiling to himself he knew Tyger had taken it with her. Still unaware of the fact that she would always have a constant reminder of him, he found comfort in knowing she had taken a piece of him with her no matter how insignificant. Walking over to the closet he retrieved another shirt, slipped on a pair of sweatpants, slipped into his shoes and headed downstairs. On the way out the door he grabbed his keys and cellphone. He heard Nico yelling behind him, "Ace, hold on!"

Ace yelled back, "It's good, I'm going out alone."

The rain was still coming down in buckets, but he needed to get out of the house. Heading toward the club, Ace decided to drink the pain of loneliness away. At the club there was an infinite supply of whatever his heart desired. It was quiet there, no Nico, no nothing,

Just Ace and his broken heart. Ace drove through the slick streets obsessing over his decision to let Tyger leave without him. He couldn't understand why he'd made such a foolish mistake. His heart ached and his head throbbed with regret. Feeling trapped inside his own mind, Ace decided to find his brother and punish him for that sacred space inside of Tyger that Aiden had ruined. Once he took care of Aiden and severed his ties with the place he called home since he was a boy, he would join Tyger. Realizing she was the part of him that made him human, that part of him that made him vulnerable and gave him life he felt like a fool for letting her go.

Arriving at the club, Ace jogged upstairs toward the office. It seemed strange to be there when the club was closed. There was usually an out-of-control party shaking the walls, but since he and Picasso had dissolved their partnership there was an empty building awaiting its next adventure. Walking into the office he looked in the chair behind Picasso's desk expecting to see him. Shaking the thought from his head, Ace walked to the wet bar and poured himself a drink.

Standing in front of the desk, Ace reached into his pocket and grabbed Tyger's engagement ring. Taking a deep breath, he took a seat and propped his feet on top of the desk. Twisting Tyger's ring around the tip of his finger, Ace watched the diamonds sparkle as the moonlight shining through the window bounced off the stones. Startled by the sound of the office door opening, he sprang to his feet. Grabbing his gun, he yelled out, "Who's there?"

A voice answered, "Damn man take it easy, it's just me. What are you doing sitting in the dark?"

"You should be on your way to who knows where right now. What are you doing here?" Picasso walked into the office and took a seat on the couch. Ace took his spot behind the desk.

"I couldn't leave without telling you the truth, I figured you'd be here getting drunk."

Ace leaned back in his chair, "The truth about what?"

Picasso was by no means afraid or intimidated by Ace, but he was exceptionally nervous about revealing that Tyger was pregnant.

Without hesitation Picasso let the truth fly out of his mouth at warp speed.

"Tyger is pregnant. She swore me to secrecy, and I promised her I wouldn't tell you before she did. On the way to the airport I asked her one last time to tell you before we left and she refused."

Picasso watched as the veins protruded from Ace's neck and his temples throbbed. Feeling like his head was going to explode, Ace was speechless, he was unable to utter a sound. Shaking his head and pounding his fist on the desk, he sprang to his feet, "Why didn't she tell me!"

"She was giving you a chance to make the decision to stay or leave without pressure. If you knew she was pregnant, you would either make her stay here or go with her out of obligation. She doesn't want either of her children growing up with a father who wants nothing that resembles a normal life."

"What is that supposed to mean?"

"Come on man! You know how it feels to live a lifetime without a good night's sleep. You can't even take a piss without a body guard standing there watching your dick flap in the wind. You need someone to taste your food before you eat it. Do you think it's fair to ask your wife and children to do the same?"

Ace sprang to his feet, "It's not her decision to make. This is some bullshit. Was she ever planning to tell me?"

"I don't know." With his face resting in the palm of his hands, Ace continued to shake his head, "This doesn't make sense to me. Did she think I wouldn't choose to be with my child?"

"Yes, that's exactly what she thought. Tyger thinks, you love the life that Ace Del Toro leads more than you love her. I mean, you did tell her you had no plans on leaving this place and moving away with her. What else is she supposed to think?"

Ace rose to his feet, "Damn man, I think she did try to tell me. She came by the house tonight. She said she needed to tell me something, but I wasn't exactly in the right headspace to listen. Letting Tyger go is the hardest thing I've ever had to do. I didn't let her go because I don't love her or don't want to be with her. I let her go because it's the safest decision I could've made."

Picasso tilted his head, " I don't understand."

"The night Tyger found Bella, we were at the house waiting for her to be loaded into the ambulance. Tyger and I had the worst argument we've ever had. We were in each other's faces as if we were strangers. She said something that struck a nerve and I hit her…"

Picasso raised up from the couch with his fists clinched, "What?"

Ace stood up and stepped toward Picasso with his hands up, "Hold on, wait. She hit me back, that's why my eye still looks like this. She punched the shit outta me."

Picasso's chest was heaving, "I don't care if she did hit you back. You had no business…"

Ace interrupted Picasso, "I know, I know I was wrong. But that scared the hell out of both of us. Tyger is the only thing I've ever had that came close to love. I love that woman with every breath in my body. She has challenged me, pissed me off almost to the point of no return and plenty of times I wanted to shake the hell out of her, but in that split second after I hit her and she instantly punched me, the look in her eye said that was it; we'd both crossed a line. With all she's done to protect Nina and the rest of us, I now know what we are both capable of; that's just too much power in one house. When is the next time we both lose control? I don't want us to turn into my parents or even her parents. I just don't think I'm good enough for Tyger."

Picasso took a deep breath and looked at Ace with contempt, "Shit man, you and Tyger deserve each other. Both of you are really full of shit. You're willing to just let your woman fly outta here because you don't feel you're good enough for her. She is willing to leave you behind because she's afraid you don't love her enough. Both of you would literally kill for each other. The two of you have been playing this stupid cat and mouse game since you were teenagers, now both of you have a chance to try and make this work, but neither of you can pull the trigger. It makes no sense to me at all."

Picasso walked over to Ace, "At first I didn't like you, but now I love you like a brother, a real blood brother. I trust you with my life and I hope you feel the same about me. So, I'm going to give you some brotherly advice. Stop being stupid. Tyger loves you and you love her; it's that simple. Now the two of you are going to have a baby, together. Man, what else could you possibly want?

Picasso landed a one-two punch to Ace's face. "I know you didn't think I would let you slide for hitting Tyger. Our flight leaves in fifty-three minutes; it's a chartered flight, so there is a little leeway with flight time. You do what you want, but I'm leaving with the only family that either of us have."

Without uttering a word, Picasso turned and exited the room as quietly as he'd entered. Lying on the floor, Ace desperately wanted to run to Tyger, but the thought of being a father terrified him. He had no idea what being a father looked like. Both his stepfather and biological father were demon spawn. He wondered if he was capable of being a good father. Ace's head swooned with ridiculously tedious questions. Unable to control the train tunneling through his brain, he screamed so loud his tonsils vibrated. Landing a punch in the wall behind the desk, Ace began to breath like an angry dragon. Trying to catch his breath, he jumped up and grabbed Tyger's ring from the desk and ran out the door.

Running to his car, he fumbled with his key fob. As he approached the car the doors unlocked, and he hoped in the driver's seat. With his tires squealing, smoke followed him as he sped out of the parking lot at top speed. He tried to instruct the Command system to call Tyger, but his adrenalin was flowing, he couldn't complete a sentence.

Running lights, swerving in and out of traffic, Ace drove like a mad man trying to make it to the airport before Tyger's plane left the airport. After risking his own life and the other drivers on the freeway, Ace arrived. Wheeling his car around to the front of the small private airport, he jumped out of the car leaving his door hanging open. Ace ran inside searching for Tyger. Scanning the crowd in the small airport he failed to recognize anyone. Looking out into the night, he squinted his eyes and discovered Nina in the distance holding on to her mother's hand. With excitement, Ace grabbed his chest and ran out through the sliding glass doors.

Waiving his hands, Ace yelled our to Tyger. Turning abruptly, her mouth flew open at the sight of Ace running out onto the tarmac. Nina broke away from her mother's grip and ran toward Ace, screaming his name. Nina jumped into Ace's arms and buried her face into the side of his neck. Holding her close to him, Ace kissed her warm cheek. Still holding Nina, Ace briskly walked toward Tyger. Finally reaching her, Ace and Tyger stood in front of each other in the midst of an awkward silence. Ace stared into Tyger's eyes. With an enormous grin, Picasso ran over and stood next to Ace.

Ace grabbed Tyger's hand, "I don't really know what I need to do right now. I just know that I can't live without you. If you will give me some time, I'll get my stuff together and meet you wherever you want. But I need you to understand that I am Ace Del Toro and I can't just up and leave town without getting my business in order. I promise, just give me a few weeks and I'll be wherever you are…" Ace leaned in closer to Tyger, "Tyger, are you listening? Did you hear what I said…"

Staring past Ace into the distance, Tyger's body grew numb, "Aiden."

Confused, Ace asked, "Aiden? What?"

Pointing over Ace's shoulder, she yelled out, "Aiden, he's behind you!"

Picasso and Ace both turned in Aiden's direction. Placing Nina on the ground behind him, Ace scowled, "What the fuck are you doing here?"

Aiden wielded a gun from his jacket. Brandishing the gun in the air, the chrome shined under the airport lights.

Pointing the gun at Ace, Aiden laughed, "You didn't think I would leave town and leave you here alive to enjoy life, did you?"

Startled by the sound of Tyger's voice calling out, "Aiden no…" He turned toward Tyger and pulled the trigger. Falling to her knees, blood flew from Tyger's chest. Looking up at Ace she placed her hand on her chest, "He shot me…" Tyger looked back down at her wound, glanced over at Picasso and whispered, "Help me!" As Tyger struggled to breath she fell over like a ton of bricks. Ace ran to her and Picasso scooped Nina up in his arms and held her close to him. Nina's screams co-mingled with shrieks of onlookers as Tyger's lifeless body lie on the cold asphalt. Falling to his knees, Ace cradled Tyger in his arms and rocked backward and forward begging her to open her eyes. He moaned and wailed in agony as he gently kissed her face. Blinded by his tears and almost paralyzed by grief, he placed Tyger's lifeless body on the hard unyielding ground.

Struggling to breathe, Ace placed his foot onto the concrete and pulled himself up from the ground. Like a crazed Gorilla, he rose up and began beating his chest with his right arm. Saliva, tears and sweat flew from his body like a violent stream. He headed toward Aiden with brute force beating his chest with one hand and waiving his Glock in the other. The world was spinning in slow motion, time had stopped, Ace felt like he was walking through a cold dark tunnel. Walking toward Aiden with his gun extended, Ace's face grew red and his eyes were like lakes of fire. Both Ace and Aiden walked toward each other at top speed, one pointing his gun at the other. With bullets flying and cries of unbearable anguish filling the sky, shots rang into the night. Searching for a final target, bullets sailed through the air.

Halting in his tracks, Ace watched his brother fall to his knees and collapse. Ace walked over and stood over Aiden. Aiden lay on his back with blood pouring from his neck struggling to speak. Like a helpless animal shot down by a hunter, Aiden twitched and shook trying to hold on to his last breath. Ace stood over Aiden waiting for the light in his eyes to extinguish. Looking down at his brother swimming in a pool of blood, Ace watched as Aiden raised his finger and pointed. In a soft whisper and smiled, "I finally got you." Taking his last breath, life drained from Aiden's body.

Puzzled by his brother's last remarks, Ace saw blood rolling down his shirt making a puddle on the ground. Picasso ran over, "Ace, you've been shot."

Ace looked down at the blood pouring from his chest. He placed his hand over his chest. Looking at the hole in his chest, Ace's hand was saturated with blood. Staggering toward Tyger's body, Ace fell to his knees and crawled toward her. Falling next to Tyger, he pulled her close to him. Laying his head on Tyger's heart, tears fell down the side of Ace's face. Holding Tyger's hand in his, Ace Del Toro took his last breath.

Tyger and Ace lie together on the blood-stained concrete in an eternal embrace. Picasso stood in silence paralyzed by the sight of his brother and best friend lying lifeless as he held Nina in his arms. As the wind blew like a raging beast and the sirens roared in the distance, the crowd continued to gather around him. Amidst the whispers, questions and stares of those that looked on, Picasso's heart broke into a million tiny pieces.

www.ingramcontent.com/pod-product-compliance
Lightning Source LLC
Chambersburg PA
CBHW070011120726
47909CB00003B/887